HOME OF THE BRAISED

"Action-packed . . . With grace and aplomb, Ollie juggles her job and sleuthing, receiving a very pleasant surprise of her own at the satisfying conclusion."　　*—Publishers Weekly*

"[Ollie is] a spunky heroine . . . The plot was dynamic, ripe with clues, and paced swiftly but not too quickly . . . A great read."
　　　　　　　　　　　　　　　　　　　　—Fresh Fiction

"Julie Hyzy never disappoints . . . This was a fast, fun killer read."　　　　　　　　　　　　　　　　*—MyShelf.com*

"Another thrilling entry into the White House Chef series . . . There's wonderful talk of food along with a great deal of tension, thrills, and intrigue."　　　*—Gumshoe Review*

FONDUING FATHERS

"Hyzy, as always, fills this novel with a clever plot and fascinating behind-the-scenes glimpses of life in the White House. But it's Ollie who carries the series, and never more so than in this moving page-turner."　　*—Richmond Times-Dispatch*

"This time [Ollie's] investigation is a personal one, as closely held family secrets are revealed. Scenes in the White House kitchen will appeal to foodies. A touch of romance rounds out this delectable offering."　　　　　*—RT Book Reviews*

"[A] mystery delight . . . This is a fantastic installment in the series . . . The White House staff is still quirky and interesting, and the recipes at the end range from really easy to needing to raise the spirit of Julia Child as a spirit guide . . . and yes, there is fondue."　　　*—Kings River Life Magazine*

continued . . .

AFFAIRS OF STEAK

"Hyzy shines in this volume. *Affairs of Steak* proves unequiv-ocally that this series burns as bright as the sun during a swel-tering D.C. summer."   —*Seattle Post-Intelligencer*

"These are wonderful books, enjoyable to read, hard to put down, and they make you really look forward to the next one in the series."   —*AnnArbor.com*

"Fun and intriguing . . . I will keep my eye out for other books in the White House Chef Mystery Series."   —*Fresh Fiction*

BUFFALO WEST WING

"Hyzy's obvious research into protocol and procedures gives her story the realistic element that her readers have come to expect from this top-notch mystery writer. Adventure, intrigue, and a dash of romance combine for a delicious cozy that is a delight to read."   —*Fresh Fiction*

"A captivating story from the very first page until the end . . . From the easy-to-recreate recipes in the back to its high-energy, ever-changing story line, this one is good enough to serve to the higher-ups . . . Great job, Julie Hyzy. Another all-around great read!"   —*The Romance Readers Connection*

"Every White House Chef Mystery is cause for celebration. The daily schedule in the White House kitchen is trauma enough, but Hyzy always ratchets up the tension with plots and danger . . . Julie Hyzy's star shines brighter than ever with *Buffalo West Wing*."   —*Lesa's Book Critiques*

EGGSECUTIVE ORDERS

"The ever-burgeoning culinary mystery subgenre has a new chef-sleuth . . . The backstage look at the White House proves fascinating."   —*Booklist*

"A quickly paced plot with a headstrong heroine and some recipes featuring eggs all add up to a dependable mystery."
                    —*The Mystery Reader*

Berkley Prime Crime titles by Julie Hyzy

White House Chef Mysteries

STATE OF THE ONION
HAIL TO THE CHEF
EGGSECUTIVE ORDERS
BUFFALO WEST WING
AFFAIRS OF STEAK
FONDUING FATHERS
HOME OF THE BRAISED
ALL THE PRESIDENT'S MENUS

Manor House Mysteries

GRACE UNDER PRESSURE
GRACE INTERRUPTED
GRACE AMONG THIEVES
GRACE TAKES OFF
GRACE AGAINST THE CLOCK

Anthologies

INAUGURAL PARADE

ALL THE PRESIDENT'S MENUS

JULIE HYZY

BERKLEY PRIME CRIME, NEW YORK

THE BERKLEY PUBLISHING GROUP
Published by the Penguin Group
Penguin Group (USA) LLC
375 Hudson Street, New York, New York 10014

USA • Canada • UK • Ireland • Australia • New Zealand • India • South Africa • China

penguin.com

A Penguin Random House Company

ALL THE PRESIDENT'S MENUS

A Berkley Prime Crime Book / published by arrangement with Tekno Books LLC

Berkley Prime Crime Books are published by The Berkley Publishing Group.
BERKLEY® PRIME CRIME and the PRIME CRIME logo are trademarks of
Penguin Group (USA) LLC.

For information, address: The Berkley Publishing Group,
a division of Penguin Group (USA) LLC,
375 Hudson Street, New York, New York 10014.

ISBN: 978-0-425-26239-9

PUBLISHING HISTORY
Berkley Prime Crime mass-market / January 2015

PRINTED IN THE UNITED STATES OF AMERICA

10 9 8 7 6 5 4 3 2 1

Interior text design by Laura K. Corless.

For Rene, with love and gratitude

ACKNOWLEDGMENTS

A significant scene in Ollie's new adventure takes place at Blair House—the president's guest house on Pennsylvania Avenue. While I was able to discover a great deal of wonderful information about the home's history and its individual rooms, I couldn't locate a copy of its floor plans anywhere. What to do? Answer: I created my own. If you happen to be one of the lucky few who have stayed at Blair House in the past, and you find yourself cringing at my depiction of its layout, let me know. I'd love to talk with you!

Several years ago, our daughter, Robyn, asked her friend Jamie Pogue for title ideas for this series. He came up with an amazing list of options and, with this book, I've finally been able to use one of them. Thank you, Jamie!

Thanks, too, to Elaine Weinmann Miller, who rose to the Facebook challenge when I requested help naming a fictional country. Thanks to Elaine, Saardisca was born.

Very warm thanks to my editor, Natalee Rosenstein, at Berkley Prime Crime. I'm so lucky to be able to work with her and her awesome assistant, Robin Barletta. Thanks, too, to Stacy Edwards, Erica Rose, and countless others who move my stories from manuscript to finished book.

Sincere thanks as well to Larry Segriff at Tekno Books, who keeps everything running smoothly and is never too busy to answer e-mails. Thanks to my enthusiastic agent, Paige Wheeler, and to my friends at Cozy-Promo.

Big hugs and smoochy kisses to my family. Love you!

CHAPTER 1

AS EXECUTIVE CHEF AT THE WHITE HOUSE, I was responsible for feeding the First Family and—whether they be friend or foe—all the home's guests. I took my duties to heart, and was exceedingly proud of my team and the small part we played in shaping our country's history.

My role at the White House had evolved over the years, much to the Secret Service's dismay. Through no fault of my own (well, most of the time) I'd been entangled in situations involving enemies of the president, international assassins, and those who attempted to conspire against the United States. Armed with stubborn tenacity and more than a bit of good luck, I'd had a hand in seeing justice served, and even saved a few lives in the process.

It had been suggested, more than once, that President and Mrs. Hyden find less of a troublemaker to head up their kitchen. But the First Family liked me and what I brought to the table, both literally and figuratively.

Several months ago, Special Agent in Charge, Leonard Gavin—Gav—and I had gotten married in a surprise ceremony here in the White House. Surrounded by friends and family as we exchanged vows, my life changed forever. After the ceremony, during the sweet reception that my assistants, Bucky and Cyan, had arranged for us, I'd endured countless good-natured barbs about how, now that I'd "settled down," perhaps my terrorist-fighting days were over.

And maybe they were.

Since our wedding day, life had been very, very quiet. And truly, I had no quarrel with that. If I never went into hand-to-hand combat, if I never faced another barrel of a gun, if I was never again left bound and gagged with no chance of escape, well, I wasn't about to complain.

I rested my chin in one hand, elbow perched on the White House kitchen's gleaming countertop. The fingers of my other hand beat out a non-rhythm of impatience against the shiny stainless steel.

It's not that I craved life-threatening adventure. Not at all. But right about now I would have appreciated a little diversion.

Unfortunately, however, we were in the middle of a government sequester. State dinners had been delayed, parties canceled, and visitors put off until our country's leadership got its act together.

Staring at the clock, waiting for Bucky to return from an errand, I reflected on the boredom that loomed ahead. I longed for a challenge. I hungered for the excitement that came from planning a state dinner—the kind that kept guests talking for years, regaling envious friends with descriptions of mouthwatering appetizers and luxurious entrees. I ached to collaborate with the florist, the sommelier, and of course, Marcel, our executive pastry chef who could dream up a dessert that was as spectacular as it was sweet.

My skin practically crawled, itching for the president and First Lady to announce that a hundred guests were expected for dinner tomorrow night. I wouldn't have minded, even if they demanded we serve a seven-course meal. I would have gone insane with preparation, of course, but that was far more appealing than the doldrums we were facing now.

Most of all, I wanted Cyan back.

Until the country's situation improved, a number of "nonessential" members of the White House staff were on furlough—among them, Cyan. I certainly didn't consider her nonessential. Quite the opposite. But when the government decided to slash salaries, they neglected to seek my counsel.

Bucky and I were doing our best to keep the kitchen operating efficiently, which—to be fair—wasn't difficult, given the ripple effect the sequester was having on entertainment. I thanked my lucky stars Bucky hadn't been sent home, too. I'd have gone stir-crazy on my own.

Because cost-cutting strategies involved eliminating most fancy dinners, he and I didn't have much to do beyond preparing the family's meals and feeding numerous—often angry—congressional leaders during marathon negotiation sessions held at the White House.

Marcel, the executive pastry chef whose French accent seemed to grow thicker with each passing day, had also been kept on. I knew why. Despite what the anti-Hyden pundits may assume, Marcel's job wasn't secure because the First Family chose to indulge their collective sweet tooth. Truth was, the Hydens weren't big fans of dessert. They preferred savory items.

What kept Marcel busy in his kitchen was the fact that the president recognized how effective a tray full of expertly crafted and lick-your-fingers-clean pastries could be at the bargaining table. While my concoctions of steak salad, lobster bisque, or pork tenderloin sandwiches satisfied appetites, Marcel's creations had far more potential to cheer up grumpy lawmakers.

In my heart, I knew I shouldn't complain. Granted, Cyan was out of the kitchen, and that wasn't optimal. But, on the bright side, Virgil was missing, too. A few months earlier the First Lady had delivered an ultimatum to our high-drama chef: Virgil would be required to seek help for his anger management issues and apologize to me and my staff or his career at the White House was over. The man had attempted to undermine my authority and sabotage my career once too often. That final, fateful time, Mrs. Hyden had witnessed his hostility and laid down the law.

Since that fateful day, we hadn't heard a peep from the dining diva. Our chief usher, Peter Everett Sargeant III, kept us informed enough to let us know that Virgil remained in town, but beyond that, no one knew what he was up to, nor whether he'd taken steps to address his problems. He hadn't apologized. I had a feeling it was that, more than the mandate to get help, that was holding him back from returning to work.

With all that in mind, I'd decided that my only option was to wait out the sequester with little to no complaint. Except for worrying about Cyan, who was living without a paycheck for the foreseeable future, we were under very little pressure. Food preparation at the White House had been the quietest and least stressful it had been for as long as I'd worked here. Maybe I should try harder to enjoy the lull.

"Good morning, Ms. Paras."

I straightened to see Peter Sargeant and his assistant, Margaret, in my kitchen doorway. He wore his customary squirrel-alert expression. She carried a tablet and blinked at me from behind large tortoiseshell glasses. Neither smiled, but that was no surprise. Having them show up in my kitchen together, however, was. The last time they had, it had been to inform me of Cyan's furlough. I braced myself, hoping Bucky wasn't about to be cut, too.

Sargeant stepped forward, his ever-eager associate close behind. "I hope we aren't interrupting your busy day." Giving a derisive look around the quiet, pristine kitchen, he added, "Or your daydreaming."

"What do you need, Peter?" I asked, ignoring the snarky comment. Over the years I'd come to accept his personality.

I appreciated the fact that I could depend on him for support when I needed it, but on a day-to-day basis, I found dealing with his persnickety attitude to be more than a bit tedious.

He turned to Margaret. "You may do the honors."

She was tiny, even shorter than Sargeant, with small fingers and big eyes. Mid-forties, she sported a short, dark bob and wore clothes that were so perfectly suited, I wondered if she and Sargeant shared the same tailor.

"We have news and important updates to share with you." She cleared her throat and read from her tablet. "The first comes from an e-mail to Peter Everett Sargeant, from Parker Hyden." She glanced up at me at that, lifting her eyebrows in emphasis, as though I wouldn't have recognized the president's name on my own.

"Share the pertinent information, Margaret," Sargeant said. "No need for dramatics."

Margaret tightened her lips at the rebuke, pushed her glasses up her nose, and went on. "We will host a Saardiscan dignitary for dinner, approximately two weeks from now." She slid her gaze toward Sargeant before continuing. "The second update comes from the secretary of state, informing us that the chefs who were originally scheduled to visit your kitchen are on their way, too."

"The Saardiscans are coming?" I repeated. "What about the sequester?"

Margaret said, "Does it matter? We were told to notify all departments. That's really all you need to know."

Even Sargeant seemed taken aback by his assistant's snippiness. "Yes, well, there is more to it," he said. "As you know, the Saardiscan chefs' visit was arranged for more than a year ago. We were loath to cancel."

I did know. This was a very big deal where our two countries' diplomatic efforts were concerned. "But you did cancel," I said. "Are you telling me they're coming tomorrow, after all?"

He nodded.

I pinched the bridge of my nose, closing my eyes for a brief second to gather my thoughts. I'd wished for this, I reminded myself. Mere moments ago.

Sargeant went on to explain, "When the sequester was first announced, everything was canceled. The problem, at least as it relates to the White House, is that negotiation can be delicate with some countries. Saardisca is one of these."

I understood, even as my mind raced. Had we planned to entertain chefs from France or Canada, the administration might have been able to rearrange things with little more than a polite apology. Saardisca, however, was an uneasy ally. A frenemy. We hadn't had a political or ideological blowup between our countries in more than a decade, but that didn't mean we agreed on everything. Truth was, we didn't agree on much.

Yet, I wasn't prepared for this sudden change. I'd had a plan in place for the Saardiscans' visit, but once the sequester had been imposed, I'd put those plans on hold. I needed to salvage my notes, pull lists together, and set up flowcharts.

Ideas banged against each other in my noisy brain; I barely registered that Sargeant was still talking.

"Fulfilling our promise to Saardisca has been deemed of the utmost importance. The decision, therefore, has been made to honor our agreement."

"I wish I would have known this was a possibility," I said.

One side of his mouth curled up. "I'm sure the president regrets his oversight in neglecting to include you in the decision making."

I ignored the sarcasm. "How long will they be here?"

"Two weeks."

"Two weeks?" I repeated, surprise jolting my voice up several notches. "I thought they were to visit for three or four days." So much for the original plans I'd made. Those notes would barely get me started.

"Things change," he said, deadpan. "In what appears to

be serendipitous timing, the delegates will be working with you for the duration of the Saardiscan presidential candidate's visit to the United States. President Hyden will host an official dinner for all of them when the candidate returns here after touring the country."

"Did you say *'candidate'*?" I asked. "You mean it's the challenger for president who's coming to visit?" That surprised me. The incumbent had been in power for decades.

"Yes, Kerry Freiberg," he said. "If you kept up with headlines, you would know that her campaign has been gaining steam."

I did keep up with headlines, but there had been no mention of her coming here. "She's the first female to run for that office, isn't she?"

"No one expects her to win, but the fact that she's the first woman to make it this far is garnering her a great deal of press." He sniffed. "And because her platform is based on improving diplomatic relations with other countries, a stop in the United States is a requirement."

"A two-week stop." I rubbed my forehead. I needed to get organized, and quickly. "Tell me what I need to know. Do you have the date that we'll be hosting her for dinner? Will there be more than one event? Do we have dietary dossiers for Ms. Freiberg and the members of her staff?"

Margaret had begun taking notes, writing longhand with a stylus, as I outlined all the information I'd need.

"We will get back to you on these matters," Sargeant said when I took a breath. "And whatever else you need to know. As you can imagine, there are other departments to be notified and a great deal that my office needs to oversee. If you'll excuse us."

Bucky returned a little while later, bringing with him the woodsy scent of autumn air. He hung up his windbreaker and came to stand over my shoulder to study the notes I was jotting as thoughts occurred to me. I would arrange these scribbles into some semblance of order later.

"What's up, chief?" he asked.

My mind twisted and flipped with a myriad of things I needed to do—hundreds of things I wouldn't have imagined having to worry about a half hour earlier. My fingers tingled; my leg bounced with impatience.

I looked up at him, grinning. "We're having company."

CHAPTER 2

WHEN THE PRESIDENT'S SON, JOSH, TUMBLED into the kitchen that afternoon for his cooking lesson, I had the unhappy duty of letting him know that the plans we'd made for the coming weeks had been canceled.

"That stinks," he said, brows furrowing over dark eyes. The kid was far too considerate to pitch a fit, but I detected a tiny whine in his tone. "I thought that this sequester thing meant that I would get to spend more time in the kitchen, not less."

"I thought so, too," I said. "I'll make it up to you, I promise."

Disappointed, he nodded.

"While the visitors are here, the Secret Service thinks it would be best to keep you out of the kitchen completely."

"Stupid Secret Service."

"Your safety is the most important thing," I said, ruffling his hair. "And we both know that's serious business."

Grudgingly, he nodded again. "We can still work together today, though, right?"

Despite the fact that I had a thousand things to get done before tomorrow, I refused to disappoint him further. "Absolutely. Let's get started."

BY THE TIME THE SAARDISCANS ARRIVED THE next morning, I'd received dossiers on all four of them as well as a little more background on why this particular diplomatic endeavor had been given the green light when so many others had not.

President Hyden and his advisers had discovered that canceling the chefs' visit would be viewed as a personal affront to the current Saardiscan government. Rather than risk a political firestorm and public-relations nightmare with the touchy country, the president had chosen to take the high road and see this endeavor through.

I suppose I should have anticipated this, at least a little. We were, whether it was acknowledged or not, putting our neck out politically by hosting the chefs here. Saardisca would have been reluctant to let this opportunity go.

Recent unpopular decisions by Saardiscan leaders had caused several other countries to give them the cold shoulder. If passive-aggressive games could be played at high-stakes tables like the U.N.'s, then those nations were doubling down for the win.

Bucky and I had gone over the chefs' dossiers the night before, discovering that the documents were light on substance. We'd been given copies of their solemn-faced passport photos—all of which reminded me of mug shots—along with information about which province each man hailed from and where they'd studied. There was almost zero in terms of personal information.

"Not much to go on," Bucky had said.

I pointed at each photo in turn. "Kilian, Tibor, Hector, and Nate," I said. "I need to memorize their faces so I don't mix them up. You know how hard it is to keep people straight when you meet them all at once."

"Not a very pleasant-looking bunch," he said.

I laughed. "My passport photo isn't much better."

"All men, too."

"According to the notes, Kilian and Tibor are the top two chefs in their country," I said, "but neither was invited to the Club des Chefs des Chefs this year. Or the year before."

"Sounds to me like Saardisca is upset that they haven't been invited to the grown-ups' table," Bucky said.

"They feel snubbed; not that I blame them. This venture may be their ticket in, assuming things go well."

Bucky stepped back and folded his arms across his chest. "No pressure on us. No way," he said, rolling his eyes. "Seems like a lot to ask of a kitchen that's operating short-staffed."

I pulled in a breath. I knew Bucky was right, that there was enormous pressure on us to make this work. And yet, I was thrilled. We had a project. An important one. I couldn't wait to meet these men.

"We're serving as kitchen ambassadors," I said. "Our job isn't to craft policy. Our job is to make the chefs feel welcome. And to keep everything on an even keel while they're here. We can do that."

"If you say so, chief."

"Diplomacy has to start somewhere."

The men arrived in the kitchen a short while later, accompanied by two Secret Service agents. After we made introductions and quietly assessed one another, I showed them around the main kitchen. They took everything in slowly, occasionally asking a question, and making unintelligible noises that could have been appreciation or disdain.

While the Saardiscans were in the White House, they'd be allowed unrestricted access to the main kitchen, pastry kitchen, two pantries, the refrigeration area, and some storage. They would also be allowed in the Center Hall

and ground floor as needed, but if they were to travel elsewhere in the building, they would require an escort.

Marcel had taken our visitors for a quick lunch before
providing a tour of the pastry kitchen. Bucky and I planned
to join them in a few minutes, as soon as we finished plating
lunch for the First Lady and her staff. The president's meal
had been sent to the West Wing twenty minutes earlier.

One of the Saardiscans returned to the kitchen. He
came around the corner with his hands balled, elbows up,
as though looking for a fistfight. Moving quickly, he strode
in, not making eye contact with either Bucky or me.

It took me a moment to remember which one he was.
"Tibor," I called to the man. Muscular and strong-shouldered,
he was systematically opening and shutting every stainless
steel cabinet in the room. The brisk clanking spoke to his
vexation. "What are you looking for?"

He spun, scowling. Tall and solid, he was at least fifteen
years my senior. His face was lined and red, like a fresh
cut of flank steak. He had thick, black hair, which he wore
brushed back and that quivered with gel.

"Nate told me to bring him a new apron." Tibor flung
his hands in the air. "How do I find anything in this place?
Every cabinet looks the same."

Bucky glanced at me. His lips twisted and he looked
away. Neither he nor I could mistake Tibor's contemptuous
tone, but Bucky knew better than to snap back, thereby
risking an international incident. He held his tongue and
waited for me to respond.

"We keep our extra linens in that cabinet." I pointed.
Tibor would have found them eventually but I saved him
about six cabinets' worth of banging. "Did something happen to the one he was wearing?"

Tibor huffed, as though I'd asked a foolish question.

Bucky made a similar noise that was probably meant
for Tibor's benefit, but the agitated man ignored it.

The four visiting chefs had only been here a few hours,

but I was already seeing personality traits emerge. Tibor was the hothead of the bunch. I hadn't yet decided whether it was me he didn't like, or women in general.

"Why do you have everything closed up?" he asked. When Tibor spoke, only his bottom teeth showed, reminding me of Jack Klugman in old reruns of *The Odd Couple* and *Quincy, M.E.* Or the cartoon dog Mutley, but without the laugh. Tibor motioned again at the gleaming row of cabinets. "Why not keep everything more easy to see?"

"That's a fair question," I said. A tuxedoed butler arrived to pick up the chicken pita sandwiches and bowls of quinoa and chicken soup we'd prepared for Mrs. Hyden's lunch meeting. "Glass-front cabinets would make it easier to find things, but a lot more difficult to hide the mess." I smiled. Tibor didn't.

Bucky and I covered the lunch items then handed them to the butler for loading onto his rolling cart. "Thanks, Jackson," I said to him.

"Thank you, ma'am," he said with a wink. "Looks and smells as wonderful as always."

Once Jackson had taken off, Tibor—having procured the apron he sought—scowled again. "I don't understand you Americans."

Bucky's face twitched. In a heartbeat, I knew this was going to be a long couple of weeks.

As much as I wanted to fire off a retort, I held back. I needed to remain tactful. More important, I needed to maintain control. Until I got to know these visitors a little bit better I couldn't risk offending them.

"What don't you understand?" I asked, keeping my tone lightly conversational. "Maybe I can help you."

"Never mind."

I'd learned early on that crusty people often used their crabby demeanor to mask insecurities. It was taking a great deal of effort on my part, but I vowed not to judge these new arrivals. They were probably as uncomfortable in a strange workspace as we were having them here.

I wiped my hands on my apron, addressing both Bucky and Tibor. "Are you ready to head upstairs?" I asked, pointing in the direction of the pastry kitchen.

WHEN WE ARRIVED, MARCEL WAS HOLDING court in his deliciously creative kingdom.

Cramped and mostly windowless, this nonetheless efficient pastry kitchen had been created by carving out space from the home's high-ceilinged pantry below.

This mezzanine-level work area, which was always tight, felt overwhelmingly warm today with the addition of four sizeable Saardiscans. Their tangy body odor made me wonder how often they bathed. Bucky and I stood closest to the exit, where I shifted from foot to foot, feeling a tingle of claustrophobia crawl up the back of my neck.

Oblivious, or merely accustomed to the compact surroundings and warm scent of humanity, Marcel was in his element. His dark, round face gleamed with pride as he showed off samples of the remarkable desserts he'd lovingly created for dozens of state events. Years before either of us had started working here, one of Marcel's predecessors had installed a glass cabinet on the wall to display the exquisite models, which sat like priceless works of art on shiny shelves.

While some of Marcel's most noteworthy accomplishments had been removed from the glass case due to deterioration, age, or from gathering too much dust, our ebullient French chef's all-time favorite item was still holding strong. It was my favorite as well. A few years back, when President Hyden had invited the illustrious author Ray Bradbury for dinner, Marcel had created sunny dandelions fashioned from pulled sugar. A fist-sized bouquet of them in an edible vase had served as centerpiece.

Kilian, the leader of the Saardiscan contingent—the top

chef, if you will—shook his head, his pale, soft face creasing into a frown. He used a chubby finger to scratch the top of his freckled crown. I put him in his early fifties, but he may have been younger. His baldness, ample girth, and cheeks blazing with broken blood vessels gave him the appearance of a well-fed, successful businessman.

"Is that not a weed plant?" he asked. While all of them spoke English far better than I would ever be able to speak Saardiscan, Kilian's command of our language seemed to be the best of the bunch. "Why would you choose to decorate an elegant dinner with unwanted shrubbery?"

"Ah, but you see, this is a very special plant," Marcel began in his mellifluous French accent. He must have anticipated the question, because as he launched into a nostalgic chronicle of Bradbury's work, he leaned over to pull a slim paperback from a nearby shelf. Holding up a well-worn copy of *Dandelion Wine*, Marcel waxed poetic about how both he and President Hyden were enormous fans of the late master's work. As was I.

The dandelions' graceful, lance-shaped leaves and their heads' luminous yellow rays, crafted from sugar and talent, never ceased to astonish me. These stunning decorations appeared so real that even though I knew the truth, it took all my self-control to stop from touching them, just to make sure. Every piece Marcel created in this cramped kitchen was edible. The work involved and level of precision required made my head spin.

Marcel often told me that he was in awe of my talents, but I believed his gifts far surpassed mine. These were masterpieces. I wished there was a way to display each and every one in the Smithsonian so that others, beyond those lucky enough to score a White House invitation, would be able to see and appreciate them.

When Tibor, Bucky, and I had gotten up here, Tibor had given the apron to Nate. Right now, the item sat unattended on a nearby countertop. I couldn't imagine why they'd needed one from the main kitchen, rather than grabbing one from the supply here.

While Marcel continued to talk about the work done in his kitchen and about the members of his staff who were currently on furlough, I studied our new additions. I was having a very tough time remembering who was who.

When the four men had originally accompanied Marcel upstairs, and before Tibor had returned for the apron, I'd mentioned to Bucky that I was afraid I'd have to rely on mnemonic devices to keep the chefs straight.

"Kilian is easy," I'd said. Short and pudgy, he was the head chef, "He's the leader of the group. No problem there."

"What about the rest of them?" he asked. "Can we come up with hints?" He pointed to one of the photographs. "Tibor the Terrible would work for this guy."

"Tibor's actually pretty easy to remember," I said. "He's always scowling and unpleasant. Whether or not it's a good thing, it makes him memorable."

"I have the hardest time with these two." Bucky tapped the photos.

"Hector and Nate." I read their names aloud. "I'm open to suggestions."

"Neither one of them seems particularly thrilled to be here," he said.

"Like Terrible Tibor does?"

Bucky shrugged, but I knew what he meant. "You can tell that Kilian can't wait to get started. And Tibor, for all his grousing, asks good questions and seems like he's, if not happy to be here, then at least willing to give it his best."

"These other two are clearly more reserved," I said, finishing his thought. "Nate takes in everything, but without comment. He's so pale, so expressionless, he practically fades into the background. I'm afraid I'll start forgetting he's even here."

"I doubt that," he said. "But you've given me an idea. How about 'Neutral Nate'?"

"Fair enough. Last up is this guy. Hector," I said. "He always seems to be smiling. What do you think?"

"Looks more like a sneer to me." When I reacted, Bucky held both hands up. "Okay, okay, that was unkind. They aren't exactly warm and fuzzy personalities, though."

"It's our job to make them feel welcome," I said. "So, how about Happy Hector?"

"Happy Hector," he repeated. "Not terribly imaginative, but it'll do."

Now in the pastry kitchen, as I surreptitiously watched our visitors, I reminded myself of the nicknames Bucky and I had bestowed on them.

Terrible Tibor's solid build, slick hair, and ruddy complexion contrasted with Nate's physical blandness and stooped posture. Nate kept his eyes low and his shoulders hunched, constantly watching, never commenting, leading me to believe he was the least experienced of the group. Tibor kept his arms crossed as he listened, his lips curled to one side. Nate shifted his weight from foot to foot.

Hector was taller and younger than Kilian. More muscular, too. He spoke very little. His extraordinarily round face, coupled with his high eyebrows and upturned mouth, gave him an expression of perpetual wonderment. Bucky was wrong when he termed it a sneer. Hector struck me as the easiest of the bunch to manage.

Now, as Marcel turned to replace the dandelion in the display case, I quietly addressed Nate. "What happened to you?" The front of his smock was stained with what looked like red fruit juice.

Marcel answered my question, his voice booming. "Ah, you see the results of our little accident," he said. Grabbing the new apron, he thrust it at Nate. "I am again so very apologetic for causing you to spill."

Nate dismissed Marcel's concerns, removing the stained item and replacing it with a new one. "Many thanks," he said to Tibor. To me and Bucky, he offered a smile. "Not a favorable way to begin our visit, is it?"

"My fault, my fault," Marcel said waving his hands in the air. I could tell he was eager to get back to his presentation. "Tibor was handing a pot of raspberry sauce to me, but it jumped from my fingers and attacked poor Nate. Again, I am so very sorry."

Curious about the raspberry sauce, because nothing on display would have required its use, I was about to ask when Marcel turned to address the group once again. "As our delightful executive chef, Olivia, so eloquently told you when you first arrived, we hope you will treat our kitchens as your home during your most welcome visit." He wiped the back of his hand across his brow.

Nate and Tibor glanced at me. It seemed the mere mention of my position startled them. Maybe I was imagining it. Marcel sniffed in deeply and blinked a couple of times as though clearing his vision. "We encourage you to share with us your particular expertise. This time we spend together promises to be a learning experience for both our countries. We—"

Marcel gripped the edge of the countertop behind him. "Oh, *mon dieu*," he said, his eyes rolling up into the top of his head. *"Je suis—"*

Pushing my way between the others who stood paralyzed in front of Marcel—who was clearly in distress—I rushed to our pastry chef's side. Too late. His mouth falling slack, Marcel toppled sideways.

His right arm reached into the air for help. Rotating as he fell to the floor, his flailing appendage hit the frame of a nearby shelving unit with enough force to make it wobble. One of Marcel's spare stand mixers, perched near the shelf's edge for easy access, listed heavily from side to side. Too far away to do anything but hold my breath, I watched as the apparatus almost righted itself one-half beat before Marcel bounced against it a second time.

He fell.

The mixer fell.

It landed, with a horrifying crunch, atop his extended arm. All I could do at the moment was thank heavens it had missed his head.

"Marcel," I shouted, kneeling next to him, searching for a pulse in his neck. I yelped at the sight of his arm, grotesquely twisted backward against the tile.

I turned to Bucky, but he was already calling for help.

CHAPTER 3

MARCEL WAS UNCONSCIOUS, BUT BREATHING. I loosened the neck of his tunic, doing my best not to move him, as I directed the visiting chefs to move toward the small kitchen's far corner.

My words were quiet, but urgent. "Marcel," I said. "Marcel, wake up."

As if in reply, our pastry chef's body jerked. His back arched and he began to convulse. I pulled at his clothing to loosen it further, trying to remember my first-aid training. Marcel coughed, spewing blood.

Kilian stared at Marcel's prone form. "What happened? Is he unwell?"

I bit back the snippy response before it escaped my lips. What kind of question was that? Did he think that Marcel had simply decided to take a nap right now, in the middle of the kitchen floor? Did Kilian not see the man's obviously broken arm? I directed my attention to Bucky, who had returned from the phone.

He took up a position next to me on the floor. "They're on their way."

I wasn't a medical expert, so I had no idea what had happened. Didn't heart attack victims usually remain conscious? Or was that just the way they were portrayed on TV? Could Marcel have suffered a stroke? He wasn't that much older than I was. It was unlikely, but possible.

While monitoring him as best I could given my limited capabilities, I was aware of the visiting chefs murmuring among themselves across the room. They were clearly as confused as I was about what to do next.

Marcel didn't require CPR, but his breathing was labored and his face glistened with sweat.

The moment the doctor and his assistants arrived, I stepped away, giving them as much pertinent information as I could.

The doctor, a slim, handsome man with prematurely white hair and a calm demeanor, turned to me. "What has he ingested today, do you know?"

"Marcel tends to taste as he works," I said, feeling profoundly unhelpful. Our pastry chef's girth was testament to the appeal of his creations. He was much too careful and too diligent, however, to accidentally nibble an ingredient he shouldn't. Yet, what if? Despite the fact that everything he produced was edible, the kitchen itself was filled with items not meant for human consumption. "I've been downstairs most of the day." A second later, I remembered, and turned to the visitors. "Did he sample anything?" I gestured the act of putting food in one's mouth. Even though these men understood English quite well, I couldn't help the instinctive movement.

The four men looked at each other, Kilian and Nate shaking their heads, and Tibor shrugging. "We stopped for the noon-hour meal. He ate with us," Nate said, as though that explained it. Belatedly, I remembered that Marcel had arranged for the Navy Mess to provide lunch for our guests.

Hector's eyes went wide. "What are you saying? There was something wrong with our food?"

"That's not what I meant," I began.

"Wait." Kilian stepped forward. "He did taste more. We did." Wiggling a finger between himself, Hector, and Nate, he said, "The raspberry sauce."

Nate made a face, then held a hand to his stomach. "Yes, you are right."

Hector stared at me. "Your Marcel had us try it when Tibor was downstairs." His eyes were wild, his tone panicked. "He said there was only sugar and fruit. What was in it?"

I glanced back at Marcel's unconscious form, hoping that what he'd coughed up might actually be raspberry sauce rather than blood. "We don't know what affected Marcel; I'm simply trying to find out what may have gone on here while Bucky and I were downstairs." Another thought came to me and I turned to one of the doctor's assistants, a young man tapping information into a tablet. "I don't know Marcel's health history. Maybe he's on medication?"

The assistant nodded, not breaking his concentration from the tablet's screen. "Accessing his White House records now."

The two Secret Service agents who had accompanied the medical personnel began herding us toward the spiral staircase that would lead us down to the Butler's Pantry. "Let's let the professionals handle this," one said.

Bucky started down first. I let the visitors go next before following. As I stepped through the doorway, I gave Marcel one last glance. "Be okay," I whispered.

There were two more Secret Service agents waiting for us when we arrived in the Butler's Pantry. They politely, yet firmly, ushered our Saardiscan guests to stand against the long countertop that lined the room. Even though I'd only known the men for a couple of hours, I could sense their agitation.

Kilian whispered to Bucky. "What is happening?"

Bucky held his hand out toward me, a deferential message that Kilian ignored.

He pressed his case to Bucky. "Why are we made to wait here? Are we to be questioned?"

Bucky and I exchanged a glance. We'd both heard stories of brutal interrogations that were rumored to occur regularly in Saardisca. The men watched us with a fear that was palpable.

I took a step forward, which had the desired effect of garnering Kilian's attention. "The doctor and Secret Service will update us on Marcel's condition when they can." My words were calm, but worry for my colleague's health made my heart race in my chest and my breath come quickly.

Bucky kept his gaze on me, forcing the other man's attention. Kilian's words were clipped when he said, "We are concerned."

"Of course you are," I said. "We all are. I promise to keep you posted when we find out what happened."

I tried to project an air of control, but I was anxious. Marcel had fainted without any forewarning. And that arm . . .

I couldn't think about that now. The White House remained charged with collaborating with our Saardiscan guests and it was up to me and Bucky to shoulder that responsibility. "I'm certain that Marcel will recover and we'll find out what's ailing him. I'd rather not speculate."

Clapping my hands together the way our former chief usher, Paul Vasquez, used to when he required our cooperation, I took charge. "We planned for most of today to be an overview, an introduction to our kitchens, and orientation," I began. "I know that the next stop on your tour was supposed to be the chocolate shop. Let's hope that Marcel recovers soon, because I know he would prefer to show you that area himself. In the meantime, let's return to our main kitchen." I held out a hand toward the doorway, encouraging the others to enter ahead of me.

Kilian took a deep breath. He nodded. As he proceeded into the kitchen, the others followed. I made eye contact with one of the two Secret Service agents. "I think we're settled here," I said. "Unless you feel the need to stay."

One of the two spoke into his microphone, waited for a reply, then turned to me. "Let us know if you need anything, Chef," he said. Two seconds later they were gone.

Bucky sidled up as we made our way into the kitchen. "You've got an uphill battle on your hands with these guys," he said under his breath. "I don't think they're comfortable with a woman in charge."

"You think it's that, or that they don't like me?"

Bucky shrugged. "Does it matter?"

Kilian talked with his group in their mother language as Bucky and I decided on a plan of action.

"It bugs me that we can't understand what they're saying," Bucky said softly. "Yet you and I don't have that advantage."

"I'm sure they're unsettled by Marcel's collapse. I know I am." I bit my bottom lip. "One of the goals for this visit is to help Kilian and his team learn more about how we do things in this kitchen. Marcel was planning to handle a good chunk of that."

"It's a good thing you came up with plans for our portion," he said. "Looks like we'll be getting started on those sooner than we expected."

"There's not much choice, is there?"

Bucky lowered his voice further. "Who's brainy idea was it to host them here for two weeks, anyway?"

I ignored that and called the group to attention. "As you know, our country is in the midst of a sequester." I caught a gleam in the eyes of a couple of the Saardiscans, giving me the impression that they wanted to ask more on that topic. We could save that for later. Right now I needed to establish order.

I went on. "Because the president is entertaining fewer guests these days, we don't have an official dinner scheduled until the one for your country's presidential candidate, Kerry Freiberg. From what I understand, she'll be stopping by briefly to visit with President Hyden before she embarks on a tour of several North American cities. We'll have more than a week and a half to plan for the dinner, and I think that's plenty of time. What Bucky and I plan to do is to take you through the steps before big events, show you what we do in advance, and explain what methods we rely on to stay organized. We're also eager for this opportunity to learn from pros like yourselves."

"You Americans," Tibor said, echoing his remark from earlier, "I do not understand you."

"What don't you understand?" I strained for politeness, but this guy's attitude was getting old.

Tibor took a step toward me. His feet were planted shoulder width apart, his arms crossed in front of his chest, and his head tilted to one side in a signal I read as condescending. He offered what might have been a smile, but it was too forced, too harsh. His eyes remained tight. "We have come to visit, to learn about your country's cooking methods, correct?"

I nodded.

"In our country, we feed our leaders using a traditional menu. Very little deviation. We order our ingredients in advance, and we prepare the food for consumption. We do not have a 'main kitchen,' a 'chocolate kitchen,' a 'pastry kitchen,' or a 'navy kitchen.'" He shook his head as though the very thought of so many options disgusted him. "You may have six more kitchens you haven't even revealed to us yet. I do not care. What I care about is pleasing our country's leaders. We have been here many hours and have not prepared a single item yet."

As Tibor was delivering his speech, Kilian grew visibly agitated. He pushed past his colleague, his attention defaulting, once again, to Bucky.

"My friend speaks out of turn," Kilian said. "He is correct in that our country's chefs do not have access to the tools and resources we're seeing here, but he forgets that we are here to learn." With that, he shot a pointed look at Tibor.

"How do we learn anything when all they do is talk at us?"

"Tibor." Kilian's voice strove for calm. "Have you no patience? We have not been here a full day yet."

Tibor pointed at the kitchen clock as he faced Kilian. "Our day is almost over." Then, with a sidelong glance at me and Bucky, he lapsed into Saardiscan, his voice rising.

Happy Hector and Neutral Nate watched their colleagues in what looked like horrified disbelief, saying nothing.

Kilian grasped Tibor's forearms, hard. "Enough," he said in English. Through clenched teeth, he added, "We are guests here. Stop behaving like a spoiled young child."

Bucky nudged me. I didn't look up at him.

"I would appreciate it very much," I said, injecting authority into my voice, "if while we are working together in the White House, we all speak English."

Tibor shot me a scathing look. "We are here one day and already you want us to forsake our home language?" If we were anywhere else, I believed he would have spat on the floor.

"I'm *asking* you to keep to English as much as possible," I said, stressing the word *ask*, "because as of today, we're a team. And in order to work together, we need to keep our communication open."

"Bah." He stared at the floor and scowled.

Kilian grabbed Tibor's arm again and squeezed. "We will try our best to speak in English." In a carefully modulated tone, he switched subjects. "One of the many things I seek to know more about is your culture. I believe Marcel was attempting to share some of that with us before his unfortunate accident."

"Yes, he was," I interjected before any of the visitors could launch into another speech. "I guarantee you will all learn much about the foods we prepare and how we plan for important events. I'm hoping that in doing so, you are encouraged to share with us some of your tricks of the trade." I took a breath, watching their reactions, hoping "tricks of the trade" wasn't too much of colloquialism, and that they'd understood. "Because we're currently entertaining fewer guests for dinner, it appears as though we don't work very hard at our jobs. I assure you, we do."

I took another look at the wall clock. Not quite two thirty. Sargeant had warned me to be mindful of the fact that our guests would be suffering from jet lag and had set our first day's schedule to end at three. "The car to take you back to your hotel will be here in thirty minutes," I said. "Why don't we go over tomorrow's schedule in our remaining time, and plan to start fresh in the morning?"

When they were finally gone for the day, Bucky folded his arms and leaned against the wall. "Doesn't ever get easier around here, does it?"

CHAPTER 4

THAT NIGHT, GAV AND I SETTLED IN AT THE kitchen table to have dinner and discuss our days. He passed the Brussels sprouts to me. "Do they have a prognosis for Marcel?" he asked as I scooped a helping onto my dish. Dinner tonight was a balsamic-crusted roast pork loin with mashed potatoes and the delicious sprouts. Comfort food. Perfect for the cooler fall weather.

"I heard from him before we left for the day. He was groggy, but lucid. He's scheduled for a battery of tests tomorrow."

"And his arm?"

"Oh, it's broken all right." I pointed to a spot halfway up my forearm. "If I understood correctly, he not only dislocated his elbow, he broke both his radius and ulna, right about here."

Gav winced. "I'm sorry to hear it."

As we served ourselves and dug into our meal, Gav told me a little bit about his day. He'd gone back to work several weeks ago, after an extended medical leave and our two-day honeymoon—most of which had been spent moving his belongings into my Crystal City apartment.

I listened as he told me about how, even after weeks back on the job, training his muscles to behave the way they had before his injuries was harder work than he'd anticipated. While he talked, I remembered our wedding day and how he'd surprised me by bringing everyone I loved together for the ceremony.

I sighed.

"Uh-oh. What's wrong?" he asked.

"Nothing at all, why?"

"You've got a wistful look on your face," he said. "You seem miles away."

"I'm sorry. One of the things you said whisked me back to our wedding day in the China Room."

"No regrets about marrying me?" he asked. "The two of us lived on our own for a long time. We're still in the adjustment period as a couple."

"I think we're handling that marvelously."

He reached over to grab my hand. "Do you?"

"Absolutely." I smiled as he ran a thumb over the backs of my knuckles. "What about you?" I asked. "It had to be tough to leave your bachelor pad for this quiet area." I thought about Gav's place, closer to the bustle of D.C. I'd loved the view of the Washington Monument from his living room.

"There's no place I'd rather be than right here."

I pulled my hand away, grinning. "Your food is getting cold."

He looked as though he was about to say more when his cell phone rang. He pulled it from his pocket, gave the display a curious, confused look, then answered. "Gavin here." He pushed back from the table and stood. As he listened, he started toward the living room.

I wondered why he hadn't answered it as "Special Agent Gavin." Must be a personal call.

He stopped walking.

"When?" he asked.

He placed a finger up against his open ear, pushing the phone closer to his head. "I can barely hear you."

I watched as confusion, then pain, crossed his expression. "Tell me where he is again." He glanced around frantically. I jumped to my feet and brought him a pad of paper and pen.

With the barest of glances to thank me, he took the pen and made his way back to the table to set the paper down. He fought to cradle his cell phone between his shoulder and ear. The corners of his eyes crinkled, but not with happiness. With his jaw set, he scribbled notes, swallowing hard as he did so. He made a couple of unintelligible noises, probably to assure the person on the other end of the phone that he was taking down all the information.

Finally, he stood straight. "Are you sure you don't need me tonight?" He waited, nodding with what looked like resignation. "All right. First thing tomorrow, then. You take care of yourself until I get there."

He hung up, dropped the phone onto the tabletop, and covered his eyes with one hand for a silent moment. From upside down, I read what he'd written: GOOD SHEPHERD HOSPITAL, ROOM 350.

I'd never heard of Good Shepherd Hospital.

"What happened?" I asked.

His hand lowered from his brow to his chin. He stroked his late-in-the-day stubble. "You remember Bill and Erma?"

I did. I'd met them several months earlier when Gav and I had visited their Loudoun County winery. They'd been kind and welcoming to me, despite the fact that years ago, their daughter had been engaged to Gav. Before the marriage could take place, however, Jennifer had become the Maryland Murderer's final victim.

Bill and Erma had made the effort to remain close with

Gav, and treated him like the son they'd never had. I knew it was their way to hold onto their daughter's memory.

"Bill suffered a stroke this afternoon." Gav tapped the notes he'd scribbled. "He's stable now but the prognosis is unclear."

"You'll go," I said. I didn't phrase it as a question.

He nodded, staring across the room. I could tell he wasn't seeing anything at all. "Erma says she's doing all right. The doctors assure her that he's in good hands, but she's staying with him tonight anyway."

"She wants to watch over him herself. I understand."

Gav's eyes met mine. "You would know something about that, wouldn't you?"

I reached out and touched his arm. "I can't get away while the sequester is on—while the Saardiscans are here."

He put his hand over mine. "I know. I'll inform my team leader, then head out there in the morning."

I remembered taciturn, watchful Bill. Where Erma had been warm and eager to connect with me, Bill had held back. I didn't blame him. "I hope he's all right," I said.

Gav gave my hand a squeeze, but didn't say a word.

WHEN MY ALARM WENT OFF IN THE MORNING, I was wrapped around Gav's warm body. My arm encircled his waist, my left leg draped over his. I blinked myself awake, pulled away, and shut off the radio. As I got out of bed, I turned, noticing that Gav hadn't moved. He was still on his back, one arm beneath his head, eyes wide open as he stared at the ceiling.

"Did you get any sleep at all?" I asked.

"Some."

"Are you okay?" I asked. If I was being honest with myself, I'd have to admit that I was wondering if last night's phone call was bringing back memories of his life with Jennifer. I wondered if Erma reaching out to Gav was reminiscent of when the older couple had reached out to him at their daughter's death. Whatever Gav was going through had to be hard for him. There wasn't much I could do beyond letting him grieve in his own way and to be as supportive as I could until he found his way back to me.

"I will be," he said.

"I know."

"It's just . . ." He bolstered himself up on one elbow to face me. In his rumpled T-shirt, with morning stubble and bed-tousled hair, he was truly the most attractive man I'd ever seen. Not only that—he became increasingly more handsome by the day.

I sat down on the bed next to him. "This brings back memories?"

His brow came together and he gave a quick headshake. "The opposite, in fact. Right before you woke up I was thinking about how difficult things have been for Erma and Bill. How they probably couldn't have made it without having each other. How lucky they are that they do. How lucky to have had one another for so many years. Life can be so full of anguish. But when sorrows are shared . . ." He reached out for my hand, and held tightly. "Thank you for being here for me."

I leaned over to kiss him lightly on the lips. "Always."

"YOU WANT A WHAT?"

Tom MacKenzie, head of the Presidential Protective Division of the Secret Service, the PPD, practically choked with laughter.

We were seated across from one another in Tom's West Wing office. I was allowed broad access to the Secret Service and to Tom because of the many situations I'd been involved with in the past. Where once Tom and his staff had worked to exclude me and even belittle my contributions, he now grudgingly accepted my peculiar talents as part of the job.

"I think it would be smart—forward-thinking, even—to post a linguist in the kitchen while the Saardiscan contingent is here. To translate what they're saying."

"Don't they speak English?"

"They do, very well."

"Stir that, bake this, pass the artichokes." He cocked his head to one side. "What more do you need?"

I sat up a little straighter, my spine zinging at the condescension. "They carry on extended conversations that neither Bucky nor I understand."

"So? They're friends. They probably have a lot of things to discuss."

"It isn't right."

"Have you asked them to speak English in the kitchen?"

"I have, but they're still lapsing into Saardiscan. Quite a lot, actually."

Tom shook his head. "Has it been too long since we've uncovered a conspiracy in the White House? Are you bored and looking for a little excitement?"

"What is up with you today?" I asked him. "Don't get me wrong, I know how sarcastic you can be when you're in that kind of mood, but this seems over the top, even for you."

He pulled at his nose, not looking at me. My words had struck home, and I watched as he collected himself.

"There is no such thing as nonessential staff when it comes to protecting the president and his family," he said. "Even though my workforce hasn't been cut during this sequester, there have been ripple effects from personnel shortages in other departments. Tensions are high."

"I get that you're under pressure, but it isn't fair to take it out on me."

"You're right. I'm sorry." The words were there, but the tone was perfunctory. "Thing is, Ollie, while the government is running shorthanded, this is a ludicrous request."

I bit the insides of my cheeks. "Hardly ludicrous," I said. "The decision was made to honor our promise to

Saardisca and host their team. Seems to me that if this ini-
tiative was so crucial that the sequester couldn't touch it,
we ought to give it its best shot at success."

"And you think a linguist will do that? Seriously, Ollie?
Don't you believe they have a right to private conversation?"

Of course I did. Yet, while we all worked together in the
White House kitchen, I needed to know what was going
on. How could I tell Tom that I had an uneasy feeling about
them? He would immediately claim I was chasing conspiracies again.

"Bucky and I don't have the luxury of private conversation," I said. "And with Marcel out, he and I are stretched
thin."

"Talk to me about being stretched thin." He shook his
head. "Your request is denied. Totally out of the question.
Besides, the visitors won't be here long."

"Two weeks."

He directed a baleful expression at me. "You've been
through tougher situations than this one. You'll adjust. Now,
if there's nothing else?"

CHAPTER 5

I RETURNED TO THE KITCHEN TO FIND BUCKY instructing the Saardiscan team on how to use one of our tilt-skillets. The four men stood around the waist-high, stainless steel device looking confused. I got the impression they'd never seen one before. That would be a shame, because the tilt-skillet was a workhorse. I didn't know what we'd do without it.

The men glanced up at my entrance, but only Bucky acknowledged me. In the middle of a demonstration, he flicked on the heat, then poured a generous glug of olive oil into the mechanism's wide, flat base. "Let's say we're making a chowder."

At their blank looks, he clarified. "Soup."

All four men nodded.

"We often need to prepare enough soup to feed more than a hundred guests."

The chefs grunted sounds of disbelief.

"More than a hundred?" Kilian seemed to be the group's spokesperson. "That is an exaggeration, no? Yesterday, your pastry chef, Marcel, showed us photos of many events held here, but the quantity he spoke of could not be accurate. Much of what your government shares with the world is propaganda, is it not?"

Bucky's mouth quirked up on one side as he spread the oil around the tilt-skillet's bottom. "Whatever Marcel showed you was not propaganda."

He reached around and pulled up a large bowl of ingredients and tossed the contents into the hot oil, making the chopped onions, green and red peppers, and carrots dance in the sizzling oil.

Tibor pretended to be paying attention to the chowder-making, but I could tell he was more interested in my presence. I couldn't fathom why, but Nate and Hector noticed him watching me and nudged one another.

Bucky could tell he was losing his audience. He raised his voice and spoke with more animation. "We've prepared dinner here for far more than a hundred guests. In some instances, we've entertained more than a thousand. I'm sure whatever Marcel showed you was from one of our many successful gatherings."

Kilian, who appeared to be the only member of his team actively paying attention to Bucky, shook his head with vehemence. "This kitchen is too small to prepare food to serve more than fifty, perhaps sixty diners." His soft face creased into a knowing smile. "We were warned before we left Saardisca that you might try to sway us into believing of your country's wealth and privilege by sharing outlandish stories."

I took a step forward. "We have no reason to lie to you about the dinners we prepare. And I have no personal motivation to try to convince you that we're telling the truth. Our goal here—at least the way we understood it—was to forge a bond between our countries by sharing foods our citizens love."

Tibor gave a haughty chuckle. "Yes," he said, "and that is why you brag about your phantom parties."

Bucky and I exchanged a look.

"Phantom parties?" Bucky repeated. "I assure you, we work very hard to bring sparkling events to life."

"What about the queen of England's visit here? Or that of Germany's chancellor? Certainly those have been publicized in your country. Do you doubt your own broadcasters?" I said it with a smile, but I was beginning to suspect that this really *was* all news to them.

"If such events took place, we would have heard about them. Of course we know that your president entertains guests from other countries, but the scope and the extravagance you're suggesting . . ." Kilian shrugged. "Let me simply say that I find your descriptions too incredible to be true."

"I understand that we approach entertaining differently," I said. It was becoming clear to me that these men came from a culture so far removed from ours that things we took for granted seemed fantastic and impossible. "But by the time you depart to return to your country, I hope you have a clearer understanding about how we do things here."

Bucky chimed in. "And we have a clearer understanding as to how entertainment is handled in your country."

"Well said." I smiled. Kilian, however, maintained his skeptical expression. Tibor glared. Only Happy Hector smiled back at me.

By now, the sizzling ingredients filled the room with mouthwatering aromas. I pulled a long spoon from one of the drawers and began to stir the bits around. From the shocked looks on the visiting chefs' faces I recognized I'd done something to surprise them.

"Is there a problem?" I asked.

Hector's dark eyes were as wide as doughnuts. His mouth opened and he made a noise that sounded like a strangled half laugh. Tibor sputtered and pointed. "That is not yours."

I'd stopped stirring when I'd noticed their reactions. Now I picked the spoon up and looked at it. "What do you mean? You saw me pull this out from the drawer. Whose do you think it is?"

"Not the spoon," Tibor said. "That is Mr. Bucky's food creation. You should not be interfering with it."

Words failed me for about two heartbeats. "In this kitchen," I began, "we work as a team."

Kilian gave me an indulgent look. "Then how is the president to know who made the *most* delicious food?" At this, he gestured to Bucky with his eyes. "And who is responsible for the lesser offerings?" He shifted his gaze to me.

I rubbed my forehead. We were in for a long two weeks, indeed.

PETER EVERETT SARGEANT FOLDED HIS HANDS across the top of his desk. "They are a patriarchal society," he said with exaggerated patience. "We knew that before they arrived."

I treated him to a beleaguered sigh. "I'm simply taken aback by their disregard for my authority."

"Are you suggesting that this arrangement is too much for you?" Sargeant raised an eyebrow. "I'd hasten to remind you that you've faced more difficult challenges in the past. Tut, tut. You're not getting soft on me, are you?"

"Of course not." Bristling, I was reminded of Tom's similar statement earlier this morning. I chose my next words with care. "I'm not here to whine and complain, but I do think it's worth your knowing what Bucky and I are dealing with."

"Indeed. Your assistant is having trouble engaging the visitors? They aren't respecting him?"

"They are, as a matter of fact. But I believe it's because he's male."

Sargeant waited. I could have sworn he was amused.

"You don't intend to help me out here, do you?" I asked.

Did his eyes twinkle? Or was it my imagination? "If there's one thing I've learned about you, Ms. Paras, it's that you rarely require my assistance."

In a flash, I heard myself and felt ashamed. Sargeant wasn't saying it in so many words, but the fractious chefs who were inhabiting my kitchen were my responsibility. It was up to me to find common ground.

Sure, Sargeant could sit these men down and impress on them—again—that I was in charge and that they needed to respect my authority. But the beliefs they accepted as part of their culture and years of chauvinistic upbringing weren't about to be invalidated by one lecture from our chief usher.

I needed to establish my authority, to lead by example, and hope they'd pick up on the lessons.

Talk about on-the-job training.

Sargeant shifted, sitting up straighter. "In other business, I understand Marcel remains hospitalized, undergoing tests."

"Have you heard when he might return?"

Sargeant shook his head. "I'd expected an update this morning. You will keep me posted if he gets in touch?"

I agreed and made ready to stand.

He sniffed loudly and stared pointedly. "Where are you going?"

"I thought we'd covered everything you wanted to discuss."

"You would be mistaken."

I resettled myself.

Sargeant sniffed again, then steepled his fingers in front of his nose. "I have additional information for you."

I waited.

"It's about the Saardiscan elections."

I remembered his jab about keeping up with headlines. "Go ahead."

Sargeant leaned forward, hands atop his blotter. "In my

position as chief usher, I am privy to some intelligence. Not a great deal of it, but from time to time, I am granted access to information I need to know in order to perform my job to the best of my abilities."

"What are you trying to tell me?"

"You understand, Ms. Paras, that I am choosing to divulge certain things to you, trusting that you'll keep them confidential."

"You know I will."

He nodded. "Our agencies' sources have reason to believe that Kerry Freiberg may have a better chance at winning the election than the Saardiscan administration is allowing the world to believe."

That *was* news. "What does that have to do with me? Or our chef guests?"

He leaned back again, watching me with his tiny, squirrel-like eyes. "As you know, Ms. Freiberg is a revolutionary in her country. She wants to establish alliances with other countries, and has expressed her willingness to negotiate on everything from arms to trade."

"I thought that was why she had no chance of winning."

"It seems the winds of change are blowing in Saardisca." Sargeant folded his hands on his desk again. "Because her chances seem to be improving, President Hyden wants to do his utmost to make her feel welcome while she's here. He's hopeful that perceived support from the United States will be enough to help her win the election."

"Sounds promising," I said.

"Our job is to ensure that all goes perfectly smoothly during her visit. I understand that working among men who dispute your authority doesn't create an optimal environment, but I urge you to put your issues aside for the greater good. If doing so requires that Buckminster Reed take charge of the kitchen for the duration of their stay, so be it."

My jaw went slack. "You didn't really just say that, did you?"

He leaned forward over his hands. "I am not suggesting that you give up control of your kitchen, merely that you do what's in the best interests of the country. If these visitors respond better to your assistant, why not find a way to make that work? Wouldn't that be better than fighting with them for the next two weeks?"

I was speechless. Struck dumb.

When I didn't respond, he lowered his voice. "Ms. Paras, I am not saying that this is your only option. If you can get these men to respect your authority in the short period of time that they're here, I will personally congratulate you. I'm merely suggesting that you see the problem logically. And that you do whatever you must to achieve our goal."

"Are you suggesting that the ends justify the means?"

"On occasion, they do. This may be one of those times."

"I will make this work. My way," I said. I felt the blood rise into my cheeks and I took pleasure in the fact that Sargeant seemed the tiniest bit alarmed. "Count on it."

CHAPTER 6

I STOLE A FEW PRECIOUS MINUTES TO PUT IN A
call to Gav, to ask about how things were going with Bill
and Erma. His phone went to voice mail. I didn't leave a
message, knowing he would return the call when he could.

I then hurried up to the pastry kitchen, taking a quick
look around for the raspberry sauce that the Saardiscans
and Marcel had all tasted. None of the other men had
fallen ill, so I didn't believe the sauce was at fault, but I did
want to get a closer look at it.

I found it in a small, open container, sitting on a countertop. This probably should have been refrigerated, but in
the excitement and chaos from the day before, no one
would have thought to put it away. Four spoons sat next to
the container, and it was clear from the smeared red mark-
ings on their bowls that these had been used for sampling.

What I wanted, most of all, was to reassure myself that the
red fluid I'd seen Marcel cough up was not blood. I dunked
one of the spoons and spread the viscous goo onto an empty
plate. Not that I could remember specifically, but the color

looked familiar. I heaved a small sigh of relief. Perhaps Marcel had simply had a moment of light-headedness and there was nothing more worrisome about his health than that.

The doctors would have a diagnosis soon, I was sure. Trouble was, I wasn't the most patient person in the world.

I spent a little time tidying up the pastry kitchen before heading back downstairs.

"How are things going?" I asked Bucky when I returned.

The four visiting chefs were hard at work around the center counter and it appeared as though they were busy with preparations for tonight's dinner offerings. We had a few guests coming this evening, including the speaker of the house and the senate minority leader. They were charged with corralling members of their respective parties to cooperate to end this sequester before we entered another week of cuts.

Everyone glanced up at my question. Kilian waved his colleagues back to work as though my return to the kitchen was of no consequence.

"Good, you're here," Bucky said with undisguised relief. To the chefs he said, "We'll be right back, don't worry." They didn't look terribly concerned. Bucky motioned me to follow. He headed out of the kitchen, through the corridors, and across the basement hall into the White House chocolate shop.

He shut the door to the little room once we were both inside. This windowless, close room was lined on one side with a countertop. Although there were cabinets, drawers, and sufficient kitchen equipment to produce fine and fancy chocolates here, the space lacked any sort of personality or decoration. It was bland, tiny, utilitarian.

"Uh-oh," I said. "What happened?"

"Got a call from Marcel. He wanted to talk with you. I thought you were upstairs with Sargeant but when they patched me through, your meeting with him was over."

"I took a detour coming back. What did he want to talk about? Did the doctors deliver bad news?"

"He needed surgery on his arm." Bucky's face was a mixture of worry and strain as he forced himself to speak slowly. "And he'll be in a cast for at least six weeks."

This *was* bad news. "Oh no."

Bucky's agitation grew. "You and I were depending on Marcel to shoulder some of the work during the Saardiscans' stay. Not that I'm blaming Marcel—of course not— but we had a structure planned that's completely blown now. It's enough work to prepare all the First Family's meals without tripping over four more bodies while we do it. What are we going to do with them? We've been able to scramble since the accident, but I don't know how you and I will be able to maintain control without help. Not to mention that there's no way we can cover desserts properly."

Bucky's words had tumbled out quickly and I agreed with everything he'd said. Not that I had any answers for him. I ran a hand through my hair. "In other news, I talked with Tom this morning about getting a linguist to join us in the kitchen."

"I can guess by the look on your face how well that went over."

"I'll talk with Sargeant about arranging to have one of Marcel's assistants return for the duration."

Bucky shook his head.

"What?" I asked.

"Not happening," he said. "When I called up there and found out you'd already left, I decided to ask Sargeant about it myself."

"And he said no?"

Bucky folded his arms across his chest. "He told us to find other ways to keep the visiting team busy."

"We'll manage. I don't know how yet, but we will." I took in a breath. "I may wait a bit then take another run at Sargeant about getting a pastry chef back on board."

"Good luck with that."

"The Saardiscans are here; we're stuck with them. Nothing we can do to change that. What you and I have to do is find a way to keep order in the kitchen and the First Family happy and well fed. In the meantime, I think we ought to try to persuade our guests to lighten up and take in the town as tourists. A little free time couldn't hurt."

"They don't strike me as the type who know how to lighten up."

I chose not to share Sargeant's suggestion about Bucky taking charge of the kitchen, with me assuming more of a backseat role. Even though I had no intention of implementing the idea, right about now my assistant was too worked up for me to mention it. "Let's take this one day at a time, shall we?"

SARGEANT SENT AN E-MAIL, DETAILING SPECIF-ics for candidate Kerry Freiberg's dinner. To my surprise, it had been decided that the affair would be hosted at Blair House.

Blair House was an opulent residence on Pennsylvania Avenue across from the White House. It was purchased by the United States during World War II when President Franklin Delano Roosevelt decided that guests were best accommodated elsewhere. Legend has it that this determination was made after Eleanor Roosevelt happened upon frequent guest Winston Churchill wandering the White House corridors at three in the morning, looking for Franklin to chat with.

From that point on, Blair House became the first choice for providing dignitaries with elegant accommodations. Through the years, adjacent buildings were acquired, walls were torn down, and renovations were made, turning four separate structures into one stately residence. Harry Truman and his family lived in Blair House for a good portion of his presidency while the White House—which had fallen into sad disrepair—was gutted and refurbished.

According to Sargeant, the location was ideal for Kerry Freiberg's visit. Blair House provided an informal and warm setting to host dinner for the visiting dignitary without raising the ire of those who would question the president entertaining at the White House during the government shutdown.

Later that day, Bucky and I presented a new agenda to our chefs, one that allowed them a bit more free time.

"Our original schedule had the four of you here every day, from about eight in the morning until about four in the afternoon." I made eye contact with them as I spoke. "And you all had rotating time off." At this point, I hadn't told them anything they didn't already know. "With Marcel out of the picture, Bucky and I have come up with a new plan, one that will give you more free time to explore the city."

I went on to cover the specifics of the schedule, with Bucky chiming in to clarify as needed.

Their reaction was mixed. Kilian nodded often. I thought I detected a gleam of interest in his expression.

"Remember," I said, "this is only a possibility. If we're able to bring back Marcel, even if he's stuck working one-handed for a while, we'll revert to our original plan."

Nate and Hector kept nodding as Bucky and I talked, but otherwise showed no reaction. I got the feeling they didn't completely comprehend.

Tibor, however, understood. He practically scalded me with a look of disgust. "We do not come here to waste time. We came here to benefit Saardisca." He flung his hands up, fingers extended like ten tense exclamation points. He cast his gaze about the room, looking for support from his colleagues.

Hector and Nate exchanged a confused glance and whispered to each other, but I couldn't make out what they were saying.

Kilian tried to quiet Tibor's rant. "This could be a very good chance for us," he said in a calming voice. He then lapsed into Saardiscan and spoke so quickly that I couldn't even get a sense of what the message was. Was he chastising his colleague? Was he in agreement with Tibor but asking the man to cooperate? There were times I believed I could understand anyone, no matter the language. Body movement, tone, and expression all combine to provide context. This was not one of those times.

When Kilian finished his speed-speak, he turned to me and asked if he and I could have a moment alone. Tibor folded his arms and looked away.

Surprised by the request, I agreed, leading the Saardiscan back toward the refrigeration area. "This should be sufficiently private," I said. "What's on your mind?"

Kilian's smile rose and fell quickly in that fake way people do when they're working hard to minimize tension. "You must forgive my friend Tibor. He is a master chef in his province, as I am in mine. It was difficult to decide between us who was to be in charge during this voyage, but the decision was made to make me our official leader. This has not set well with Tibor."

That explained a good deal of the man's surliness. "Go on," I said.

"If he were in charge of making decisions for all of us, he would never agree to take time away from working."

"And if we didn't allow you access to the White House? What could he do then?"

"With Tibor in charge, he would no doubt find work for us to do in our hotel rooms. You must forgive him. He is driven to succeed. He will stop at nothing to see that we achieve many goals here."

"I have no doubt that success, whatever you take that to mean, will be yours as long as we work together," I said. "Our goal here, remember, is to exchange knowledge and forge a bond. We don't intend to submit a report to your government on any of you. A little time off isn't going to hurt anyone."

Kilian's expression shifted in a way that I didn't understand. He glanced back the way we'd come, as though to assure himself that no one else was nearby. Lowering his voice, he stepped closer. "You, Bucky, and Marcel have been kind to us. I realize we have only been here for little more than a day, but I sense no animosity from any of you."

"Did you expect to?"

His expression was earnest. "Of course." He held both hands out. "The kitchen is a place of great competition. Only he who works hard to be the best will survive."

"Or she."

His brow furrowed. "May I speak plainly?"

"Of course."

"You are female."

"So I've noticed."

He either didn't understand the humor or chose to ignore it, and continued without missing a beat. "In our country, females rarely hold such a position. We expected to encounter more difficulty with you. How is it that you have come to this level? How is it that you are above men in your field?"

"I don't understand your confusion," I began. "I may be the executive chef here, but there are many women—hundreds, if not thousands—who hold positions far more impressive than mine. Not only chefs, of course. There are female lawmakers, scientists, artists, ambassadors, and businesswomen all over this country. All over the world, in fact. You can't possibly be surprised by that. Saardisca has a woman running for president, for heaven's sake. You do know that, don't you?"

He waved that away. "She will not win."

I thought about my discussion with Sargeant earlier. "How can you be so sure?"

"If she were to gain the presidency, it would be only because many men have helped put her in that position. And when she is there, they will demand a share of her power."

"That's very cynical. Maybe her message is resonating with voters more than you realize."

"The changes she speaks of would be wonderful for our citizens," he said. "But how can I believe that she is not merely a puppet?"

"I don't know," I said, for I truly didn't. "All I can tell you is that when I vote in an election, I choose the candidate whose views most closely align with my own. Maybe I'm naïve, but I tend to believe that most men and women running for office do so because they hope to improve the world."

"We should all be so naïve," he said. "When we have access to your news," he said in a hushed voice, "we are told it is propaganda. That none of it is true. And yet . . ." He held his palms up. "Here you are."

"Are you telling me that your government sent you here, not knowing that you'd be working with me?"

"We were told that your presence in the kitchen is a publicity stunt to allow women to believe that they have potential. Giving them such hopes encourages them to work harder at their jobs. We were told that life here is much the way it is at home: Women work but they cannot achieve positions of power."

"I think that's deplorable," I said.

I don't know what it was—the look on his face at that moment, or some vague sense that he agreed with my pronouncement—that spurred me to ask, "What do *you* think about that?"

Kilian's eyes grew wide. He looked as though he was about to share a confidence, but stopped himself with three fingers to his lips. "I will appreciate the chance to see your city and make good use of this 'time off' you have described. My colleagues may not agree with your decision, but I am in charge and they will abide by my instructions."

"I'm sorry our schedules had to change."

He said, "I am not so sorry," which surprised me. His expression grew troubled. "You will keep this conversation in confidence?"

"Yes," I said, "no worries."

He held out his hand for me to shake. I did.

Maybe I was reading a lot into the gesture, but I said, "I hope you find more about our country to appreciate. I wish you luck in your exploration."

This time his smile was genuine. "I will look forward to discussing further experiences with you."

CHAPTER 7

I MET CYAN FOR A QUICK BITE AFTER WORK
that evening. My young red-haired assistant with the ever-
changing-color eyes agreed to meet at a local salad place
before we visited Marcel in the hospital.

"So, wait," she said after we'd started eating. "These
guys—coming from a country that prefers to keep its citizens
in the dark about the rest of the world—are angry because they
have *more* free time to explore the capital of the United States?"

I speared a thin slice of Parmesan cheese and a bunch of
arugula. "I think it's more complicated than that. They're in
a new environment, with new rules. I think they're simply
uncomfortable here and they're taking it out on me because,
well, I'm the woman in charge."

"Which is also a point of contention."

I nodded and took a bite.

"Maybe I'm glad I'm not working there right now."

After chewing and swallowing, I took a drink of water.
"I'd love to have you back, Cyan. Right now, especially.
How are things going?"

"Without a paycheck? Without knowing how soon I'll be back at work?" She shrugged and snagged a big chunk of salad. "Nerve-wracking. I've offered to substitute or to take temporary work at some of the local upscale places, but no luck. So many people out of work these days. The competition is tough."

"You'd think with your resume that restaurants would jump at the chance to take you on, even temporarily."

"That's the thing. The transient nature of my status makes them leery. They know I could get called back at any time."

"Leaving them with an opening to fill, again," I said.

"I have to tell you, this situation makes me wonder." She fiddled with her fork without looking up. "About where I'm going."

The greens in my stomach twisted into a knotty ball. "What do you mean?"

Still not meeting my eyes, she said, "Bucky is your first in command. Believe me, I get it. He deserves that. But he's not moving. And you're not, either. Not that I want you to." Shaking her head, she finally looked up. "This is coming out wrong."

"Not if it's what's on your mind," I said. "If something is bothering you about the workplace, I need to hear it. What's going on?"

"You're only a few years older than I am and you're the executive chef at the White House. Where am I?"

"You're an essential member of the White House kitchen team. You're well-respected and you've got amazing talent."

"But where, exactly, is my career going?"

She had blue contacts in today, and when she stared across the high table at me, I could see behind them into the depths of her eyes.

I put my fork down. "This conversation hasn't come up solely because of the sequester, has it?"

She shook her head.

"You've been thinking about this for some time, haven't you?"

Nodding, she put her fork down, too. "I look at you, Ollie. You have it all. You're at the top of your career, you have the love of your life, you're content and settled and strong. I'm still struggling to find my place in the world."

"And that place isn't the White House kitchen?"

She wrinkled her nose. "I need to broaden my horizons. This job takes everything from us. Our time, our lives, our hearts. I don't know that I have any more to give."

I started to say something, but she reached across and patted my hand, stopping me.

"Not you, Ollie. You're always generous with compliments and you do, truly, make those of us working for you feel valued. Best of all, I know you believe what you're saying. But maybe I don't believe it. Maybe I need to prove to myself that I'm capable of more."

My heart sank with every word out of her mouth, but I had to admit I understood. Perhaps that's why it cut me to hear it. Cyan was leaving us.

"How soon?" I asked.

"I've been wanting to talk to you about this for quite some time," she said with a tiny smile. "I've only finally found the nerve. But because I want to take my time and find the right fit, probably not very soon. Don't tell anyone, okay?"

"What about Bucky? Does he know?"

Cyan gave a breathy laugh. "Yeah."

"I figured. You two have become pretty tight over the years."

"We all have," she said.

"That's absolutely true." Though her decision made me profoundly sad, I would do whatever I could to help. "We will miss you, Cyan. More than you can ever know. Take all the time you need, okay?"

The bottoms of her eyes had gone red. "Thanks for understanding."

MARCEL HAD SEVERAL FRIENDS VISITING WHEN we arrived, so Cyan and I didn't get a lot of time to talk with him alone. His surgery had gone well and his arm was expected to heal even though they'd had to insert metal pins for stability.

We'd brought him some chocolate from a local shop. When Marcel opened the wrappings and saw the store name, he turned up his nose. "I make confections far superior to these," he said.

Cyan and I shared a grin.

"Looks like you're back to normal," I said.

His distaste for the store-bought chocolates didn't stop him from sampling one. He popped it into his mouth, then snagged a second piece before offering the box to his guests to share.

"What happened?" I asked Marcel as his friends talked among themselves. "Do the doctors have any idea why you passed out?"

Still enjoying the first chocolate, with great mouth movements and an appreciative eye roll, he shook his head. "Thank you so much, my Olivia and Cyan. You are both too kind to come visit. Yes," he said, with a sheepish look, "we know why I lost consciousness."

Cyan and I waited.

Again, a flash of embarrassment. "I have not made a habit of sharing medical information."

"I don't mean to pry," I said.

"No, of course not. What I mean to say is that I had not yet informed you, nor the White House doctors, that I have recently been prescribed a medication for high blood pressure. Unfortunately, I miscalculated the dosage." He gave an elegant shrug, considering he had one arm jammed into his chest. "I must stay here until they ensure that my vitals remain stable." He took a deep sniff, then popped the second chocolate into his mouth. "Dark chocolate. My favorite."

"It sounds as though you'll be discharged soon."

"We are hopeful for tomorrow morning. That is, assuming the results from today's tests come clear. You know as well as I do, Olivia, that we who cook for the president cannot be found to be carrying illness. They have run extensive tests."

Cyan had gone to the other side of Marcel's bed. "It's good to be careful," she said, patting his uninjured arm. "Like Ollie, I never want to pry, but I hope you'll keep us updated."

"I certainly will," he said. "And you may repeat this information to Monsieur Sargeant and to Bucky, and others in the staff. If word of my misstep helps to prevent someone else from making such a mistake, I am happy to share."

He smacked his lips, eyeing the box of chocolates, which were now being devoured across the room. "This is not how I anticipated my week."

"When you're feeling better," I said, "I hope you'll be able to return to the White House."

He held up his right arm—at least as far as he was able to. "With this? How can I be of any use to anyone?"

"We're putting in another request for one of your assistants to take the lead while you're out, but you know how much more we'd love having you back. Even if all you do is oversee the visiting chefs' efforts from time to time during the day, that would be a huge help."

Marcel's dark face split into a deep grin. "Then I shall look forward to returning to work as soon as the doctors and our esteemed chief usher allow."

I felt a great weight lift off me. "Wonderful," I said.

Cyan and I made a little more small talk, but because Marcel's friends seemed to be eager to get back to their visit, and because any further delay might result in Marcel being deprived of more chocolate, we said good-bye and promised to check in on him again soon.

CHAPTER 8

MRS. WENTWORTH STEPPED OUT OF HER APART-
ment as I was unlocking my door. "And how are things at
the White House during this sequester?" she asked.

"Has it been that long since we've talked?"

Twisting her mouth to one side, she gave me a long,
appraising look. "Seems to me now that you're married,
you don't have time for us old folks anymore. I don't think
I've talked to you more than twice since my wedding."

She and the apartment building's handyman, Stanley,
had tied the knot shortly after Gav and I had. Just as I had
kept my name, Olivia Paras, she'd kept hers. I was happy
about that. To me, she would always be Mrs. Wentworth.

"The sequester is keeping me busier than I'd expected,"
I said.

"Where's your ball and chain?"

I laughed. "I'm not sure he'd be too thrilled with that
moniker."

"That's what they are, though," she said. Even across

the corridor, I could see the twinkle in her eyes. "Always keeping us home, slave to the stove."

"You and Stan eat out almost every night," I said.

She brushed a stray white hair off her forehead, causing her cascade of bracelets to jangle down her arm. "*Pfft.* If we don't complain about our husbands, they'll think we have it too easy."

I crossed the short space between us and spoke softly. "But you and I both know we are the two luckiest women on the planet, don't we?"

"Shush." She slid a glance toward her apartment, as though afraid Stanley might hear. "Don't want him to catch on."

"I'm sure he already has."

My cell phone buzzed in my purse. As I dug it out, I bade Mrs. Wentworth a good night and pulled the device out to answer. It was Gav.

Part of me was thrilled to hear from him. Part of me was disappointed. A call this late in the evening meant that he probably wouldn't be home tonight.

I shut the apartment door before answering. "Hey," I said.

"It's good to hear your voice, Ollie." He sounded tired and worn, but not distraught.

"How is Bill?" I asked. "Any change?"

Gav took an extra second to answer. "He's stable," he said, but something in the way he hesitated made me wonder.

"But you're staying out there tonight?"

Again the hesitation. "I am. That okay with you?"

"Of course. You need to be with them right now."

"It seems I do."

"There's something you're not telling me."

He expelled a quick breath. "Nothing that can't wait. I'll be home as soon as I can. You know I love you, right?"

"Yeah, I do. And I love you back."

As much as I wanted to bring him up to speed about

Cyan and Marcel, and get his read on both matters, I could tell from the sound of his voice that he needed rest. And probably a clearer mind than he had at the moment.

"I'll see you tomorrow, Ollie. I promise."

"I'll hold you to it. Take care of yourself, okay?"

I could almost see him smile. "You, too."

"MS. PARAS? MR. REED?"

Bucky and I glanced up—as did our four guests—to see our chief usher and his assistant in the doorway.

We'd been in the middle of learning how to put together a Saardiscan dish involving cabbage, ground chicken, and rice. I wiped my hands on my apron and made my way over to him. "Peter, Margaret," I began, "I'm surprised to see you down here."

Margaret nodded acknowledgment, but remained mum.

Keeping his hands folded in front of his waist—a Peter Everett Sargeant move if there ever was one—he raced his gaze over everyone in the room. It took only a second or two, but he settled on Kilian. Lifting the edges of his lips in what should have been a smile, he continued, "Good morning, everyone. I trust you are enjoying your experience here in our kitchen?"

All four men nodded, but didn't reply.

"Ms. Paras and Mr. Reed approached me about the difficulties we're facing here with Marcel's absence." Again, the non-smile. "It is unfortunate that due to circumstances beyond my control, and despite multiple impassioned requests, I am unable to reinstate Marcel's assistant, even temporarily."

"Peter," I said, "isn't this a topic we ought to discuss in your office?"

Or *anywhere* more private than this? Such an announcement should not be made to the visitors without informing staff first.

His eyes flashed at the interruption. "What you are

unaware of, Ms. Paras, is that your colleague here, Kilian"—
he rolled his hand toward the Saardiscan chef—"is a man of
many talents."

"Don't you think we should—"

Sargeant talked right over me. "Not only is he considered
the top chef in his country"—at this, Tibor made a disagree-
able noise, then tried to cover it with a cough—"he is an
undisputed master with regard to pastries and desserts."

"That's good to know—" I worked to get a word in
edgewise.

Sargeant nodded to Margaret. "We can thank my assistant for her diligence in discovering this information."

Margaret beamed at Sargeant, then cast her eyes around
the room expectantly, her smile fading ever so slightly at
the lack of reaction. Did she assume we'd all burst into
applause?

Hector and Nate stared at us with uneasy expressions.
Tibor shifted his weight, sending hard glances at Kilian,
whose red cheeks grew ever brighter.

Sargeant turned to me. "We're very fortunate to have
Kilian with us, aren't we, Ms. Paras?"

In a wordless demand to know where this was going, I
glared at Sargeant. "Yes, very."

Facing the group, he continued, "Of course, our fervent
hope is that Marcel rejoins the kitchen soon, but until he is
given the all-clear, we're hoping that you, Kilian, will take
over the pastry kitchen in his stead."

Whether these men knew what "in his stead" meant or
not, didn't matter. I did. Unable to stop myself, I gasped.
"Peter."

He turned to me again, speaking quietly through clenched
teeth. "I know what I'm doing."

I pulled my lips in tightly. I really would have preferred
to shout.

"A word, Peter?" I asked.

He ignored me, continuing to share details about how

the teams' schedule would change—yet again—and how much everyone was looking forward to sampling the Saardiscan national delicacies. All the while, Margaret glowered at me with a steely imperative to back off.

So tightly wound and laser focused on what was wrong with this picture, I barely heard what Sargeant was saying. The Saardiscans listened with rapt, occasionally confused, expressions. Finally, the chief usher's cadence alerted me that he was winding down.

"If you have any questions," he said, "please feel free to contact my assistant. She'll bring your concerns directly to my attention."

When they turned to leave, I touched Sargeant's arm. "I need a moment of your time."

He blinked at me, eyes glinting. "I thought you might. One minute, Ms. Paras. That's all I have." To his assistant, he said, "Margaret, I will meet you upstairs."

She still hadn't said a word, but her body language communicated her disappointment at the dismissal. Being the perfect assistant, however, she did as she was told.

I followed Sargeant through the pantry and into the Center Hall. "Map Room," I said.

He didn't argue.

The Map Room's soft, ivory-toned walls and understated décor suited the mood I strove for. Plus, it was one of the closest private rooms across from the kitchen.

The minute the door closed behind us, I exploded. "What was that all about?"

"I'm certain I don't need to remind you that as chief usher, I manage personnel issues among White House staff. Are you questioning my authority in this matter?"

"Of course not," I said. "Everyone knows you have every right to hire and fire at will. But just because Kilian is a chef with pastry experience doesn't necessarily mean he ought to take over. Do you really believe it's a good idea to hand over that level of control? To a stranger?"

"This was not my decision."

"Whose was it?"

"This came down from the highest levels."

"Quit with the ambiguous-speak, Peter. It's me you're talking to. Are you saying President Hyden made this decision?"

He flexed his chin. "No. This comes from the chief of staff."

"Do you have any idea what kind of security breach this is? It's one thing to have visitors *assisting* with food that the president and his guests consume. It's wholly another to have them in charge of an entire course with no oversight. Am I the only person who sees this?"

"Certainly not, Ms. Paras, and I'll thank you to calm yourself. You and I don't set policy here. Nor are we ultimately in charge of decisions such as this. The team you're working with has been vetted by both Saardiscan authorities and by our Secret Service."

I paced in a small circle, my anger compelling me to move, to fight for what I knew was right.

"What about the way you handled the situation?" I flung a hand toward the kitchen. "You didn't think I deserved a heads-up before you announced it to the Saardiscans?"

"Would it have made a difference?"

I wanted to take him by his perfect lapels and shake some sense into him.

He tilted his head in what could have been condescension, but in the moment, looked more like solidarity. "We would have had this fight in my office before I talked with the group instead of afterward," he said.

I scratched an eyebrow, realizing that Sargeant wasn't arguing with me. That he'd been put in the same situation, and we were both stuck dealing with it.

"I would have preferred a heads-up," I said in a quieter voice.

He gave me a withering glare. "I imagine you would

have. But this was out of my hands and I'm tied up with meetings until nightfall. It was now, like this, or let you swing in the wind all day without answers."

I was so full of fury I didn't know where to begin.

"Let's hope Marcel is able to return to duty soon, which would render this decision moot," Sargeant said, and I recognized it for what it was—an attempt to find common ground. "Until then, I have faith that you will find a way to make this situation work to the best of your abilities." He pushed up the sleeve of his suit jacket and showed me his watch. "Your minute is up. I have other matters to attend to."

I let him go without further argument. What if? I thought. What if Kilian decided to put a little something special in President Hyden's chocolate soufflé? Starting now, Bucky and I were the last line of defense where food was concerned.

Time to step up my game.

CHAPTER 9

ONCE I'D SETTLED MYSELF SUFFICIENTLY TO BE able to mask my unease around the visitors, I departed the Map Room and returned to the kitchen. Not that anyone would have cared whether I was upset or even bothered. No one seemed to notice when I slipped back in. Bucky was talking with Kilian and Tibor, while gesturing toward a simmering pot on the massive stovetop. All three had their backs to me.

Hector and Nate had teamed up across from each other at the far end of the center countertop. They'd returned to working with leaves of cooked cabbage, filling them one at a time and wrapping them up. This dish reminded me of Polish cabbage rolls, or *golabki*, but featured a far spicier mix.

The rolls themselves, according to Tibor, who had been our main instructor before Sargeant's arrival, were to be folded and rolled tight so that they could be placed in neat, uniform rows in a pan to bake.

Tibor had given us a quick lesson, impressing me with

his quick movements and obvious expertise. The four rolls he'd produced in less than a minute each told me that he'd made this dish many, many times in his life.

Before Sargeant's interruption, no one else had attempted to put one together. With Bucky, Tibor, and Kilian at the stovetop, the filling process had been left to Hector and Nate.

Hector dug a cabbage leaf out from the pile, ripping it in two. As yet unaware of my presence, he smirked and flung the wet, droopy leaf at Nate, who was spooning rice mixture into a leaf of his own.

The projectile hit Nate straight in the nose. He looked up with instant anger that, a half second later, morphed into amusement. Grinning now, he blurted out a couple of words in Saardiscan and reached for the offending leaf, intending to throw it back.

When he spied me in the doorway, however, he hesitated. He shot a snarly look at Hector, then placed the leaf next to the partially filled one he'd been working on, as though that had been his plan all along.

Hector bit his bottom lip, grabbed a new leaf, and began stuffing it with filling. Both men seemed determined to pretend they hadn't been horsing around, but the quality of their rolls fell short of those Tibor had made.

By this point, Bucky and the other two had turned around. "You're back," Bucky said unnecessarily. His tone was cheery but his eyes were filled with questions. Not something I was ready to deal with right now.

"What are we doing?" I asked, glancing at the stovetop. It was clear to me that the three of them had begun another concoction that had nothing to do with the wrapping assembly going on behind me.

Bucky hesitated. "I suppose that's up to you. We were about to embark on stage two of the traditional Saardiscan celebration meal, and I'd asked Kilian about preferred desserts." He gestured toward the other man.

Kilian hadn't had the chance to utter a word when Tibor

spouted a strangled cry. He slammed his hands against the sides of his legs and bolted away from our small group. A second later he was practically on top of Nate, banging the steel countertop and shouting in Saardiscan.

Taken aback, I turned to Kilian. "What's happening?"

Kilian's face reddened. "Nate is not performing properly." He nudged my arm with his elbow. "Neither is Hector, but it seems Tibor hasn't yet taken notice of him."

I leaned forward to see better, as Tibor's flying fit tapered off into angry scolding. The four expertly wrapped rolls Tibor had made sat in the baking pan, waiting for the next step. Outside the pan were Hector's and Nate's attempts to duplicate Tibor's efforts. Eight cabbage lumps lay there in an uneven pile. They weren't as perfect as the samples, but they weren't so bad as to warrant such a scene.

"Not pretty," Bucky said.

I didn't know whether he was referring to the rolls or to the fit Tibor was throwing. "He's worse than Virgil," I said under my breath.

I thought I heard Bucky say, "No, he isn't," but I couldn't be sure.

I strode across the room to take Tibor by the arm. "Enough already."

He spun.

"Stop," I said. "That's not how we do things around here."

He shrugged out of my grasp. "What do you think you're doing?"

We'd caused sufficient commotion to draw the attention of ground-floor Secret Service agents. "Is there a problem, Chef?"

"We're fine here, thanks," I said, even though that wasn't entirely true.

The minute the two men raced into the kitchen, Tibor went pale. By the time the agents disappeared around the corner again, the Saardiscan's attitude had transformed. He waved his hands over the misshapen rolls and backed away from the worktable. "These will be fine. I am in error." He ducked his head. "My apologies."

I exchanged a glance with Bucky, who looked as confused as I was. "What's going on here? How can you be outraged one minute and timid the next? I don't understand."

Tibor didn't look at me. He shifted his shoulders and edged sideways to get past without touching me, eager to get back to Kilian's side. "I made an error," he said again.

Kilian patted his colleague on the shoulder. "Perhaps it would be best if you, Hector, and Nate took one of those breaks." He shot me a look, giving me the sense that he wanted to talk with me, but not in front of the other men.

"Taking a break" had been another American tradition they hadn't understood. While Bucky and I were usually too busy to take breaks, we endeavored to be mindful of our guests' needs. At first, they'd been astounded by the idea of sanctioned time to relax, but once they got the hang of it, seemed to enjoy the custom.

"That sounds good," I said. "Bucky, why don't you take everyone to the Navy Mess for coffee or whatever anyone wants."

Bucky gave a quick nod. "Let's go, guys. We can come back and finish up here shortly." He turned to me. "What do you think? About ten, fifteen minutes?"

I glanced up at the clock. We had plenty of time before needing to prep for lunch. "Perfect," I said.

Bucky led them away. Kilian followed them to the door, patting the other men on the back and speaking what sounded like encouragement. He turned to me when they'd exited. "I apologize for my friend," he said. "We are finding life in the United States to be far different from what we expected. You are very . . . open . . . here. Surprisingly talkative."

I waited, not sure where this was going.

"Even when we are in our hotel rooms at night"—he gestured vaguely in the direction of where they were staying—"we can't believe the freedom we've been granted here. No one comes to check on us."

"Why would they? You're adults, professionals."

His soft face creased into a wide smile. "There is much that is different between our cultures. We heard rumors that America was a place where one could say and do whatever one wanted, but I confess I didn't believe it. I don't think my colleagues believed it, either. From the time we're little children, we're taught that the activity and happiness we see coming from the United States is all propaganda."

Again propaganda. Not for the first time, I wondered why—if Saardisca was as extreme in controlling their citizens as it seemed—these men had been allowed to come here to work. And for two weeks. There was certainly no way to shield them from American ideals, from our culture, or from our freedoms while they were immersed in it. If the Saardiscans were as anti-freedom as they seemed to be, then what had persuaded the government to send a delegation here to visit?

I asked Kilian that. He pondered the question. "I believe our government has begun to sense that there is change in the world. I think they are worried that if they do not send envoys out to test the waters, they will suffer later." He gave me a wry look. "Or it is, perhaps, a test of our loyalty. They may suspect that some of us are not happy with the rules and regime."

"Are you one of those people?"

He glanced both ways and peered into the corners of the kitchen where the walls and ceiling met.

"There aren't any cameras in here," I said. "No microphones."

"Are you sure?"

"Yes. Very."

Kilian took a deep breath. "Tibor is a man with much grief to bear. He does not wish to see the happiness here in America."

"Why not? How can our lives here possibly affect him?"

"His mother and father were outspoken rebels. Both parents were arrested and incarcerated when Tibor was a mere child. He never saw them again."

"*Were* they criminals?"

Kilian shook his head. "They were not terrorists, if that's what you're asking. They simply attempted to bring people together to effect change. Unfortunately for them, and for Tibor, they were not successful."

"That's terrible."

Kilian got a faraway look in his eyes. "Tibor became a ward of the state at a young age. As such, he was indoctrinated into the government's belief systems. He is a product of this regime. That is why he was allowed to enter into the field of his choosing."

"The culinary arts?" I asked.

Kilian nodded, clearly on a roll. "He has been granted privileges that others only dream of, and he has been elevated to his position due to his drive and eagerness to defend the tenets we are required to uphold. He believes it all." Raising his hands, Kilian encompassed the room, but I realized what he was really doing was encompassing all of the United States. "What we see here makes us question what we have been taught."

"What about you? How are *you* allowed to visit here? You seem to have adapted better than your friend Tibor. What do you think of America?"

Kilian smiled warmly. "I come from a long line of distinguished chefs. I was born into this life," he said. "It is a good thing that I love what I do."

"What about the other two?" I asked. "Hector and Nate?"

"The provinces they come from are less industrialized, less modern. Tibor and I have met and worked together on several occasions. Hector and Nate have not been schooled to the same extent and have not had the opportunity to apprentice the way Tibor and I have." He gave a resigned shrug. "They are doing well enough, considering their backgrounds."

I took a deep breath. "Thank you," I said. "I appreciate the insight."

He nodded.

I realized Kilian hadn't answered one of my questions. "What do you think about all you're experiencing here? I understand that some of what you're seeing must be eye-opening, but how is that affecting *you*?"

Again, Kilian looked around as though certain some-one was spying on us.

"If you'd rather not talk about it, I understand," I said.

"No, it is not that." He pulled his lips in and in the quiet couple of seconds that followed I sensed he was coming to a decision. When he did, he pointed at me. "As we have discussed, in Saardisca, it is very unusual for a woman to be the boss."

"Does it bother you that I'm in charge here?"

He made a so-so motion with his head. "At first, yes, I admit that it did. But I am seeing you not solely as a woman, but differently. I can't explain why, but I am less uncomfortable than when we first arrived."

"Go on."

"Tibor is less uncomfortable, too."

"He certainly doesn't show it."

"No," Kilian said. "The way he is acting today tells me how uncomfortable he is about *not* being uncomfortable." Tilting his head, he asked, "Am I conveying my meaning correctly?"

"You are," I said. "And now that you're not uncomfortable—and you believe your colleagues may be settling in as well—what does that mean for all of you?"

He got a wistful expression on his face. "The govern-ment has been very good to my family for generations. And yet." He sighed. "I long for more. You have so much to offer here in this country."

"What about Kerry Freiberg?" I asked. "If she wins the election, she promises sweeping changes."

When he laughed, it was a sad sound. "She will not win. This I know."

"Then why have they allowed her to make this trip to the United States? Is it all for show?"

Kilian dropped his voice. For all my assurances that we weren't being listened to, he still opted to take no chances. "That is exactly why she is here. For show," he said. "You do not understand how things work in my country. Our leaders desire to be respected by other countries—a goal they have yet to achieve. Ms. Freiberg's revolutionary position sends a message to the world that Saardisca is open to change and growth."

"But it isn't true?" I asked.

He winced. "There is much unrest in Saardisca. The government would have you believe that all is well and the people are fed, happy, and enjoy fulfilling lives. That is true for only very few of us. I'm one of the lucky ones." He looked around the room and sighed again. "And yet . . ."

Acting on a hunch, I asked, "You wouldn't consider requesting asylum, would you?"

His gaze flew to mine.

At that moment Bucky, Hector, and Nate returned.

Kilian's glare was razor sharp. He leaned in close and whispered, "Do not ever say that word aloud again. Please."

CHAPTER 10

I LEFT GAV SLEEPING, BUT MADE SURE THAT HIS alarm was set. He had to be in for training by eight. He was in for a long day because he'd missed so much by going out to see Erma and Bill.

I was excited to get to the White House this morning. Marcel had called to tell me that he was returning to work, causing yet another adjustment to our plans for the Saardiscans. This time, however, I welcomed the change. It would be great to have him back.

I'd been asleep when Gav had gotten home the night before, but I'd roused myself enough to hear him say that everything was okay, and that he was tired. He promised to bring me up to speed when I got back home tonight. I was really looking forward to our time together. After so many years of living alone, I'd expected that adjusting to life with another person to be difficult. What I'd discovered, instead, was that the more time I spent with Gav, the more I wanted. Best of all, I knew he felt the same way. We'd taken so long to find each other that we didn't want to miss a single minute.

I drew a deep breath as I stepped into the White House kitchen. I appreciated the silence—the solitude. Making my way into the dark room, I turned on the light and inhaled the faint scent of disinfectant. The surfaces were swiftly cleaned between projects and left sparkling every evening. Preventing illness from food-borne germs was of utmost importance.

Making my way to the cabinet where we kept fresh smocks and aprons, I donned mine for the day and surveyed the quiet scene with a sigh, longing to get back to normal with Bucky and Cyan. And yet, after Cyan's admission the other day, I knew the three of us would never again experience the same carefree normal we'd had. The impending loss of my spunky assistant weighed heavily on my heart.

As I wiped down the kitchen surfaces in anticipation of preparing breakfast, I forced myself to focus on the positive. Marcel was coming back. Even if he didn't have the use of both hands to prepare his fabulous desserts, he would be another stabilizing presence here. Another set of eyes.

"Good morning."

"Morning, Bucky," I said. "You're in early."

He pulled out a smock and apron. "Pot calling the kettle black?"

"I guess we both need a little quiet time before today's fun, don't we?"

He finished tying on his apron. "Have you ever noticed that things are never really quiet around here for long? I mean, we're in the middle of a government sequester. Shouldn't this be a time when nothing happens? And here we are, entertaining a brigade of foreign chefs who don't even seem to like us very much."

I stopped wiping things down. "Have you noticed that we work in the capital of the United States, reporting to someone who could arguably be considered the most powerful man on earth?"

"Peter Everett Sargeant?"

Laughter burst out of me, spontaneous and loud. "Good one," I said. "But I was referring to a man who might *actually* hold the power. I didn't mean the man who only believes he does."

"Oh," he said with a smirk, "my mistake."

We talked a little bit about Cyan's future as we pulled together ingredients for the First Family's breakfast. The president always tried to make time to enjoy the morning meal with his family on weekdays before the kids went to school. We had about an hour before the butlers would arrive to pick it up. Plenty of time.

"She was anxious about telling you, Ollie," Bucky said. "It wasn't easy for her."

"It wasn't easy for me to hear."

"What do you think she'll do?"

Preparing to make a veggie frittata, I broke eggs into a wide bowl. "She can probably do anything she wants. After working here, she could find a position as executive chef at any number of top restaurants or hotels. She could write a book. Make speeches. Go on tour."

"Is that what you plan to do when you're finished here?"

I held an egg aloft, stopping myself from cracking it as I mulled the question. "I can't say that I've thought that far ahead."

"You? Not think ahead?" Bucky dug out a cast-iron skillet and began warming it on the stovetop.

I struggled for the right words, "I've never planned for more because this really is the job I've always wanted. In fact, it's more than I could have hoped for."

"You can say that again. Speaking of which, what did you and Kilian talk about yesterday?"

As I beat the eggs, I thought about everything Kilian had said. "Sounds to me as though their government is a lot more oppressive than we know." Because Kilian had spoken to me in confidence, I didn't reveal what he'd told me about Tibor. Nor did I bring up Kilian's reaction to my mention of seeking asylum.

Granted, I knew little about the actual process of requesting political asylum. For all I knew, Kilian lived a happy, productive life in Saardisca and it was simply a passing interest in our culture that led him to appear so wistful. And yet, I sensed that there was more beneath the surface.

"*Oppressive* isn't the word I'd use. Hector was telling me a little about life in Saardisca," Bucky said.

"They're from four different provinces. I get the feeling that life can vary greatly from one area to the next."

"I've gotten that impression as well, but I have to tell you that Hector and Nate don't seem to have any complaints. They're more lighthearted than the other two."

I got the feeling that Kilian could be lighthearted in the right circumstances. "More than Tibor, that's for sure."

"What is up that guy's craw, anyway?" Bucky asked. "You'd think that two weeks in a different country would be a vacation for him. Or at least a new experience he'd choose to embrace. I get the feeling he doesn't care for the United States in the least."

"His loss." Tempted to speak on the man's behalf, I held my tongue. If what Kilian had told me about Tibor was true, I was willing to cut the guy a little slack. As much as I didn't abide a bad attitude, given Tibor's past, I needed to exercise patience when dealing with him.

Bucky wasn't looking at me, but wore a thoughtful expression. "What if he's got family back there that he misses?" Now he looked up. "A wife. Kids. You know, people he cares about. I could see how two weeks away might not be such a coup after all."

I tossed chopped bell peppers into a frying pan, causing the bits to sizzle and jump, releasing the vegetable's sweet, green aroma. Stirring, I said, "We don't really know anything about these men. The Saardiscans provided resumes about their work and no more. They may *all* have families."

"Nate's a single guy who lives on his own," Bucky said, looking pleased to be a source of information. "I guess he got lucky to get a culinary internship. The state of cooking in Saardisca, at least in his province, is way behind that of Kilian's and Tibor's. Hector and Nate are both surprised at how much more we can do here than they can there."

"That's good that you're getting to know them. Good that they seem eager." I was curious as to whether Tibor talked about family, knowing what Kilian had told me. "Did Hector and Tibor talk about their backgrounds, too?"

Bucky shook his head. "Tibor was tight-lipped. Hector talked about his younger brother, who apparently also works in the culinary arts. I guess there is a little sibling rivalry going on because only one chef per province was allowed to come here. Hector's brother worked hard, but ultimately washed out. Hector seems really proud of the kid."

I poured the beaten eggs into the frying pan and stirred until the bottom was evenly coated. "They're going to be here for another week and a half. If the past days are any indication, we're in for a bumpy ride. The more we get to know these fellows, the more we'll discover common ground."

Sounds of movement rolled in from the corridor and two Secret Service agents escorted our four guests in for the day.

"Good morning," I said to them.

"Good morning," they chorused in heavy Saardiscan accents. Hector and Nate smiled and raised their hands in greeting. Kilian, behind them followed suit. When he met my eyes, I could have sworn he was silently asking if I'd kept his confidence. I gave what I hoped was an assured smile and a quick nod. Tibor must have caught the movement because he scowled at me.

The group opened the cabinet, grabbing their share of today's smocks and aprons, just as Bucky and I had done when we'd first arrived. I liked the fact that we were establishing routines.

At that very moment the butlers arrived to take breakfast up to the First Family. Bucky and I put the finishing touches on the dishes, plated and garnished everything, and sent the food on its way. Perfect timing. Good omen.

For the first time since the new people arrived, I felt optimistic and confident.

Sargeant stepped into the kitchen, this time without his faithful assistant in tow. "Good morning," he said. A genuine smile creased the chief usher's features, making me instantly wary.

As everyone responded, I took a preemptive step forward, hoping to halt him from making any more pronouncements without informing me first.

"Peter," I said, effectively blocking his way into the rest of the room, "what brings you to our kitchen this fine morning? Something we need to discuss in private?"

"I understand that Marcel is returning."

"You understand correctly."

His gaze was direct, slightly impatient. I knew he wanted me to move, but I didn't budge.

"We will be having a visitor today," he said.

"Oh?"

He gave me a pointed look, clearly asking me to step out of the way. "May I?" he asked.

Grudgingly, I obliged him. "Be my guest."

He placed his hands together, fingers close to his lips, as though praying. "We have received word that the esteemed Saardiscan candidate for president, Kerry Freiberg, will be arriving this morning to meet with President Hyden."

The Saardiscan chefs murmured their surprise. From what I could tell, all but Tibor were pleased.

"Are we preparing lunch for them?" I asked.

Sargeant continued. "No need to stop what you're doing. Ms. Freiberg will be dining in the West Wing, with the Navy Mess providing meals for all guests. And yes, the Navy Mess has already been notified."

"Thank you," I said quietly.

Addressing the group, he went on. "Ms. Freiberg has expressed her desire to come visit you." Sargeant spread his hands out, gesturing toward the four Saardiscans. "Because she wasn't expected to visit for several more days, we don't have an exact time for her arrival yet. I wanted you to be aware, however, that at some point during her visit today, she will come down here to see the kitchen. I will keep in touch with Chef Paras to update her as needed. If you have any questions you can direct them to her."

Eyes sharp, Sargeant turned to me. "That wasn't so bad, was it?"

"It could have been worse," I admitted. "What changed?"

"She's chosen to add a stop in Philadelphia to her itinerary, after her visit here but before New York. It was easier to adjust the first few days of her schedule than to rearrange everything else."

"Anything else I need to know at this point?"

"You may have very little advance notice," he said. "It's unfortunate, but we're all scrambling. Be prepared."

"You got it," I said.

CHAPTER 11

"MY OLIVIA," MARCEL EXCLAIMED WHEN HE came in. Wearing a sling around his casted arm, he could grab only one of my shoulders as he pulled me in to kiss me on both cheeks. "I would kiss you, too, my good friend," he said to Bucky, "but I believe you would—how is the word?—slug me. No?" He winked.

Bucky pulled his lips to one side as though annoyed, but I knew better. "Good to see you back, buddy."

Marcel had a coat draped over his shoulders, which he managed to shrug off one-handed. Beneath it he wore a pristine White House–embellished smock, and he'd even managed to work his injured arm through its sleeve. Pointing, I asked, "Since when do you keep these at home? You know they aren't supposed to leave the building unless we're on official duty."

His bright white teeth contrasting with his dark face, he looked around the room as though ensuring he had an audience. The four Saardiscans watched him with patent curiosity. "It is difficult to smuggle things *into* the White House, no? But not so difficult to smuggle such things out."

He patted my cheek with his free hand and winked again. "One never knows when there will be an emergency. I keep two at home for just such uses."

Truth was, I kept a smock at home, too, just in case. "Great minds think alike."

I brought Marcel up to speed about the change in Kerry Freiberg's schedule and let him know that she would be visiting our kitchen today.

"I understand," he said. "Perhaps we will provide her a tour?"

"If she has time that sounds like it would be a wonderful idea. Incidentally," I said, broaching what could turn out to be a touchy subject, "in your absence, Kilian generously agreed to step in and direct the dessert efforts. Now that you're back . . ."

Marcel patted me on the hand. "Mr. Sargeant has already informed me of the changes made during my convalescence. He was right to name someone in my place." To Kilian, he said, "Monsieur, I very much look forward to sampling your delicacies."

Kilian blushed. "Nothing I create would be able to compare with the fantastic centerpieces you've shown us."

Marcel smiled at the compliment. "You are too kind."

"It would be my honor to work alongside you," Kilian went on, "and take your direction. The pastry kitchen is your home, after all. I am a mere visitor."

"We shall work side-by-side, *mon ami*."

I smiled to myself, remembering my early morning optimism. Today was shaping up to be a very good day, indeed.

While Bucky took over the kitchen, Kilian and I decided to work with Marcel to sketch out yet another updated schedule for the rest of the week. We made our way to the library, where things were a little more quiet.

"You say these rooms are open for tours?" Kilian asked when we first entered. He ran a hand along the bookshelves and wandered the room's perimeter.

"Most of the time, yes," I said, "as are the state rooms upstairs. During this sequester, however, nonessential government services have been scaled back. Unfortunately, allowing visitors to tour the White House is one of those nonessentials."

I took a moment to try to see the library as Kilian might be viewing it. I'd been working here for years now, and although I always appreciated the beauty around me, I'd probably begun to take the opulence in the White House for granted.

"And *anyone* can come in here?"

"Well," I said, "there are rules. Tour participants have to arrange for their visits ahead of time. They need to submit information about themselves so that they can be vetted by security. And there are a whole bunch of personal items that aren't allowed inside the building."

Kilian nodded absentmindedly as though restrictions didn't surprise him. "Do very many people come through the doors?" he asked. "When there is no sequester, I mean?"

Marcel guffawed. "Hundreds," he said. "Thousands."

"Every year?" Kilian asked.

"Every day the house is open," I said.

Kilian stood near the center of the room. His expression was a mixture of disbelief and satisfaction. "I am overwhelmed."

I took a seat in one of the chairs and gestured for the two men to do the same. "Time to get started."

"We will explore the White House chocolate shop today," Marcel said with unrestrained glee. "I believe you will find what we do there truly amazing."

Kilian clapped his chubby hands together. "Excellent."

"Marcel, why don't you take our guests to the chocolate shop around two o'clock? Would that work for you?"

"Absolument."

The three of us decided on a few other plans for the rest of the week, including having Marcel accompany the group to the florist shop. Another day, Bucky would take the visitors to the calligraphers' office in the East Wing to observe how thematic elements were carried through from invitations to dinner.

I planned to take the Saardiscans into our storage area to show them the china collections we had at our disposal. The butlers and waitstaff had also agreed to share their knowledge with our visitors.

Marcel, Kilian, and I finished up and returned to the kitchen to find Bucky and the other men huddled over the center countertop, leaning forward, elbows perched on the stainless steel, studying a flurry of paperwork before them.

"And right there," Bucky was saying, "is our seating chart from when the queen of England last visited the White House."

Hector looked up and smiled at me as we entered. "We have never seen so much preparation," he said to Kilian. "We are learning very, very quickly."

Tibor's head wagged back and forth. Not as though he didn't understand, but as though he didn't approve. "I do not believe any of this." He shoved at the papers—not hard enough to send them flying—but enough to punctuate his words. "I believe that you have fabricated much to convince us that you are superior. But Saardisca is not unworthy or less capable."

"No one is saying anything about your country." Bucky looked to me for support.

"The fact that we do things differently doesn't make us better," I said as I made my way over to the group. "We happen to have had a great many guests here over the years. We've organized so many dinners that we've learned what works and what doesn't. These notes help us continue to improve."

Kilian and Marcel flanked me. "I believe this is good knowledge," Kilian said.

Tibor bared his bottom teeth, barely containing himself. What made this man so constantly angry? Despite what Kilian had told me about Tibor's past, his reactions were out of proportion.

"We hope to learn from you as well," I said. "Remember, that's one of the goals of this visit."

Tibor's eyes narrowed. Hector touched him on the arm, speaking softly in Saardiscan. A few tense moments later, Tibor's shoulders relaxed and his posture softened.

"I had a plan to teach all of you one of our traditional desserts," Kilian said with a pained smile on his face.

"Yes? That would be kind of you," Marcel said in an unusually high voice. It seemed everyone in the room, with the exception of Tibor, was striving to lighten the mood.

"The dinner for our country's candidate will provide us an opportunity to see for ourselves how events are organized here," Kilian said. He walked over and placed his hands on Tibor's shoulders. "You don't want to believe any of this is true. We've been taught that Americans have produced nothing but propaganda. We've believed this all our lives because we did not know better. Tibor, my friend, you are uncomfortable because all that we were taught now seems to be what is faulty. Perhaps *we* have been mistaken. I do not want you to lose out on this opportunity to learn because your mind is closed. You may have to begin to consider the possibility that our government has been lying to us all our lives."

Tibor shook Kilian away. "You talk blasphemy," he said, and stormed out of the kitchen.

Hector moved to follow, but Nate grabbed him back.

Kilian said, "Let him go. You do not know the man as well as I do. Everything he believes in is crumbling before his eyes."

"Why did they send him with us?" Hector asked.

That was a good question. I waited for Kilian's reply.

"I don't know," he said. "Perhaps they are testing him."

WE WERE IN THE MIDST OF A DISCUSSION
when Tibor returned a short while later. He mumbled what

might have been an apology, but sounded to me more like a low-toned complaint.

"Chocolate," I continued. "That's the next stop on your agenda. I know Marcel can't wait to show off his magnificent designs there. You won't believe the beauty this man is capable of."

"Ah, you exaggerate." Marcel waved his free hand toward me, but he beamed, enjoying the compliments.

I decided to indulge him further. "You remember the gorgeous centerpieces Marcel showed you your first day here?"

The four men nodded.

"Be prepared to be amazed. Chocolate creations are, without a doubt, among the most popular desserts we serve. But you won't believe your eyes when you see how it can be presented."

Marcel lifted his broken arm up enough to call attention to it. "I may not be able to show many of my tricks, but I am happy to share the magical workshop with you. Would you all care to join me?"

Kilian spoke for the group. "Of course."

I glanced up at the clock. Right on schedule. Bucky and I had the First Lady's afternoon meeting to prepare for. Getting these four swarming bodies out of here and into the chocolate shop would be a great boon to us while we put together the snacks and savories.

"This way then," Marcel said, and led them out.

"Our job is becoming more traffic cop than chef," Bucky said when they were gone. "Timing is critical and moving them from place to place is a challenge." He waited a beat, then asked, "What's with that Tibor, anyway?"

I decided it might be best to share a little of what I knew with Bucky. Enough to give him insight, without divulging specifics. "From what Kilian's told me, Tibor has had a rough life. Sounds like he sees the Saardiscan government almost as a father figure. It's got to hurt if all of a sudden you realize that figure has been keeping you from learning the truth about the world."

Bucky perched his fists at his waist and stared out the way the team had gone. "Then why send him here in the first place? There has to be a reason."

"I can't tell you how many times I've wondered that myself." I shrugged. "With any luck, they'll be back in Saardisca soon and we'll never find out."

Bucky gave me the oddest look. "This from you? I thought you got your kicks out of digging into things that don't make sense."

"As long as our kitchen is shorthanded and as long as I'm responsible for the actions of these men—one of whom seems determined to make trouble—I'm keeping my nose as clean as possible." I held up both hands. "I never go looking for trouble. You know that. This time, I'm doing my best to avoid it, too."

LATER, MOMENTS AFTER WE'D SENT THE FIRST Lady's meeting fare upstairs, a Secret Service agent appeared in the kitchen's doorway. He spoke quietly, barely moving his lips. "Candidate Kerry Freiberg is on her way," he said.

Instinctively, I glanced up at the clock, even though I'd done so moments earlier. "Should we bring the Saardiscan chefs back in here?" I asked.

"I was told to alert you," he said. "Nothing more."

"Thank you. How long before she gets here?"

I heard the elevator open. "They're here." He motioned toward an unseen person. "This way," he said. He held his other hand out toward me.

Kerry Freiberg came around the corner, peering into the kitchen, a wide smile on her face. She was accompanied by President Hyden, who followed with his hands in his pockets, his voice booming. "And this is the kitchen where our wonderful chefs keep us happy and healthy, and oftentimes safe." He winked at me. "Hello, Ollie."

"Good afternoon, Mr. President."

"Kerry," he said to his guest, "I would like you to meet our incomparable executive chef, Olivia Paras, and her outstanding assistant, Buckminster Reed."

"How do you do?" I said, reaching to shake the candidate's hand.

After we greeted our guests, Bucky whispered that he would let the Saardiscans know that she was here.

Kerry Freiberg was even more lovely in person than her newspaper photos had led me to believe. Her blonde hair, worn loose and long, curled into perfect waves around her shoulders. She had an inquisitive, authoritative quality, yet looked to be a person accustomed to smiling, and who enjoyed doing so.

If that astonished me—and it did, considering that her fellow Saardiscans rarely smiled at all—that surprise was eclipsed by the fact that she wasn't alone. In her arms, Kerry Freiberg carried a fluffy white dog with perky ears and bright brown eyes.

"And who is this?" I asked.

"Her name is Frosty," she said, with a light roll to her *r*.

"She's adorable," Reaching my hand toward the little pet, I asked, "May I?"

"Of course." As I scratched Frosty's neck, the dog nosed my hand. "She is a West Highland white terrier," Ms. Freiberg said.

"A Westie."

"You know them?" She seemed delighted by this.

"A good friend of mine back in the Midwest has a sweetheart about this same size named Duncan Tryon." I gave Frosty a final pat on the head. "They are wonderful dogs, aren't they?"

Ms. Freiberg nuzzled the top of Frosty's head. "She

accompanies me everywhere. Her presence is a calming influence in a rapidly changing world."

I wondered how our chef guests would react to Frosty, and why Sargeant had neglected to mention the four-legged visitor.

President Hyden had remained quiet during our interchange. Now, he said, "Ms. Freiberg was interested to see how her countrymen were getting along here in the kitchen with you." He made a show of scanning the area. "Don't tell me you sent them home early today?"

"Not at all," I said. "Bucky went to let them know that you're here. Marcel is in the middle of showing them the chocolate shop. You know how much enjoyment he gets out of showing off his handiwork."

President Hyden nodded. "Yes, I do know."

"Chocolate shop?" Ms. Freiberg said. "Inside your home? Amazing."

"I'm sure Marcel will be delighted to show it to you after you meet with your countrymen." The chocolate shop comfortably fit two, maybe three people. At the moment, there were five full-grown adults in there. I had an image of what would happen if we added two more, plus Secret Service, plus a dog. "How about if we wait for them here?" I suggested. "There's not a lot of elbow room in there."

"Good thinking," the president said.

"I'm sure you'll have the opportunity to sample some of the chocolate, if you wish," I said. "I wouldn't want you to miss out."

She smiled. "You are most kind."

I turned at the sound of fast footsteps to see Bucky rounding the far doorway. His eyes were wide. "Ollie," he said. A half-beat later, he added, "Mr. President."

"What is it?" I asked.

He was breathless. "It's Marcel. He collapsed."

CHAPTER 12

MY BRAIN TOOK PRECIOUS SECONDS TO PRO-
cess Bucky's words.

All I could think was, *again*?

The Secret Service agents immediately began to shepherd President Hyden and Ms. Freiberg from the kitchen.
The president touched my arm as he was led away. "Keep
me updated."

"Yes, sir."

Bucky and I hurried out of the kitchen, where we encountered another Secret Service agent. "We need you to take
the visitors out of here," the agent said to me. "There's too
much commotion and the doctor needs room."

He didn't need to explain. But what was wrong with
Marcel? Had he taken the wrong dosage of his blood pressure medication again?

"Follow me," the agent said as he led us to the chocolate
shop. Like we didn't know the way.

The Saardiscans were stumbling out of the little room
as we arrived. I peered in through the door. Two things I

noticed at once. The room was heavy with stale body heat, and there was blood on the floor.

"What happened?"

The White House doctor knelt next to Marcel, barking orders to his assistant. At my question, he glanced over his shoulder. "Get all these people out of here."

"Kilian," I called. "Let's go."

I didn't like the idea of leaving Marcel, but there was little I could do, and I took comfort in knowing that the doctor was there. We trooped back to the kitchen, the Saardiscans chattering among themselves in their native language. I wanted to know what they were saying. Darn this sequester and Tom's refusal to approve a translator to help us out.

"What happened?" I asked.

Tibor was as pale as I'd ever seen him. He set his lips in a thin line and didn't make eye contact with any of us. Instead he made his way to a stool we kept at one end of the kitchen. He didn't sit on it, exactly. More like leaned on it for support.

Kilian noticed and sidled up to me. "When Marcel collapsed, he grabbed at Tibor before he fell. Tibor tried to help, but Marcel hit his head and . . ." He let the words hang.

"Is Marcel okay?" I asked.

Kilian shrugged. "I do not know."

Of course he didn't. How could he?

"Did he wake up before you left?" I knew I was grasping at straws, but I was desperate for hope. "Was he able to talk?"

Bucky stood behind our guests facing me. They couldn't see the fear for our friend in his eyes. I could practically read his thoughts across the room.

"What happened?" I asked again. Even as I forced myself to speak calmly, I realized my heart was racing and I could tell my face was flushed. "What was he doing when he lost consciousness?"

Kilian tightened his face as though working to remember clearly. "He wanted to show us how he made small rabbits and ducks for an Easter centerpiece," he said. Holding a hand out to Hector, he asked, "Marcel seemed fine, didn't he? There was nothing amiss."

I desperately wanted whatever was afflicting Marcel to be a temporary problem, not a life-threatening illness. I hoped it was as simple as him having taken that extra dosage again, but my gut told me otherwise. For Marcel to have made that mistake even once was unheard of. To have done it twice—nearly impossible. I considered other possibilities: an allergic reaction, a momentary sugar spike. "Did any of you notice him eat anything?"

The men exchanged uneasy glances. Kilian said, "Marcel offered us samples. Nate had some. And Hector did." He pointed to Tibor. "He did, too."

"What about you?"

"No, nothing. I don't care for sweets all that much."

And yet he was the master of desserts in his country? I'd think about that later. "How are you feeling, Tibor?"

He didn't answer. Still leaning on the stool, he waved my question away.

"Hector?" I asked.

He gave me a confident grin, pounded on his chest with both fists, and said, "I am fine."

Nate nodded. "I am well."

"What was it that Marcel ate?" I asked.

Tibor was the one who answered. "Not ate. Drank. A chocolate drink he was very proud of."

I knew exactly what Tibor was talking about. One of Marcel's specialties was a warm chocolate drink. Richer and thicker than traditional hot chocolate, it went down like liquid silk and left a whisper of spice in its wake. "Did he add anything to it?"

Tibor shrugged and looked to his colleagues.

Hector nodded. "Schnapps."

"And he drank some?" I asked to confirm. "Several of you did?"

"Yes," Tibor said. He pointed as he spoke. "Marcel, Hector, Nate, me. We all drank it."

"And you all feel fine?" I asked.

Tibor didn't look fine. He rubbed his forehead. "I am sorry I could not stop him from injuring himself again," he said when he noticed my scrutiny. "I hope he will recover quickly."

"I don't know what's going on," I said. "The doctors put Marcel through a battery of tests and found nothing amiss."

"Doctors are not always right," Tibor said.

BUCKY AND I WERE BACK IN CHARGE OF THE kitchen, again without Marcel. We'd gotten word later that afternoon that he'd been hospitalized, but this time they intended to administer more tests than they had the time before. The Secret Service agent who delivered the news tried to reassure me, "They'll figure it out. You'll see."

I hoped so. For all our sakes.

"Well, then," I said, my brain scrambling for order in what was becoming yet another chaotic day, "let's regroup. Until we know more about Marcel's prognosis, let's focus on some traditional Saardiscan food. Do any of you have a specific dish in mind you'd be willing to teach us how to make?"

Kilian said that he did.

"Would you be so kind as to write down the ingredients?" I asked, "I'll have the agents pick them up for us. It may take a day or two until the order comes in, though," I added, belatedly remembering that the sequester might cause a delay, "but Bucky and I would very much enjoy learning from you."

While Kilian did as I asked, Bucky got the other men started on planning for the dinner at Blair House.

I was about to pick up the phone, intending to contact

Sargeant to ask if Kerry Freiberg and the president were willing to return to the kitchen for the visit they'd missed, but before I could lift the receiver, the phone rang.

"What in the world is going on in your kitchen, Ms. Paras?"

"Peter," I said, "I was about to call you. If Ms. Freiberg is still available, we have returned to the kitchen and I know that Kilian and his team would very much like to meet with her."

"Is everything under control there?"

I took a brief look around. "Seems to be."

He sniffed. "The president and Ms. Freiberg are touring the state rooms as we speak. I do not believe there will be time for them to return downstairs. If that changes, I'll let you know."

He hung up before I could reply.

"Kilian," I said when I returned to the group, "you and I need to chat about the pastry kitchen. If you're to be in charge of desserts again, Bucky and I can take turns joining you there to serve as your assistant."

He got a peculiar look in his eyes. "Why would you or Bucky join me, when it would be more efficient to have Tibor? He has much experience with desserts. You have stated that for you and your assistant, this would be more difficult."

It was a valid question. "The whole purpose for your team's visit here is to share knowledge and experience. We can't share very much if we don't work together."

"I had not thought of it in those terms." Satisfied, he nodded. "Yes, you're right."

He and I hashed out a plan of how we might divvy up time, resources, and responsibilities between our two kitchens. Even as we talked and he became more animated—I could tell that the idea of being able to run his own section of the kitchen energized him—I couldn't help but worry for Marcel.

Bucky took the other three out of the kitchen to visit one of the other departments.

As Kilian and I put the finishing touches on our plan for the next several days, I decided to do a little fishing. My vow to not get involved danced in my brain, but after this last episode with Marcel, I couldn't help myself. "It's a shame you didn't have a chance to meet with Ms. Freiberg today."

Kilian nodded. "I would have enjoyed the chance to speak with her."

"With any luck, she and the president will have time to try again."

Kilian's pink cheeks flushed. "Perhaps."

I kept my voice low. "Tell me more about Saardisca."

He glanced around the room. "What do you want to know?"

I answered him truthfully. "What do the four of you talk about when you speak Saardiscan here?"

"Nothing so terrible," he said with a smile that brightened his entire face. "Tibor and Nate have a tendency to discuss politics and religion. Hector and I know better than to join in."

"Why? Do Tibor and Nate get into arguments?"

"Not at all. They are both loyal Saardiscans."

I found his phrasing interesting. "And you and Hector are not?"

"I cannot speak for Hector. I know little of the young man. But I am not a fervent believer in our system, and far less vocal." He was quick to add, "This does not make me a bad person. I am not a rebel. But I am not so sure that what we are told is good for us, is really what's best. I have begun to see that there is more to the world than what has been taught to us."

"Your visit here has something to do with that?"

"I had been having doubts for a long time before this trip was even announced." Kilian's gaze jumped in the furtive way it tended to do when he wanted to ensure no one was listening in. "I am not as loyal as the government believes I am. The government knows not what is in my heart." He patted his chest with his fist. "If they did, I would never have been allowed to leave."

"Surely, you're not the only one," I said. "I mean, there have to be others who share your doubts."

He smiled. "There are. Yet, it is difficult for us to find places and times to discuss questions or seek answers. We all know of insurgents who have suffered greatly because they dared to doubt what the government decreed."

"That must be difficult."

He shrugged. "You get used to it."

"And here? In such close quarters with the other three men? Do you find it easier or more difficult?"

His brow furrowed. "I would never let any of these men know of my doubts. In an instant they would turn on me and have me sent back."

"Wouldn't they believe the same of you? That you would turn on them if they expressed doubts?"

"Yes."

"Then how do you know that none of them are simply being as clever and careful as you are?"

He blinked at me. Took a deep breath. "I had not considered such a thing. I believe what I believe, though. I think I am right." With a wry grin, he said, "We are getting to know one another better each day. Time will tell."

"That's good."

He made a face—one I couldn't parse.

"What's wrong?"

"If I get to know them, then perhaps they will get to know me. I do my best to keep my opinions secret, but if my guard comes down . . ." He let the thought hang. "I must be careful never to let that happen."

I held a finger to my lips. "I won't say a word."

CHAPTER 13

I WAITED TO EAT DINNER UNTIL GAV GOT HOME that night. After years of dining alone at my kitchen table, the prospect of cooking for someone I loved seemed like a great gift. I looked forward to the time we spent together, no matter what was on the menu and no matter what we had planned.

Tonight was one of our leftover nights. He showered when he first came in and returned to the kitchen just as I was setting out our plates. It wasn't all that late, but the shower had given him the opportunity to switch clothes; he'd opted for his striped pajama pants and gray T-shirt. His hair was wet and his eyes tired, but his smile was warm.

"Hey," he said, placing an arm around me. "What can I do?"

My kitchen was small and everything was almost done. "Sit," I said with a smile. "Relax for a few minutes. Talk to me."

"Everything smells wonderful."

"Good. After today's craziness at work, I didn't have it in me to concoct anything new. Hope you don't mind."

He sat at the kitchen table, one corner of his mouth turned upward. "Am I here with you?"

"Yes, you're here with me."

"Then I'm very happy."

I brought a bowl of vegetables to the table, and as I turned back toward the stove, he put his hands around my waist and pulled me to him.

I laughed. "What are you doing?"

He sat me on one of his knees. "It was tough, being out there with Erma and Bill."

I'd expected that we'd talk about his visit with them, and that he'd update me on Bill's prognosis, but just as he'd hesitated when we'd talked on the phone, he hedged again now. The look in Gav's eyes told me there was more to the story than I expected.

"What happened?" I asked.

"Not much more than what I've already told you."

"Then what's bothering you?"

He rubbed my back. "They have no one else."

I put an arm around his neck. "I know. This has got to be tough on you."

"Tough on them. They already feel alone."

I tried to guess what was going on here. "Does it bother them that you and I are married?"

He looked away, but shook his head. "Not in the way you're asking. No. They've come to terms with their loss, and I believe that they're both truly happy for me. For us."

"Then what?"

He got a sad, thoughtful look in his eyes. "I want to be able to help them."

"Okay," I said, still not understanding. "How?"

When Gav didn't want to continue a conversation, his eyes became unreadable. He put up a protective wall. Sometimes, as he struggled to sort things out for himself, he would even put physical distance between us before he was comfortable enough to share. I was much the same way, and we'd learned to give one another the space we needed, whenever we needed it.

I watched the smile in his eyes dim. "We'll have to talk about that."

Even though he continued to rub my back, the moment was over. I could tell that he had something big on his mind, but apparently this was not the time.

"Okay." I stood back up, kissed him on the forehead, and returned to the stove to finish pulling dinner together.

"Tell me about Marcel," he said. "What's going on with him?"

Over dinner, I told Gav all I knew: Marcel was conscious, lucid, and angry to be hospitalized once again.

"Did you talk to him?"

I nodded as I forked a mouthful of green beans.

Gav pressed on. "And he hasn't told you that he's suffering from any ailment?"

I swallowed. "He swears he didn't take the wrong dosage this time and I believe him. He has no reason to lie about that. You know, of course, that the White House isn't taking any chances. They've ordered a bunch of tests."

"And the doctors don't believe this could be related to the first incident?"

"Doubtful. He's had days to allow that medicine to get through his system, and they even cut back on his dosage temporarily, just in case. They're monitoring him closely," I said, "but he was being monitored just as closely before he was released the first time. Nobody has answers."

"He has to be so frustrated."

"Tell me about it. It looks like he may have suffered a concussion when he hit his head. He's out of commission at the White House until he's fully recovered."

I asked Gav about his day at work, and his training. I knew how much he wanted to get back into the field and into the action, but they didn't want him to take on more than he could handle and so were taking it slow until they knew he was back up to full speed. His superiors had suggested extra training, and he'd been at that for a couple of weeks now.

"You've heard of muscle memory," he said with a humorous expression. "Seems as though my muscles have forgotten everything they'd ever learned. I'm more out of shape than I've ever been."

"I beg to differ. You're in great shape."

"Thanks," he said, "but not compared to where I was. I don't remember being this sore in my life, ever. Even during basic training."

"But you can feel things getting better, can't you?"

He smiled across the table. "Days like this make me wonder if I'm getting too old for field work."

"Old?" I nearly choked on my food. "You're in your early forties."

"Secret Service agents need to be nimble, agile, and fast. At this point I'm none of these things."

If only he could see himself the way I saw him. Compared to most men his age, Gav was a fine specimen. He was tall, slim but not emaciated, and when he took his shirt off my breath caught at the sight of muscles the rest of the world didn't get to see. The man was beautiful. In every sense of the word.

"But you're working to get back to where you were," I said.

"I hope I get there."

There was something in his eyes that made me believe he wasn't really hearing me. That there was more on his mind. More doubts about himself, perhaps?

"You will," I said.

I was about to say more when my cell phone rang. I reached for it, making a face of surprise when I read the display. "It's Lyman Hall Hospital," I said, then answered, "Hello?"

Marcel's booming, French accent greeted me. "Ah! Olivia!"

I held the phone away from my ear.

"How are you?" I asked, but he was still talking and didn't hear the question.

"I am calling from the phone in my room," he said. "My cell phone will not work here." He made a *tsk*ing sound and continued without pausing for breath. "Olivia, you must help me. I need your assistance."

With the phone a good six inches from my head, and Marcel speaking so loudly, Gav could hear every word. He and I exchanged a look of confusion.

"Absolutely, Marcel. What do you need? You sound very good, by the way. Are you feeling better?"

Again, he ignored my question. "Olivia, this is very important and I do not like speaking on the telephone about this."

"Okay," I said, this time with hesitation. "What's on your mind?"

"Are you in a place where it is safe to talk? You are not at the White House, correct?"

"I'm home," I answered, wondering what was going on. "Gav is with me."

"Good. He is safe," he said. "I cannot leave this room because the phone is attached to the wall." He made another noise, this one of disgust. "Why is it that they diminish power for cell phones in hospitals? Is this not where most people will need to make important calls?"

I didn't have an answer for that. "What's going on?"

"One moment," he said.

What I heard next sounded like wind, or perhaps fabric movement. A couple of seconds later, Marcel was back. "Are you able to hear me?" His voice was lower, muffled.

I pulled the phone closer to my ear. "What are you doing?"

"I have covered myself with the sheets and my pillow," he said. "I want no one other than you and your agent to hear what I have to say."

"Marcel, I don't understand."

"Olivia." He took a deep breath, the sound of which was magnified from being under wraps. "I was drugged."

"What?" The useless question escaped my lips instinctively. "Are you telling me that's why you collapsed?"

"It is. There is no doubt."

My mind reeled. "How did your doctors discover this? What were you drugged with?"

"No, no, you misunderstand," Marcel said quickly. "My doctors claim to have no idea why I lost consciousness. They have ordered toxicology tests but the results of those are not in yet."

"Then how do you know you were drugged?"

"My friend Franco brought me my laptop and I have been doing some investigating. You would be proud of me, no?"

I could tell from the look on Gav's face that he was following the conversation. He looked as confused as I was.

"Tell me everything," I said into the phone. "What are you talking about?"

Marcel adopted a patient tone, which, for him, was an enormous exercise in restraint. "I do not faint," he began. "Except for that single incident with a mistake in my dosage, I am not a person who loses consciousness, nor do I have any illnesses that might cause me to suffer such indignity." He gave a vexed huff.

"I understand," I said. "And so you want answers."

"Which these doctors do not seem willing to provide." He made another *tsk*ing noise. "It isn't that they are hiding information from me. It is that they don't know. So I took it upon myself to find out. I put my symptoms into that Google box and voilà!"

I bit my lower lip. "What did you find?"

"It is classic," he said. "Smooth and silky, like a dark ganache, there is a drug that works to render individuals unconscious. It works very quickly and is virtually undetectable."

"What is it?"

"GHB," he said, enunciating the letters carefully.

Gav mouthed the words as Marcel spoke them aloud. "Gamma-hydroxybutyrate."

I knew a little about the drug. Enough to know how unusual it was to screen for. "They tested you for GHB?" I asked.

"They did not."

"Then how do you know that's what happened?"

Marcel let loose a sigh that conveyed exasperation. "I have every symptom. I am, what you call, a textbook case. There is no doubt in my mind that one of the Saardiscan men put this into my drink."

"I don't understand," I said again.

"Have any of them experienced these symptoms? Have any of them needed to be taken to the hospital?"

"No."

"You see," he said. "I was targeted. They did this to me."

"To what end?" I asked. Not because I wanted to argue the point with Marcel. Our pastry chef was clearly troubled by this theory. "What would they stand to gain with you in the hospital? GHB knocks people out temporarily. What would that do for them?"

"How should I know?" Marcel asked, his voice so shrill at that point that I'm sure everyone on the hospital floor heard it, pillow over his head or not. "That is why I need your help. You must find out why they would do this."

Words failed me.

"He wouldn't have been tested for GHB as a matter of course," Gav whispered, close to my ear so that Marcel wouldn't be able to hear. "Chances are his body has already metabolized it. That is, if there were any there to begin with."

"How's your head?" I asked Marcel. "Did you need any stitches?"

"Fourteen," he said. "It is very hot under here." I could tell, from the noises in the background, when he pulled the sheets and pillow away. "Ah. There. Better."

"Any updates about the concussion?"

"Our chief usher believes that my impairment renders me unable to work in the kitchen. He has prohibited me from returning until I complete certain examinations."

"I'm sorry, Marcel," I said. "But I understand Peter Sargeant's directive. Concussions are serious. We don't want you to rush your recovery and possibly make things worse."

"Do not think that my head injury is affecting my judgment, Olivia," he said. "I know you would suspect that I am feeble-brained right now."

"Not at all," I said, though the idea had crossed my mind. "But I am worried for you."

"If you want to help, then you must investigate this. I know that my chocolate had a more salty taste than it should have. I was disappointed even though I knew I had not erred while assembling the ingredients. GHB has a salty taste. You see?"

"Have you brought this to the attention of the Secret Service?"

"Your handsome new husband is now aware, yes?"

"Yes," I agreed, though I wished I didn't have to. Rather than look distraught by my admission, Gav looked thoughtful. He continued to pay close attention as Marcel went on.

"I will, of course, tell Agent MacKenzie, but you must promise me," he said. "Of everyone at the White House, you are the person who is best at uncovering the truth."

"I wouldn't go that far."

"I would," he said with more than a touch of enthusiasm. "You have unmasked killers and have put yourself at great personal risk for many people you do not even know. Will you not help a friend?"

At that I had no choice. Marcel was right. He was my friend and I owed it to him. What might be even more to the point was that if the Saardiscans *had* sabotaged his chocolate, then everyone in the White House was at risk. The chances of that were slim, of course. I hoped all of tonight's drama had more to do with our pastry chef's concussion than any real threat.

"I'll look into it, Marcel."

"My dearest Olivia, I knew I could count on you."

"I'll be in touch. Don't worry another minute." Gav regarded me with an odd expression. I shrugged. "You concentrate on getting better so that we have you back in the White House as soon as we can."

When I hung up, Gav asked, "How, exactly, do you plan to look into this?"

I didn't know, and admitted as much. "I couldn't refuse him. Not when he was so distraught."

"I understand."

"Do you think he's imagining all this?"

"The man suffered a concussion. It's possible. The bigger question is, what do you think?"

"Marcel is fond of drama, but he doesn't make things up." I was reasoning aloud, which often helped. "I understand the concussion could be causing him to imagine such a scenario, but—like I asked him—what would the Saardiscans stand to gain by taking him out?"

"Nothing comes to mind?"

"The only thing," I said, "and this is a stretch, is that after the first incident, when we didn't know how long Marcel would be out, Sargeant asked Kilian to take over as pastry chef. When Marcel returned to the kitchen, those plans were scrapped."

"That's a fairly extreme action to take."

"It is," I said, "and Kilian doesn't strike me as the sort of person who would do anyone harm on purpose."

"What about the other men? Would they take Marcel out to help elevate their leader's position?"

"No," I said. "They don't seem like they're all that close. I'm at a loss here. I told Marcel I'd look into it, but I don't have the first idea of how to do that."

"Keep your eyes open," he said. "There's really not much else you can do."

CHAPTER 14

BUCKY AND I HAD ABOUT AN HOUR ALONE together the next morning before our Saardiscan guests arrived. In that short amount of time we not only prepared the First Family's breakfast, we also set up another schedule for the remainder of the Saardiscans' visit. Again.

"This schedule has changed every single day since they've been here," Bucky said as we plodded through the process. "I've lost count of the iterations."

"Can you imagine how scatterbrained we must look to them? They came here to learn about our methods and we haven't had a single normal day since they arrived."

"Whose bright idea was it for them to stay for two weeks?" Bucky asked. "Three days would have been plenty."

"What do you think about Marcel's suspicions?" I kept my voice low. Even though we usually had a bit of advance notice before the team showed up, I didn't want anyone to overhear.

Bucky stared out the doorway as though he expected the Saardiscans to tromp through at any minute. "We've seen stranger things happen around here," he said. "I can't rule it out." ·

"Neither can I."

"What do you plan to do about it?"

"There's not much that can be done. However, *we*," I said, emphasizing the word and wiggling a finger to link us both, "can find out more about the men. Who they are. If they're capable of this kind of attack. Look around here." I perched my fists at my waist and did a slow circle around the room, seeing it all as though for the first time. "A kitchen is a dangerous place. Chefs have knives and chemicals at their disposal. Most powerful of all, they have knowledge. If one of our visitors is a bad egg, we might be in serious trouble."

I took a closer look at the schedule we'd set up. "How about we take turns working with them one on one?" I asked.

"I'm not sure what you're going for."

"Here." I pointed to the first task of the day. "We divvied the men up so that two work with you while two work with me. What if you take one, I take three?" I penciled in lines to show what I meant. "That way you can get to know that one person better. Maybe if we're able to establish rapport with them, one on one, they'll start dishing on one another."

"You really think so?"

"Unless you have a better idea?" I asked, not meaning to speak so sharply. "I think our best chance to find out if there's a hidden agenda is to get them to drop their guard."

"And if they don't?"

I held up my hands. "I don't know."

"The idea of an attack on Marcel is preposterous," he said. "I mean, why? What possible good could come from drugging the guy who's supposed to be showing you around the place?"

"I've been asking myself that question all night. The only

explanation I came up with is that with our pastry chef out of commission, that puts Kilian as the front-runner for desserts."

"Lame," he said.

"You think? I mean, there was no way they could have predicted that Kilian's expertise would be tapped in Marcel's absence. And think about this: If Marcel is right and they used GHB, that causes only temporary unconsciousness. There was no way to engineer it so that he'd hit his head. Even if Marcel collapsed, he could be back within hours. What good could that possibly do any of them?"

"Unless," Bucky said, "whatever they needed to do is done now?"

"What do you mean?"

"While Marcel was unconscious, they had the run of the chocolate shop, right? Could they have stolen something? Purloined a recipe, or done something like that?"

"Maybe," I allowed, "but that seems extreme."

"I don't have the answers. That's your job."

"How about I take a run at the chocolate shop, just to make sure nothing seems amiss?"

"Have at it, boss," he said. "I'll hold down the fort."

I headed out through the refrigeration room and crossed the basement hall, saying hello to a couple of staffers along the way before walking into the chocolate shop. The room was quiet and dark. I turned on the lights. Fitted with stainless steel appliances and countertops, the room was efficiently laid out. Good thing, because it was even smaller than the mezzanine-level pastry kitchen. Again, I marveled at how Marcel could produce delicious artistry in such limited space.

As I looked around, I realized that I so seldom visited this area, I'd have no clue if something was out of place. Still, it wouldn't hurt to spend a couple of minutes checking. Focusing, I blew out a breath of frustration as I made a slow circuit around the room.

The cleaning crew had been in here since Marcel's

collapse, and the place sparkled. On a whim, I opened up the refrigerator and peeked inside. As was his habit, Marcel had everything precisely labeled and neatly stacked in containers and jars.

I closed that unit and opened the next one. Same thing. Shelves filled with ingredients, every single canister sealed and marked for easy identification.

About to close the refrigerator door, I noticed a demitasse cup on the bottom shelf. The top of it had been hastily covered with clear plastic wrap, and the cup shoved in front of two jars of blackberry jam. I picked up the small vessel and examined it. The cleaning people had probably put this away. Peeling off the plastic wrap, I sniffed the contents.

Marcel's famous chocolate drink. About halfway full.

Holding the demitasse cup at eye level, I turned it to one side, then the other, noticing small, chocolate dribble marks down the otherwise pristine white porcelain. Someone had been drinking from this, no question about it. Whether it had been Marcel, I didn't know.

I replaced the plastic film over the top and, taking it with me, made my way back across the basement hall into our kitchen's refrigeration room, where I pulled open the right-hand unit. Tucking the cup behind a bin of Brussels sprouts on the top shelf, I thought about how best to broach the idea of getting the contents tested. I knew my request wouldn't go over well, but I didn't see that I had any choice.

I returned to the kitchen just as the Saardiscans arrived. "Good morning," I said. "How was your evening?"

Nate grinned. "We went to a bar last night where they were playing disco."

All of Washington, D.C., to sightsee, and visiting a disco was what made him happy? "That's great," I said. "I hope you'll be able to explore some of the monuments and the Smithsonian while you're here."

Hector waved his hand. "Plenty of time. Nate and I met two American women at the disco."

I didn't really want to hear more. "What about you?" I asked Kilian.

He shrugged. "I spent time at the bookstore. So much to see, to read."

Tibor was the only one of the group who hadn't chimed in. Not that I wanted to pry—all right, I admit it, I did want to pry—but I asked him, "What about you? Did you do anything fun last night?"

"We are not here for fun." He turned from me and made his way over to the cabinets where we kept our smocks and aprons. "It is time for us to work. Not to stand around and chatter."

So much for the niceties. I faced the group. "With all the changes we've had to work around, we need to make certain we haven't overlooked any details. Kilian, as you and I discussed, you're probably taking over the pastry kitchen in Marcel's absence. I want to ensure that both the chief usher and Secret Service are still in agreement with that decision."

"I am not happy about the circumstances," he said, "but I am delighted to be able to share with you some of my expertise. Is Marcel expected to return at some point?"

"Yes," I said. "This is a precautionary move."

"Then I will do my best to stand in for him."

"Great. Let's get started."

Bucky's expression grew increasingly more grim throughout this discussion. If I thought I was distrustful, Bucky was ten times more so. He also had a harder time hiding it. To the point that Tibor frowned, and pointed directly at my assistant. "You do not approve? What is the reason you are angry? You do not think that Kilian can do as good a job as your Marcel?"

Caught in the spotlight and still wearing his expression of distaste, Bucky simply shook his head. "Don't read anything into it." He patted himself on the stomach and shot me a conspiratorial look. "Onions in my omelet this morning," he said. "Not setting so well."

I took control again. "Bucky and I have come up with a new schedule that we hope appeals to all of you." I pulled out the sheets we'd been working on before the team arrived. "Even though you will be guests at our dinner for Kerry Freiberg, we want to learn more about Saardiscan dishes so we can add a bit of your country's traditional flavor to our menu."

Tibor made what sounded like a snort.

"What's wrong? Don't you like Ms. Freiberg?"

Tying his apron around his back, he didn't answer.

"Tibor," I said, waiting until he made eye contact. "Why don't you care for Ms. Freiberg?"

His gaze skimmed over his comrades, one at a time, as though seeking support. From what I could tell, he found none. Hector and Nate stared back without expression. Kilian looked confused.

"We are not here to discuss politics," Kilian said, with a pointed look at Tibor. "We are here for learning."

I recognized a lead-in when I saw it. "But don't you think that discussing politics is a way for us to learn more about each other?"

Kilian paled.

"I understand if you don't care to discuss such matters in front of one another," I said. "Forget I asked."

"There is only one answer," Tibor said. "Our current president is the only candidate qualified to rule Saardisca." He raised both hands in a movement that spoke of frustration. "How this Kerry Freiberg has become so popular so fast is suspect."

Kilian placed a hand on his friend's arm. "She is not expected to win, remember."

But Tibor was on a roll. He shook Kilian's hand off. "If she wins, Saardisca will be in ruin."

"Why do you say that?" I asked.

By this time, Tibor's side-of-beef face had gone redder than usual. His bottom teeth nearly chomped his words. "She is a woman," he said. "In our country, women do not achieve such levels. To have her running for office is a joke. She will not win."

"But what if she does?"

Tibor glared at me. He was so close to me that his eyes, a deep green with pale flecks of brown, seemed to shoot sparks as he spoke. "Then I pity her. No one will stand for such a travesty."

"Pity her?" I was pushing this man's buttons, but I couldn't help myself. "Are you saying that there are people in your country who would do her harm?"

He shrugged. "What do I know? I am only a chef. Important decisions are made by those who rule our country."

"You mean by those who are threatened by her," I said.

He scoffed. "No one of merit is threatened by her. She is being given room to fail so that her followers see how useless she really is." He waved a hand in front of his face. "Why do we talk about such things when there is work to be done?"

Kilian came between us. "It will be best if we do not continue down this path," he said.

I took a step back. "You're right, Kilian. I allowed my temper to get the best of me. My apologies." Taking a deep breath, I recollected myself. "Back to work, shall we? Bucky, how about you take everyone upstairs to the pastry kitchen, to get started up there?"

"Where will you be?" Kilian asked me.

"I have a meeting with our chief usher."

CHAPTER 15

"AND YOU EXPECT ME TO ACT ON THIS?" TOM asked, his voice strained as he leaned forward on his desk. "With no proof?"

We were in Tom's office in the West Wing. "I don't *expect* anything," I said. I turned to Sargeant, who was seated in the chair next to me, both of us across from Tom. "I do, however, believe that this is enough of an unusual situation to warrant attention."

Tom blew out a breath. I knew I wasn't the sole source of his frustration; the stress of this sequester was wearing on us all. The last thing anyone in the White House needed was another task to deal with. Yet here I sat, requesting special assistance.

Taking another breath, Tom composed himself. "What exactly are you asking for?"

"Simple, really. I'd like to have the chocolate Marcel made tested for GHB."

"You don't even know if that's the cup Marcel drank from, do you?"

"No, but if it was Marcel's and if we find out the drink was drugged—"

"That's a lot of ifs."

I drew a breath. "Wouldn't it be better to be safe than sorry?"

Tom's neck pulsed, and his lips were pale from the pressure of keeping them tightly clamped. Sargeant kept his fingers steepled in front of his lips. His brow furrowed, but he didn't say a word.

"Yes, it is," Tom said finally. "Where is the chocolate now?"

"I have it refrigerated."

"You know as well as I do that Marcel hit his head," Tom said very slowly. "He suffered a concussion. This could all be wild speculation on his part."

"I understand why this seems an outlandish allegation, but Marcel and I have finely honed palates. We're trained to discern tastes. That's not bragging; I'm stating a fact."

Tom shot a glance at Sargeant, who nodded.

Emboldened by their wordless agreement, I went on. "Our careers depend on our expertise in these matters. That chocolate is one of Marcel's signature creations. If he claims the chocolate tasted salty, you can bet that it was."

"That doesn't prove it was laced with GHB," Tom said. "Marcel doesn't know what caused the change in flavor."

"Which is why I'm asking for it to be tested."

Tom leaned forward, folding his hands on the desk. In all the time I'd known him, I'd never paid much attention to the long vein that ran from his hairline down to the inner edge of one brow. Now that vein throbbed white.

"I take threats to the residents and staff of this house very seriously." His voice was low, too low. "And even though I suspect Marcel's imagination has gotten the best of him, I can't risk being wrong." Almost as though he was afraid of being overheard by staff outside his office, he added, "We don't want this leaked to the press. Give me a little time to arrange it. I'll send someone to pick it up."

"Thank you," I said.

"I will be in touch."

Sargeant watched us, his eyes alert and interested. He'd been glancing between us as we'd traded barbs.

"You've been quiet. Do you have anything to add?" I asked him.

One eyebrow cocked up. He lowered his steepled fingers. His nose twitched. Patting his breast pocket, where a yellow handkerchief square peeked out to match his precisely knotted tie, he took his time answering.

"I may have an element of interest to contribute to the discussion."

I waited. Tom did, too.

Sargeant pinched the creases of his dress slacks, running his fingers down the length of his legs to his knees. He didn't make eye contact with us as he gathered his thoughts.

When he did look up, he turned to Tom first, then me. "What I am about to tell you is not classified information." He gave a deferential nod toward Tom. "You would be better prepared to handle that protected information, of course. What I have is, for lack of a better term, a suggestion that was offered to me. My counterpart in Saardisca—though heaven knows they don't have a counterpart who actually shoulders the same responsibilities I do—asked me to keep a close eye on our guests while they were here."

"Why didn't you tell me?" Tom asked, sitting up straight. "What is he worried about?"

"Tut, tut, young man." Sargeant was the only person in the world I knew who could get away with saying, "Tut, tut."

"If there is a security concern, I ought to have been informed."

"This is not a security concern. Not precisely." Sargeant cleared his throat. "It seems that the leader of the group,

Kilian?" Sargeant looked to me for confirmation of the man's name. I nodded. "Kilian is not as strong a defender of their nation as they might expect someone in his exalted position to be."

"Go on," Tom said.

"I know you are fully aware of Saardisca's military strength. I also know that you are up to date on such things as treaties, embargoes, agreements, what have you." Sargeant twisted a hand in the air as though none of this was of any importance. "What I bring to the table is an awareness of the mood of the country. An awareness of its citizens' mores, traditions, and belief systems."

"I am not unaware of such things." Tom's words were clipped.

"True enough. However." Sargeant leaned forward, propping one elbow on Tom's desk. "There are times when everything isn't black and white. When one needs to be sensitive to the needs of others. I hope you haven't forgotten that before I was chief usher, I was the White House sensitivity director."

I bit my lip. Contradiction in terms if there ever was one.

Sargeant was gaining momentum. "Agent MacKenzie, you are charged with the safety of those in the White House."

Tom nodded.

"As such, you see things as a threat or a non-threat. Hence, my black-and-white comment." Sargeant scratched the side of his nose with a fingertip. "My Saardiscan counterpart knows the heart of his people. That's why he relied on me to be his eyes and ears while the contingent is in the United States."

"Where is this going?" I asked.

Sargeant favored me with a withering glance. "There is some concern that, when their visit is complete, Kilian might not wish to return to Saardisca with his colleagues."

I thought about how much Kilian seemed to be enjoying his visit, and how much he valued the freedom he was experiencing here. How he'd panicked when I'd used the term *asylum*. And how he believed the government knew nothing about the doubts he harbored.

"You think he's going to want to stay?" Turning to Tom, I asked, "Would he be required to find permanent employment in order to be allowed to remain here? I don't know what the rules are."

Tom waved my question away. "Rules are different for Saardiscans," he said. "Their idea, not ours. They don't allow their citizens to travel as freely as most countries do. There are lots more hoops to jump through. That's another reason why Kerry Freiberg's visit is making headlines. We're hoping it portends favorable changes for its citizens and better relationships between our two countries."

"Would it be easier for someone like Kilian to defect now that he's here?" I asked.

Neither man answered me.

Tom went on, this time addressing Sargeant. "The timing is curious, in light of Ms. Freiberg's visit," he said. "Do they really believe Kilian might request asylum?"

Sargeant's eyes glinted, and he gave a fractional nod. "I see you grasp the enormity of the situation." Turning to me, he continued to explain. "My Saardiscan counterpart said that he had no idea that Ms. Freiberg's visit would coincide with that of the chefs. The fact that they will be here together gives Kilian an opportunity he might not have otherwise had."

"I don't understand," I said.

Tom held his hand out toward Sargeant, inviting him to continue. I got the impression that I was the only one in the room who didn't understand the ins and outs of Saardiscan law. Not that I should. I was a chef, for goodness' sake, not an ambassador.

"Kilian will connect with Ms. Freiberg at some point during her visit here," Sargeant said. "She stands for the relaxing of military rule and for the easing of restrictions on her countrymen. She could use Kilian as a pawn to further her agenda. If she encourages him, and he requests asylum, Saardisca will be forced to allow it. Otherwise, they risk Ms. Freiberg using Kilian as a political weapon."

"Then why," I asked, "did they decide to allow her to visit while the chefs were here? You and I both know that their visit was set up more than a year ago. If they have the power, and it sounds as though they do, why not delay her leaving Saardisca for a couple of weeks? They could have had their dessert and eaten it, too."

Sargeant sniffed deeply. "You evidently have no idea how difficult it is to schedule events."

I had a very clear idea of how difficult it was to make arrangements around government officials' lives. "Seems to me that if the situation was so dire, they would make every effort."

Sargeant's eyes widened. "This was the only time her schedule allowed a visit to the United States. It seems that diplomats in charge of the government and those in charge of the chefs did not communicate."

"One part of the government not knowing what another is doing?" I asked, with a little bit of a smirk. "I suppose that happens in all countries."

Visibly annoyed by my light-hearted comment, Sargeant glared. "What's important here is that we take the information we have and use it wisely." He turned to face Tom. "Agreeing to have the chocolate tested is a wise move."

Tom worked his jaw. "Let me play devil's advocate for just a moment: Why would any of them poison Marcel? If Kilian does intend to defect, Marcel's collapse blew his first chance to meet with Kerry Freiberg, didn't it?"

I didn't have an answer for that. "Desserts are Kilian's specialty," I said. "Maybe he thought that with Marcel out of the way, he'd have a chance at taking over as pastry chef—permanently."

"That," Tom said, "would be one heck of a leap."

"*We* understand that such a scheme wouldn't work. But does he understand that?" I asked. An idea popped into my head. "Or maybe the chocolate was meant for one of their own, and Marcel consumed it by mistake?"

"Another leap." Tom looked at his watch. Our time was up. "One of my team will be in touch to retrieve the chocolate."

I thanked him again.

Thus dismissed, Sargeant and I made our way back to the residence. "I appreciate the update about Kilian," I said. "He may be dissatisfied with life in Saardisca, but he doesn't strike me as the sort of person who would poison another for personal gain."

"It's a long shot, I agree," he said.

"Yet something isn't quite right."

Sargeant nodded. "Are Agent MacKenzie's doubts valid? Could this be nothing more than unfortunate coincidence? Or have you and I become eager to find conspiracies where none exist?"

I thought about it, but didn't have an answer.

CHAPTER 16

BUCKY AND THE SAARDISCANS WERE STILL
busy upstairs when I returned to the kitchen to prepare the
First Lady's lunch. Mrs. Hyden had three visitors this
afternoon, all of whom were volunteers leading the efforts
to decorate the White House for the holidays. They were
being joined by two of the White House florists, and Peter
Everett Sargeant.

We were still weeks away from the actual installation,
but plans for themes and discussions about color choices
had been ongoing for months. The sequester should be
over by then. Or so we all hoped.

I had just finished plating the meal for the First Lady
and her guests when my cell phone rang. As the butlers
whisked the food away, I pulled up the device to determine
who was calling. "Marcel," I said. "How are you?"

"Olivia! I am well. Where are you?"

I told him, mentioning that the Saardiscans and Bucky
were upstairs.

"Are you alone?"

"I am. What's wrong, Marcel?"

"Olivia, you are the only one who sees the truth. You must listen to what I have to say."

"Of course, I will. What's up?"

"Tell me again, Olivia. You are alone?"

"Yes," I said. "No one is around. What's going on?"

"I have proof," he whispered. "Proof that I was poisoned."

My hand tightened around my cell phone's casing. I whispered in reply, "What is it? What proof?"

"It was Kilian, I'm sure of it." Lapsing into French, he began talking so quickly and with such agitation that, even though I was familiar with the language, I could make out only two words: *chocolate*, and *drink*.

"Marcel," I said, trying to keep quiet, yet raise my voice enough over his deafening grievances to be heard. "Please. In English."

He stopped his rant, took a steadying breath, then continued, speaking more slowly. "My apologies. This truth has dawned on me merely moments ago and I am beside myself. Why would this man choose to do me harm? Would he truly expect that he could take my place at the White House as pastry chef? Certainly not."

I thought back to my discussion with Tom and Sargeant about this very matter. "Tell me your proof," I said.

"It is so obvious, I am ashamed to have not noticed earlier. Do you remember when I lost consciousness in the pastry kitchen?" he asked.

"Of course."

"Did the visiting chefs tell you that I had shared my raspberry sauce with them?"

"They did. Kilian, in fact, was the one who told me."

"See? See? It is Kilian who is behind all this."

"Please, slow down. I thought you told me that you took a double dose of your blood pressure medication."

"Yes, but I am now convinced that it was the raspberry sauce."

"Hang on, Marcel," I said. "Did you or didn't you take the wrong dosage of medicine?"

"I did, but now I believe it is possible that Kilian tried to poison me, and that is the real reason I collapsed."

I bit my lips together tightly. Marcel's desperation was palpable, yet I began to wonder if I'd made a mistake by bringing his suppositions to Tom's attention. "If you made the raspberry sauce, then why would you think it was poisoned?"

Marcel made another noise. He was growing impatient with me. "I passed around the container with spoons for sampling, yes? I handed it to Kilian, who shared with his colleagues. They seemed to enjoy the taste and used all but one spoon. Kilian held the plate out to me. I urged him to take it but he insisted that I should share as well. I thought he was being polite. Now I know better."

I'd been afraid of this. Marcel's deduction was hardly proof. "And the second incident?" I asked.

"That," he said with emphasis, "is what made me realize that it had been Kilian all along."

"Go on."

"We were sampling my famous chocolate drink. You know how much everyone adores that particular creation."

"I do," I said. And I did. Marcel's chocolate drink was the stuff of pure bliss.

"Not to boast, but it is such a spectacular concoction that even I cannot resist its tempting aroma. I had made enough of it for everyone to have more than a small sample. I poured it into demitasse cups and, again, passed the tray around. Again, I took the last one remaining."

"And?" I asked. "Did you see Kilian, or anyone else, add anything to the chocolate before you drank it?"

"Of course not. If I had, I would never have brought it to my lips."

"Then how—"

"I was instructing them. I was busy with preparations

for our next item. My back was turned and my attention was drawn elsewhere."

"There's no real proof then, is there?" I asked.

"The salty flavoring," he said. "I tasted additional salt in my chocolate, remember? I have a very discerning palate, you know."

"I know you do. But if you didn't actually see anyone add anything, then there's no way for us to make an accusation."

I measured my words before I continued. "I know that Kilian is to take over some of the pastry chef responsibilities while you're out, but there's no way he could have predicted that. Why would he have taken such a risk? Don't you think he would have been better off with you remaining in the White House? It would have provided him the opportunity to impress you with his knowledge."

Marcel made a faint noise of agreement. "I cannot explain another's motivation," he said after a beat. "Do not expect me to do so."

"What *do* you expect me to do?" I wanted to help him, but he was presenting me with little more than speculation and far-out accusations.

Marcel was quiet for a moment. "Let me ask you this, Olivia. What do you believe?"

I thought about it. "I don't know."

"Have I ever been a person who fabricates stories, or who seeks attention? Other than for my exemplary creations, that is?"

Marcel could be overly dramatic from time to time, but he didn't create stories out of whole cloth. "No. That isn't you."

"I make two requests of you, Olivia: Find out why this was done to me; and, more important, be careful. There is no telling what else these men are capable of."

THAT NIGHT AFTER DINNER, GAV SWIRLED THE wine in his glass as he listened to me talk. We were seated on the sofa with the television off, the way we did most nights since we'd gotten married. It was a lovely, quiet way to bring our busy days to a close and to decompress as we shared those parts of our lives that the other wasn't always privy to.

"What?" I asked, after I'd told him about Marcel's phone call. "You look as though you have something on your mind."

"I do." He placed his glass on the low coffee table, then leaned forward, elbows on knees, hands clasped. "I'm not liking this," he said.

"What part?"

"Any of it." Two small lines formed between his brows and he broke eye contact. "I was comfortable with the thought that Marcel might have been imagining things until this additional information from Sargeant."

"Tom is not convinced that Marcel was poisoned, but at least he's agreed to test the chocolate."

"How soon?"

"No idea. He said he'd send an agent to pick it up."

Gav scratched the side of his face. "Tom's PPD isn't suffering cutbacks the way the rest of government agencies are, but I'm hearing about rampant backlogs and delays just about everywhere else."

"What are you saying?"

"Even if Tom rushes the testing, he'll have to go through official channels. I'm not sure how long that will take." He waved the thought away. "Let's not worry about that right now." He sat back to watch me again. "Now that you know that Kilian is under scrutiny from Saardisca, what do *you* think about Marcel's allegations?"

I wasn't sure how to answer. "I have no doubt that there was something wrong with the chocolate. The question is, who tainted it? And why? Poisoning Marcel makes absolutely no sense. Why do that? If it were simply to cause mischief, then I have to ask—again—why? They're our guests here. I wouldn't think that they would want anything to go wrong during their stay."

"Keep going," he said. "Reasoning aloud is helpful."

"The only other possibility I can think of is that the tainted chocolate wasn't meant for Marcel. That one of the visiting chefs has it in for a colleague."

"Okay," he encouraged, "that's a reasonable theory. Have you noticed any hostility between them?"

"Not really. Yet, there's a nagging feeling here." I pointed inward. "Something is wrong with these visitors. I can't put my finger on it."

He listened, deep in thought. I waited. Finally, he broke the silence and looked up. "You know I have great respect for Tom. He's in a tough spot these days, what with the government sequester and zero room for error where security is concerned."

I leaned forward. "So you think I should chalk all this up to a sequence of unfortunate events?"

His eyes narrowed. "Here's the thing, Ollie. There's one very important variable we have to consider."

"And what's that?"

He pointed to me. "You don't rush to judgment. You're not hysterical. You have an eye and ear—a sense—for when things aren't quite right. The way you believe Marcel when he insists the chocolate was tainted, is the same way I feel hearing you. If you tell me that you sense something is wrong, then I know it is."

Gav's grave look of concern and his unwavering faith in me made my heart skip a beat. He never shut me down, never told me I was being foolish. Quite the contrary: He actually encouraged my curiosity. I'd hoped that once we'd settled down, we wouldn't have to deal with criminal or conspiratorial issues anymore. But given our jobs, I supposed there were hundreds of things going on around us every day that I was unaware of. I should be grateful that we only became involved in the few we did.

"What do you suggest?"

His lips tightened. "That's a tough one. It's virtually

impossible to investigate these chefs personally. The government of Saardisca isn't about to send you birth-to-present-day dossiers on their citizens, just because you ask nicely."

"I asked Sargeant about that after our most recent meeting with Tom." I shook my head. "We've gotten all the information we're going to get."

"Where is Marcel's chocolate right now?"

"I put it in the kitchen refrigeration room for safekeeping—behind a bin of vegetables. No one ought to dig that deeply into cold storage unless they're looking for it."

Gav rubbed his jaw. "I might be able to pull a few strings."

"You mean, have it tested? Independently?"

"We can send out two samples. Give half to Tom, the other half to me."

"That would be fabulous."

He gave a self-deprecating grin. "I've made a few friends in forensics labs over the years. I'm sure I can coerce one of them to help us out here. And because I'll be working outside official channels, there's a chance I can get this done a little bit faster."

"You are, without a doubt, the most thoughtful husband on the planet."

"All I'm doing is offering to help my wife."

I got a little tingle of joy every time he referred to me as his wife. Leaning forward, I wrapped a hand around the back of his neck and pulled him close. "You know that flowers, candy, and jewelry don't make me swoon. But *ooh*, when you whisper words like *forensics*, I get goose bumps." I leaned forward and placed a soft kiss on his lips.

"No doubt about it," he said when I sat back. "I've still got the touch."

That settled, I took another sip of my wine and studied Gav. My husband. It had taken me a little while to get used to that label, and the first time Gav had introduced me as his wife had taken me off guard. Still so new.

He'd picked up his glass and seemed to be memorizing it. The man hadn't swirled his wine this much in a long time.

I leaned toward him, placing a hand on his forearm. "You've been wonderful at listening to my troubles at work. But I can tell there's more on your mind."

He looked up. What did I read there? Relief? Worry? A combination?

"Is it Bill and Erma?" I asked. "Is he worse off than we first thought?"

Gav shook his head. "His prognosis is good. Erma is convinced that as long as he takes it easy and follows doctors' orders, he'll be back to normal in no time."

"Will he follow orders?"

Gav made a so-so face. "If he were on his own, no. But Erma will make sure he toes the line."

"Then what is it?" I asked. "You may as well tell me because you know I won't give up until I get answers."

That garnered me a half-grin. "I do want to talk to you about this, but I'm having a difficult time finding the words."

This sounded serious. When I leaned back, he reached over and placed a warm hand on my knee.

"Sorry. I'm going about this all wrong. It is about Bill and Erma, but not in the way you might imagine."

"Then tell me," I said. "No need to watch your words. It's me, remember?"

He flashed that half-grin again.

Gav refilled both our glasses and then held the bottle aloft.

"Do you like this wine?" he asked.

He turned the label to face me, but I already knew what we were drinking: a lush cabernet from Spencer's Vineyards. It had been one of several bottles Erma and Bill had given us when we'd visited their winery several months back.

"I love it," I said. "I've enjoyed every one of their wines."

"How much do you love it?"

"I don't understand."

He took a deep breath. Replacing the bottle on the table, he turned to me. His face was devoid of expression; he'd adopted his "agent demeanor." Different from his mood when he simply needed time, this side of him was impenetrable. Unyielding. I knew he was capable of assuming his hardline persona at any time, but I didn't expect him to do so with me. Not anymore.

Before he could speak again, I interrupted. "What is going on? What are you so afraid to tell me?"

I thought I detected a crack in his armor, but in a flash it was gone. Whatever he'd been about to say, he clearly didn't want me to read the emotion behind it. I envied him the ability to close that part of himself off, but I was miffed that he was doing it.

"Gav." My voice was a warning to him. "We're in this together, remember?"

My words hit some invisible target.

"That's what makes this so difficult," he said, shutting his eyes for a long moment. When he opened them again, he pulled in another deep breath, solidifying his resolve. The steel-faced agent was back. "Bill and Erma," he began slowly, "want me to take over the winery."

I don't know what I'd expected him to say, but it certainly wasn't that.

"Take over?" I repeated. "You mean while Bill is recovering?"

"No." He continued to stare at me, and I realized how much I pitied suspects forced to endure Gav's interrogations. If I hadn't known him, I would have been terrified. It was clear he was waiting to gauge my reaction before sharing his own.

"Then what?" I asked.

"Jenny was Bill and Erma's only child," he said, referring to his former fiancée, the young woman who had been murdered shortly before they could be wed. "I'm the closest thing to a son they've ever had. They want to leave their vineyard to me. To us," he added with a nod.

My jaw went slack and my mouth opened. I said the first thing that came to mind. "But their vineyard is hours away. How would you commute?"

He took to swirling his wineglass again. "That's the problem. I couldn't."

Like a swarm of ideas condensing together to create a whole, I felt a cloud forming in my brain. A storm cloud. "You would give up your work in the Secret Service?" I asked. I was shocked and taken aback, and not certain what to do with all the thoughts ricocheting in my brain. "Is that what you want?"

Gav rubbed his face with his free hand, and in that instant, agent Gav dissolved, and my caring husband was back. "I don't know what I want," he said. "But before I can even consider it, I need to know what you think about all this."

"I . . . I . . ." Speechless, because I had no idea how to answer, I stopped trying. "When would this take place?"

"They were planning to have this talk with me a few years from now," he said. "But Bill's stroke changed their timeline. They don't expect me—expect us—to drop our lives here and move there immediately. They want us to take our time and think about it."

I tried to digest without panicking. "That would mean me leaving the White House."

"There may be options we're unaware of."

"Like what?"

"Erma and Bill employ a good group of workers, people they trust. There may be an extended period of time where I wouldn't have to be there at all. And don't forget, Bill and Erma don't plan to retire yet. They fully intend to keep working there and to keep running the place themselves for years to come."

"But they want to know now if you're willing."

Gav nodded, but said nothing.

My mind raced. "What did you tell them?"

"Nothing," he said quickly. "They knew I needed to talk with you, first."

I nodded, buying time. We'd been married less than six months. Wasn't this the sort of major upheaval that cropped up after the first anniversary? Not that major changes respected timetables, of course.

The biggest question hung between us. "What do *you* want?" I asked. "I mean, if you're bringing this up in this way, you must be considering it."

He frowned, but nodded. "It's not my nature to reject an opportunity out of hand. I need to at least consider what this means."

"I thought you were already where you always wanted to be. You told me that you'd turned down other opportunities because working with the Secret Service in the capacity that you do is what you've always wanted."

"It is."

"You'd give that up?" I couldn't help it. Silently, my selfish side asked, "And you'd be asking me to give my career up, too?"

He looked directly into my eyes. "What I want is what's right for both of us." He placed his glass down and motioned for me to do the same. I complied. After I did, he took both my hands in his. "I will never ask you to give anything up that's important to you for something that's important to me."

"But"—I knew I was arguing against myself here—"isn't that what people do in a marriage? And if we don't take it on, won't you be giving up this chance for me?"

He let go of my hands. "I will never ask you to give up your life here in D.C.," he began again, "but what if? What if when the next president comes in, you tender your resignation, and he or she accepts it?"

That was a constant fear I harbored in my heart.

"Would you be content working in a hotel kitchen?" he asked. "Would you start your own restaurant?"

"I don't know yet."

"Which is why I'm hoping you and I can talk about this. I can't work in the field forever. Even though I'm recovered from my recent injury, I know that agents don't have lengthy careers in positions where physical stamina and prowess are requirements. There are always younger, stronger, savvier young recruits eager to take our spots." He stared away for a moment, and I wondered what he was seeing. "I would feel claustrophobic in a desk job. I've always known that, and I constantly fight the demons that warn that my days are numbered."

I reached forward to touch him. "You're nowhere close to being finished in the field."

"I know," he said, turning to me again. "I plan to push myself for as long as I can. But this recent injury has been my wakeup call. I can't deny the fact that there will come a time when I'm no longer assigned to hunt down the bad guys. What then? I've never allowed myself to think that far ahead."

He gave me a sad smile. "Future plans and I never seemed to get along very well." He grasped my hands again. "Until you came into my life, Olivia Paras."

I swallowed at the emotion laid bare in his eyes.

"Now," he said, "I'm less afraid of making plans, but I've avoided the whole issue for so long that I don't know where to begin." His shoulders raised up, ever so slightly. "This situation with Bill and Erma came out of the blue. I need your help to decide what we ought to do about it."

I still didn't have an answer and knew I wouldn't for what might be a long time. "What will happen if you turn them down?"

When he let go of my hands again, he smiled. "Apparently, they've already written their will, leaving everything to me. Whether I choose to run the winery or not is completely immaterial. They hope I will, of course—they want me to—but once ownership transfers to me, the property is mine to do as I see fit. I can sell it, lease it out, hire others to run it—whatever I choose. They made it clear that this was a gift with no strings attached."

"They are incredibly generous people."

"And if I had my wish, they would run Spencer's Vineyards forever. But they're making future plans, and that's causing me to assess mine, which means ours." He lifted my glass and handed it to me, then picked his own glass back up. "For now, we can put this on the back burner. No pressure, Ollie. None at all." He raised his glass as though in a toast. "To our future together. Whatever it holds."

We clinked our glasses.

"To our future," I said.

CHAPTER 17

"YOU LOOK EXACTLY LIKE CYAN DID WHEN word came down about the sequester," Bucky said when he walked in the next morning. As he removed his windbreaker and began donning his smock, he added, "She wasn't thrilled to be temporarily laid off, but she knew this was the kick in the pants she needed to assess her future."

Bucky was far more astute than I sometimes gave him credit for. I'd been thinking about my conversation with Gav the night before, but wasn't ready to share this new dilemma with my assistant. "I desperately want her back," I said, "but I know that her best direction may lie elsewhere."

"Don't change the subject." Bucky crossed his arms. "Your eyes are animated, yet your expression says dread."

"Is that so strange?" I asked, feigning innocence. "We finally have an event to plan—at Blair House, which makes it special—and Virgil might be gone for good. Why wouldn't I be upbeat about that?"

"You skipped over the 'dread' part of my comment. What's bothering you, chief?"

I told him about Marcel's chocolate. "I managed to find the leftovers in the chocolate shop. It's safe in our refrigeration area." I pointed in the general direction. "Top shelf where no one ever looks," I said. "I'll take half of it home with me tonight so that Gav can have it tested."

The Saardiscan foursome walked in. "Good morning," I said, hoping they hadn't heard any of the prior conversation. What with Marcel's allegations about Kilian, Tibor's unpleasantness, and the reluctant cooperation from Hector and Nate, I didn't fully trust any of them. I made a mental note to pull the chocolate out from its top-shelf position and hide it elsewhere, just in case.

"Good morning," Tibor said, surprising me with his cheery tone and the hint of a smile on his craggy face.

Three of the men appeared to be in particularly jovial moods. Kilian was the lone exception. He barely met my eyes. I wondered what was up. "How are you all this morning?"

With their backs turned to me, the others donned aprons and I couldn't see their expressions, but Tibor continued the conversation. "Today is looking to be a strong and good day," he said.

"What happened?" I asked.

Tibor scowled. "Nothing of consequence to you." He must have read my reaction because he hastened to explain, "We are happy because we have successfully completed our first week. Kilian has submitted reports to our superiors, and all have been approved."

"I'm glad to hear it," I said. "That must be a relief. Is it, Kilian?"

The doughy-faced man glanced up, his normally pink cheeks pale and damp. "Yes," he said. "Yes."

LATER THAT MORNING, AFTER WE'D FINISHED preparing breakfast, I pulled them all together. One of the items we intended to serve at Kerry Freiberg's dinner was a traditional Saardiscan dish that, based on the ingredient list Kilian had provided, resembled a version of my squash soup.

"The Secret Service delivered the final ingredients we needed," I said to Kilian. "Apparently the first several establishments they visited were out of pears."

"I am looking forward to instructing you both." His mood had not improved greatly. As he addressed his colleagues, I got the impression he had his game face on. "We have all made a variation of *bazadyn*, no?"

The three men nodded.

"And we all have our unique touches that make *bazadyn* our own." Kilian held a pencil aloft, like an orchestra conductor holding a baton. "We will all share our secret ingredients and methods so that we are all *bazadyn* brothers." He nodded to me. "And sisters."

The men nodded again, though I noticed Nate did so hesitantly. The peculiar look in his eyes led me to believe that he was worried. I would even go so far as to say there was a flash of terror there. A chef caught without his tools. As though he didn't have a secret ingredient or method to share with his brethren and was worried they might think less of him.

We took up positions around the central counter, forming a rough circle. This way. we could follow along with every step and be able to compare, contrast, and learn as we went along.

Kilian stood with his back to the westernmost door and I stood directly across the stainless steel workspace. Bucky and Nate were to my left along one side, Hector and Tibor to my right. "Shall we begin?" I asked.

Kilian's chubby cheeks, still pale, grew ever more pink as he began the instruction. "Have you ever appreciated the beauty of the lowly squash?" he asked as he hefted a ridged green globe. "You Americans call this the acorn squash. And this"—he picked up one of the other gourds in front of him—"the butternut squash, yes?"

He looked to me for acknowledgment. I nodded.

"As ingredients go, the squash is not especially attractive.

But it is solid." He knocked his knuckles against the pale sitar-shaped vegetable. "And delightfully versatile."

If Kilian planned to wax poetic about every ingredient and every step, we could be at this countertop all morning. Good thing the First Lady was out today, and the president was lunching in the Navy Mess. There were still a few things I needed to do before dinner tonight, however. I made a mental note to keep an eye on the clock.

The rotund man leaned forward, eager to corral our attention. "Let us talk further about these menu mainstays. As our esteemed hosts know, there are many varieties to choose from." He smiled at me and at Bucky, then turned his attention to his colleagues. "I have tasted Tibor's version of *bazadyn* but have not had the pleasure to sample yours, Nate. Nor yours, Hector." His head turned from side to side as he addressed the men. "I know that your provinces are not always as well stocked as ours. Which types of squash have you had the opportunity to work with?"

Put on the spot, Hector opened his mouth. Instead of an answer, he made a strange gargling noise. His eyes went wide, and he grasped at his neck.

"Are you all right?" Kilian asked.

I started for Hector, who was now gasping and coughing. He sat on the floor, one hand still at his neck, the other pressing against his forehead. "I'm all right," he managed to say. "I was dizzy for a moment there."

"Do you need us to summon the doctor?" I asked.

"I will be fine." He put his face down and wrapped both hands around the back of his head. "Please. I need only to sit."

I crouched next to him. Bucky came around the other side. "Let's get you somewhere more comfortable," he said.

Kilian came around the counter. "What is wrong?"

"Have you eaten today?" I asked Hector.

He shook his head. Swallowed, with difficulty.

Kilian lowered himself to the floor. "You had only coffee this morning, yes?"

Hector nodded.

"Maybe he's feeling faint then?" I asked. Turning to Bucky, I said, "You'd better get the doctor here, just in case."

Hector put a hand out as though to stop him, but Bucky paid him no mind.

In an effort to keep Hector alert and talking, I asked, "Nothing besides coffee? Do you need to eat?"

Kilian answered for him. "We all had coffee. At the hotel. Nothing more."

"Were you feeling ill this morning?" I asked. "Is that why you didn't have breakfast?"

Kilian was perched on the balls of his feet, knees bent, so close I could touch him if I wanted to. He leaned forward, pressing a hand to the ground in front of him, as though stopping himself from losing his balance. "Oh," he said.

His face had gone white as bleached flour.

"Are you all right?" I asked.

He didn't answer. Struggling not to topple over, he thrust a hand upward, grasping the side of the countertop. "I must have moved too quickly," he tried to say. "My head." But his words had begun to slur.

"Kilian," I said. "What's going on?"

I looked around for help. Tibor edged away and Nate stared down at me, blinking as though confused. I was crouched between two ailing men in a particularly narrow portion of the kitchen, wedged between stainless steel cabinets. To my right, Hector groaned. His head dropped forward, and he toppled sideways.

Kilian coughed, then sat on the ground, hands at his head. He'd grown even more pale and his skin was shiny with sweat. His mouth opened and a deep gurgle erupted from within. "I am—" he said, then froze.

"Kilian," I said, but the unfocused look in his eyes stopped me. I reached to grab him as I called to Nate to come around the other way. "Help Hector," I said. "Get behind him and pull him into the corridor. We need to get him some air."

Tibor had backed into the doorway, the horror in his expression making it clear that he'd be no help at all.

Nate was attempting to drag Hector out where he could be more easily administered to, whispering what sounded like assurances to the stricken man.

Hector was conscious at least, looking frightened, but alert.

I couldn't say the same for Kilian. The portly man had passed out, falling backward and hitting his head against a metal edge. He'd clutched his chest with one meaty hand, but as I leaned over him, his grip loosened and his arm fell slack to the floor.

I turned Kilian's face toward mine, but his fixed gaze confirmed the worst. Bucky rushed in with the doctor close behind, as I desperately tried to bring Kilian back by sheer force of will. "Kilian." I leaned forward to begin CPR. "Breathe," I ordered him.

The doctor pulled me to my feet, taking my place in the small space between cabinets. He began CPR compressions as he called for resuscitation equipment. I stared down at the motionless chef at my feet.

Kilian was gone. I had no doubt.

Shaking myself back into awareness, I forced myself to think, to prioritize. "Hector was struck down, too," I said to the doctor. Pointing toward the small group now outside the kitchen's walls, I added, "He's still alive. Help him."

The doctor acknowledged me. He continued to try to revive Kilian, as I knew duty required, while I made my way to where Bucky was helping Hector. To my great relief, the young Saardiscan was still alert. Someone had brought him a glass of water, and although color hadn't returned to his face, he was able to answer each of the medical assistant's questions.

Bucky nudged my arm. "Kilian?" he asked.

I kept my lips tight and shook my head.

"First Marcel, now this. What is happening here?"

"I wish I knew."

CHAPTER 18

HECTOR WAS BACK ON HIS FEET BY THE TIME the Secret Service took Kilian's body away. Nate stayed next to his shaky colleague, looking ready to leap into action if Hector so much as swayed. Tibor steered clear of them both, informing us that if they were contagious, he didn't want to get close.

It took some time, but staff members who'd come running finally dispersed, with strong admonitions from Tom and the other Secret Service agents to avoid discussing the incident with the press.

Tom pulled me aside before he left. "Let us handle this, Ollie," he said.

"A man dies in my kitchen, another is stricken and almost passes out, and you expect me to pretend it didn't happen?"

"I'm not asking you to pretend anything," he said. "Let's just try to keep things quiet."

"What about the chocolate?" I watched his face as I

pressed the issue. "After this, don't you think we ought to put a rush on the test?"

He stepped closer, giving quick looks around to ensure no one could listen in. Quietly, he said, "I have already asked them to run scans on Kilian's body for GHB, is that what you want to hear?"

"Good," I said. "It's too much of a coincidence. There has to be a connection."

"For all our sakes, I hope there isn't. I intend to check." He started away just as Peter Everett Sargeant approached.

Following Tom, I asked, "What about Hector? What did he tell you?"

"He takes medication and believes he may have accidentally double-dosed this morning. Exactly the way Marcel did." Tom raised both eyebrows. "Does that satisfy you, Sherlock?"

I was about to ask Tom what kind of medication, but he anticipated the question.

"The man's medical history is not my business," he said. "I didn't ask because I don't need to know. Neither do you."

"Wait," I said, as he turned to leave again. "What about GHB? You're having Hector tested for that, too, aren't you?"

Tom worked his jaw, settled himself, then said, "The only reason I'm answering is because I know how difficult you can be when you think people are hiding the truth from you. Yes, we will request that he submit himself for testing." Tom straightened to his full height, towering over me. "Anything else you need to know?"

"No," I said coolly. "Thank you."

"Ms. Paras," Sargeant said when Tom was out of earshot, "marriage hasn't changed you a bit, has it?"

I graced him with a withering glance, which he chose to ignore.

"Yet again we have an international crisis on our hands," he said. "The Saardiscans may be surprised to find the White House chef at its epicenter, but clearly, no one here is even raising an eyebrow."

"What do you need, Peter?"

He scratched the side of his mouth. "Your cooperation, of course. There will be questions, many of them. I wouldn't be surprised if the Saardiscan government ordered its delegates home immediately."

"I hope they do," I said under my breath.

"Oh? And why is that?"

I obviously hadn't muttered quietly enough. "It wasn't until these chefs showed up that strange things started to happen."

He almost smiled at that. "The same could be said of you, Ms. Paras." Without giving me opportunity to respond, he went on. "You and I will need to discuss all that transpired here, but first I need to contact the Saardiscans and offer our sincere condolences. I have no idea how this incident will affect their decision to allow Ms. Freiberg to return." He sniffed, glanced around the room, and added, "Margaret will be in touch with you to set up a meeting time. I trust you will make yourself available."

With that, he turned and left the kitchen.

When he was gone, I made my way into the middle of the room, where Nate and Bucky kept watch over Hector. Tibor studied them from across the room. Kilian's death, so sudden, and in my kitchen, made my knees weak with sadness, but there wasn't time to grieve now.

Nate and Hector were talking quietly in Saardiscan when I approached. Although I couldn't understand their words, I sensed the tone and could read their body language. It seemed to me that Nate was warning Hector to be more careful, or perhaps to take the day off. Hector wore a distressed expression, and nodded a lot.

"What happened, Hector?" I asked.

His puffy lower lip jutted out like a four-year-old's pout. "Is Kilian dead?" he asked.

I locked eyes with Nate, whose expression was grim. I would have thought the answer obvious by now. "I'm sorry to say that he is."

Hector's chubby lip pulled in and for a moment I thought he might cry. Instead, he clenched his eyes shut for an extended moment. When he opened them again, he pushed his lip back out. "He was always very kind to me."

"What about you?" I asked Hector. "Are you all right now?"

He ducked his head and didn't answer right away.

"Hector," I prompted, "what happened?"

"My medication is new. I am supposed to take only one per day. The old medication was two times per day." When he looked up at me again, his mouth twisted downward. "I will not make that error again."

The explanation, the same one he'd given Tom, and one that made sense, tied this coincidence up a bit too neatly for my tastes. My gut told me that Hector was lying—although I couldn't imagine why he would.

That conviction made me consider an entirely new possibility. One that would be—in my opinion—the worst alternative of all.

"I don't know," I said aloud. "This is too much of a coincidence."

Hector's expression shifted from regretful to panicked. "It is my fault," he insisted. "I will be more careful in the future. I give you my word."

"That's not what I mean." I looked up and read the same doubts on Bucky's face, which gave me enough confidence to continue my thought process. "Marcel has been incapacitated, Hector has suffered ill effects, and now, tragically, Kilian is dead. What if there's something present—here—that's making us ill?"

Tibor stepped into the group. "What are you saying? You believe we are being poisoned?" His large eyes bulged. "Do you think it is anthrax? Sarin?"

I held my hands up. "No, no," I said, "nothing like that."

Heaven help us—I hoped that wasn't the case. "I'm simply concerned that we may have all come into contact with an ingredient or substance that could do us harm."

Nate and Hector weren't as panicked as easy-to-agitate Tibor seemed to be, but they were alarmed nonetheless. Before I did anything, I needed to contain this situation. And to do that, we needed help.

"Listen," I began, "Kilian was your friend, and this has been a shock to us all. Why don't the three of you take the remainder of the day off?"

The men exchanged looks that I would characterize as shocked. "But we were sent here to work," Tibor protested. "Our leaders will be disappointed if we do not fulfill our obligation."

"Then tell them I changed your obligation. Today, at least, you're free from responsibility. I'm certain our people are already in touch with your people about Kilian, but I'm sure you'll be required to report to them, too." I expected that the Saardiscan government would waste no time in recalling the surviving men home. "Kilian was one of your countrymen and I know you all cared about him. I think an afternoon to yourselves is fully in order."

Dismissing their assertions that they were capable of carrying on despite their grief, I called for a Secret Service escort to take them back to their hotel.

"While you're gone," I said as they gathered their belongings, "I'll have a cleaning team do a thorough sanitizing of the kitchen and all the areas we work in. Although we maintain a spotless environment, there is always the risk of germs getting in. If there's any bacteria or germ at fault, we'll have it eradicated by the time you return."

Once they were gone, Bucky turned to me. "You really think that's what it is?" he asked. "Something either airborne or contagious?"

Fatigue swept over me. "I don't know what to think anymore, Bucky. You know as well as I do that we keep things spotlessly clean around here. We've never had a problem like this before. Not until these Saardiscans showed up."

"Earlier today, you thought Kilian might be responsible for Marcel's troubles. I get the impression that's changed?"

"I feel terrible about that," I said. "The poor man."

"At least we know he's probably innocent of lacing the chocolate drink with GHB."

"I knew Marcel's accusation was far-fetched," I said, "but I had to look into it for him." I shook my head. "What a shame about Kilian. I really was starting to like the guy."

"I was, too." Bucky chucked me on the shoulder. "While they're gone, maybe you and I can discuss what we plan to do about Cyan."

We called in one of the cleaning teams and instructed them to go over every surface where any of us may have worked in the past few days, including pantries, other kitchens, and storage areas. We asked them to do the main kitchen first, with the understanding that Bucky and I would go over it ourselves and conduct a second cleaning before preparing any meals.

In the meantime, he and I had time to kill. "You hungry?" I asked.

"A little."

"Me, too." I washed and hand-dried two plates and some silverware, then made my way over to the refrigeration room, where I dug out a couple of apples and a few hunks of cheese. "Grab some of that bread we baked yesterday," I called over my shoulder to him. "Ooh, we have leftover spinach salad here, too. I'll bring that as well. Is there anything else you'd like?"

He came up behind me, baguette under one arm. He'd brought along some butter and two bottles of water. "A feast fit for a president's . . . staff."

We decided to find a quiet place to enjoy lunch, which is a fairly difficult thing to do in the White House. "Come on," I said when the third spot we checked was occupied. "I know a secret place."

"Why am I not surprised?" Bucky asked, but he trooped along, good-naturedly. "Where are we going?"

"The B-M," I said, referring to the basement-mezzanine level. The area's nickname wasn't one we shared in public, for obvious reasons.

Arms loaded, we made our way eastward across the Center Hall until we reached the stairwell beyond the Library. I made a left and started down.

"Ollie," Bucky said, behind me, "I'm looking at all this stuff we're carrying."

I spoke over my shoulder. "Yeah?"

"What if these items are what affected Marcel and Kilian?"

I stopped my trek down the stairs and turned to face him. "Cheese, bread, salad, fruit." I let my gaze rest on each one as I listed them. "All of these supplies came in after Marcel fainted the first time, so they couldn't have affected him."

"What about his second episode?"

I thought about it. "We may have had the apples at that point, but none of the rest of this. I think we're safe."

"Safe enough to bet your life on it?"

"Don't joke."

He shrugged. "I wasn't."

We continued down the stairs that curled down into a wide, half-round room at its base. This spot, and the adjacent rooms and washrooms, served as greenrooms for visiting performers. I could only imagine the famous people who'd traipsed through this place over the years, changing clothes, donning makeup, and rehearsing lines and songs.

We always kept this area open and ready for our next guests. With the sequester going on, however, this section of the home wouldn't be used for quite a while. It was away from the busy areas of the house, and secluded. Perfect for us to talk and recollect ourselves after the morning's tragedy.

"So," Bucky said as we set all the food down on one of the tables, and began arranging it, "what do you plan to tell Marcel?"

I shook my head. "I really ought to call him, but I can't. It's too soon."

"You seem to be taking Kilian's death pretty hard for someone who barely knew the man."

I stopped what I was doing. "He died in front of me. In my kitchen. And . . . I'd suspected him of harming Marcel. At the same time, I had my doubts about Marcel's accusations. Now, I don't know what's going on."

"So you feel guilty for suspecting him."

"Not really."

"You don't?" He sounded shocked.

"You think I should?" I gave a sad laugh. "I didn't know Kilian. I mean, really know him. Marcel, however, is our friend, and you know how perceptive he is when it comes to taste. If he truly believes someone spiked his hot chocolate, I'm not about to scoff at the idea. Especially in our jobs, where keeping people safe is of paramount importance. Suspecting Kilian was the right thing for me to do."

"Then what *is* getting to you?"

"I feel as though I've fallen down on the job somewhere along the line. There's a connection here I'm not seeing. Kilian's death ups the stakes and I'm worried that because I missed it the first time, someone else—another one of the Saardiscans, you, me, the president—could be next."

Bucky sat, pulling the Gruyère from the plate and slicing off a slim chunk. "You could be overreacting, too."

"I suppose." Antsy, I remained standing, rearranging the food to make it look more attractive.

"Hey, it's just the two of us here," he said. "No need to make it fancy."

He was right. I was futzing when I should have been relaxing. "My coping mechanism for nerves, I guess."

With the Gruyère between his thumb and forefinger, he used the rest of his fingers to point to the chair opposite his. "Sit," he said. "You always tell me that it helps to talk things through."

He was right. I'd learned that from working with Gav.

The happenings from over the past week had been racing through my brain, and had jumbled atop one another to the point where I couldn't see where one ended and another began.

"Good idea," I said. "If we start with when they first arrived—"

I stopped short.

"What?" Bucky asked. "Did you figure it out?"

"The chocolate," I said. "I meant to move it."

I could tell from the look on Bucky's face that he didn't know what I was talking about.

"This morning," I said, "I told you that Gav offered to have some of the chocolate tested for me, too. But I was talking about where I'd hidden it when the Saardiscans walked in."

"You think they heard?"

I bit my lower lip. "I can't be sure. I'd intended to move it to a new hiding place, just to be safe. In all the chaos, however, I didn't have a chance."

Bucky gestured toward the stairs with his eyes. "Go," he said. "You won't be able to relax until you confirm it's still there."

"Thanks," I said. "I'll be right back."

CHAPTER 19

I TRIED TO IGNORE THE DEEP PULSE OF ANGER building in my chest as I made my way back to the B-M–level dressing room. The chocolate was gone. Gone from what had been—to my mind, at least—an unequivocally secure hiding spot, the substance no longer offered a chance for answers. On the contrary: Its sudden disappearance created more questions.

Frustration weighing on me, I tried to picture what had happened to the small covered cup. Tried to come up with an innocuous reason for it having been moved. But I came up empty. Just like the shelf behind the Brussels sprouts.

My hands clenched into fists as I started down the stairs, eager to share the news with Bucky. I'd left him alone far longer than I'd anticipated. He'd understand, of course, once he heard the reason why.

Turning the curve in the stairwell, I was about to launch into an explanation for my delay, when I halted, mid-step.

"Margaret," I said.

She and Bucky were seated at the small table. "Look

who joined us, Ollie," Bucky said with a pasted-on smile. "I guess we're not the only people who know about this hiding spot."

I continued to make my way down, but at a much slower pace. "I guess not."

"Hello, Olivia," Margaret said. Her tortoiseshell glasses were perfectly placed on her tiny nose, but she adjusted them just the same. "I hope you don't mind me crashing your lunch."

I pulled up another chair from a nearby table. "Not at all," I said, lying through my teeth. I glanced down at the halved, crustless-bread sandwich she had before her. She'd centered it on an open napkin and, from the looks of it, had taken only two tiny bites. On another napkin she'd laid out a cellophane-wrapped package of carrot sticks. Next to it, a store-bought brownie.

She lifted half the sandwich and took a dainty bite. I guessed it was Braunschweiger.

"Looks delicious," I said. I wasn't lying. It had been years since I'd had what my mom called a liver sausage sandwich, and—despite the bad press the meat had garnered over the years—the smell brought back memories of childhood.

She gave a disinterested shrug, chewed the bite in six seconds flat, and took a sip of water. "Bringing my lunch saves a few dollars. It's expensive to eat out every day."

"Have some cheese," Bucky said, pushing the platter toward us.

Disappointed that I wouldn't be able to bring Bucky up to date until we were alone again, I sighed, and began helping myself.

Margaret patted her lips with yet another napkin. "Have you heard anything more about the dead guy?"

"Kilian?" I said, feeling oddly protective.

She gave a little smirk. "Unless there's more than one dead Saardiscan today."

Bucky chimed in, "We haven't heard anything more. Have you?"

She took another bite—her pinkie fingers aloft—and shook her head.

"How do you like working for Sarge—er—Mr. Sargeant?"

Bless Bucky for keeping the conversation going.

She smiled for the first time. A genuine smile, all the way up to the eyes. "He's the best boss I've ever had," she said with absolutely no guile whatsoever.

"How long have you been in the workforce?" I asked.

She missed my sarcasm and, confused, answered, "All my adult life."

Bucky sent me a look of amusement. "What makes him such a great boss?" he asked.

She put her sandwich down. "The man understands rules," she said. Raising her fingers and wiggling them, she continued. "Of course, that's to be expected here. Which is why I really love my job. So many people nowadays believe rules don't pertain to them. I'm tired of it."

"Where did you work before this?"

"I served as assistant to a high-ranking senator." Her eyes took on a conspiratorial glow and she leaned forward. "The man was utterly disorganized and forever making excuses. I'm happy to be away from him." Raising the napkin on her lap to pat her lips again, she added, "I'd rather not say who."

"No problem," I assured her. "We wouldn't want you telling stories out of school."

"If there's one thing people can say about me it's that I'm trustworthy."

"I know," I said sincerely. She'd helped me out several months ago when a situation had developed with national security at stake. From what I could tell, she'd never spoken a word of it to anyone, beyond those who needed to know.

"Has Mr. Sargeant gotten in touch with the Saardiscans

about Kilian's death?" I asked. I carved a slice out of one of the apples and popped it into my mouth.

She'd finished half her sandwich. "He did," she said. "They were appalled, of course."

"Do you know if there are any plans to recall the rest of the team?"

She'd taken another little bite, and shook her head instead of answering.

"Maybe they haven't had time to make that decision yet," Bucky said.

Margaret swallowed. "You mean cancel the visit? Oh, no. They definitely talked about that. The visiting chefs are staying at least until Ms. Freiberg's visit."

"That's still on, too?"

She nodded. "Mr. Sargeant was curious as to whether they would cancel this portion of Ms. Freiberg's trip, but his counterpart in Saardisca said that there would be a revolt in his country if she wasn't allowed to complete her itinerary."

"I'm surprised," I said.

Bucky nodded. "Me, too."

Margaret hastened to add, "The Saardiscan official said that a final decision would depend on how Kilian died, of course. Right now they're assuming natural causes." She looked at me and then at Bucky. "You don't think differently, do you?"

"Not at all." Bucky answered so quickly that Margaret's eyes narrowed.

"What aren't you telling me?" she asked.

"Not a thing," I said, striving to keep this conversation from spiraling into speculation. "We're still reeling from the shock of Kilian's death, and while the kitchen is undergoing maintenance, Bucky and I came here to discuss what to do next." I directed my attention to the knife and apple in my hands. "We're going to run into problems for Ms. Freiberg's visit."

Her eyes lit up. "Problems?"

"Don't get me wrong, the biggest thing on my mind right now is Kilian's family. They're going to be devastated. But I can't neglect my duty here, and with Marcel out and now Kilian removed, we don't have a pastry chef. I hope Peter brings back one of Marcel's assistants. Unless he does, I don't know what we're going to do for dessert for the candidate's visit."

Wrinkling her nose in a way that pushed her glasses tighter against her face, she asked, "You mean that with all your experience, you can't come up with a suitable dessert?"

Bucky and I exchanged a glance. "Of course we could 'come up' with something," I said, with a little snippiness in my voice, "but there are two things to keep in mind. One, dessert is not our forte. The expectation is that every single person who visits the president for dinner will be treated to the best we have to offer. Bucky and I can whip up amazing dinners, and our desserts would be fine, but not . . . not . . ."

"Masterpieces," Bucky finished. "And the second thing, if you don't mind me jumping in here, Ollie, is that we simply don't have the staff to pull this off. Dinner will be enough of a challenge without Cyan here. To maintain our standards and create a dessert—an endeavor we're not accomplished in—would be asking for trouble."

Margaret took a prim sip of her water. "Sounds to me as though somebody—or a couple of somebodies—have gotten too big for their britches."

Bucky's face turned as red as my apple. My hand shot out beneath the tabletop and I grabbed his arm, squeezing to keep him from exploding.

"I understand how this must look to you, Margaret," I said, doing my best to ignore Bucky's splutters of indignation. "As a person who has no knowledge of our industry, all this must sound like excuse-making, or professional high-handedness. All my assurances to the contrary won't make a difference to you. So I won't even try." I'd let go of Bucky's arm and now used my other hand to pat hers. "It's a wise person who can expand her mind enough to appreciate another's challenges, even when they differ from her own."

It took her a half second to understand that I'd mocked her. In the heartbeat in between, I turned to Bucky. "You ready? The cleaning staff should be out of the kitchen by now."

He was already on his feet, gathering up our leftovers. "On it, chief."

"My, my. You admit you lack the talent necessary to prepare the full dinner." Margaret's lips pursed. "I'll be certain to let Mr. Sargeant know about these shortcomings of yours."

A deep, genuine burst of laughter blasted out of me, and I could tell she hadn't expected that. To be honest, neither had I. "Don't bother. Peter Everett Sargeant is the one person in this world who's fully aware of all my shortcomings. Trust me, he keeps a list."

She returned to her liver sausage sandwich.

Bucky and I had our arms full. "Let's go," I said.

We were back upstairs in the Center Hall when Bucky glanced over his shoulder to make sure we wouldn't be overheard. "Good for you, boss. Where does she get off telling us our jobs? I'd give her one day—no, one hour—in the kitchen. She'd be reduced to a useless puddle of whining goo in no time."

My hands were too full to do more than wave my fingers, dismissing him. "I probably should have kept my mouth shut."

"I disagree. It wasn't like you were rude. You were almost polite in pointing out what a fool she was to make judgment calls on topics she doesn't understand."

I wasn't regretting standing up for myself and Bucky, but the realization that I'd caused Margaret to go on the defensive bothered me more than I cared to admit. "My goal wasn't to belittle her; it was to open her eyes."

He stopped in the middle of the hall. "Why do you care, Ollie?" He shifted his weight. "She was clearly intent on belittling *you*. Which is something Sargeant did for years until you turned him to the dark side." A corner of Bucky's mouth quirked up. "Or, I suppose in this case, we'd call it the light side."

I stopped walking, too. "I suppose that, somewhere deep inside me, I realize that I don't want to be part of the negativity in this world. There's too much of that. Why demean someone when perhaps the only reason they're attacking is because they don't understand? Why not use that moment to teach, to help open their eyes?"

"You tried," he said. "She took it wrong."

I shook my head. "No, this was my fault. My tone was condescending and that little pat on her hand didn't help." I was angry with myself for stooping to that level. Starting for the kitchen once again, I said, "Next time I'll try harder."

He followed me. "Ollie, you try harder than anyone else I know."

The cleaning crew was dispersing as we arrived.

"Looks wonderful," I said to them. "Thank you."

The team leader walked me through the steps they'd taken and, once I was satisfied, they left.

"Hey," Bucky said. "We never got the chance to talk about Cyan because Margaret showed up while you were moving the chocolate."

I plunked my stuff down on the glistening countertop and shot Bucky a furious look. "Yeah, about that," I said.

"Uh-oh."

"It's gone. Completely disappeared from the top shelf, where I'd left it."

"Maybe someone moved it?"

"First of all, nobody uses that refrigeration unit but the kitchen staff." I shook my head. "Still, I thought the same thing—maybe it had been moved. That's why it took so long for me to get back downstairs. I started looking for it. I looked under things. I looked behind things. Nowhere."

"You think someone took it? Deliberately?"

I held my hands up. "I hadn't remembered to retrieve the chocolate until after we'd asked the cleaning crew to come in. It occurred to me that—unlikely though it might be—one of the team members may have thought it was garbage and tossed it."

"They know better than to do that."

"I know, but I asked them anyway. To double-check."

"And?"

"I talked with all four of the crew," I said. "No one threw anything from refrigeration away. No one even remembers seeing the demitasse cup."

"So . . ." he began, "either one of the cleaning crew is lying, a staffer from another department snuck in and took it, or . . ." He let the thought hang.

I nodded. "Or one of our Saardiscan friends has something to hide."

CHAPTER 20

MRS. WENTWORTH MET ME IN THE HALL AS I made my way to my apartment that evening. "They say you were right there when that Saardiscan chef died today, Ollie."

Mrs. Wentworth was an Internet junkie. Times like these I longed for the good old days, when news came out only twice a day: once in the morning paper and again during the evening broadcast. "That's true," I said with a sigh.

"You are always in the middle of things, young lady. How do you manage it?"

Her white hair was perfectly coiffed, as always. She wore sparkling earrings in both of her saggy lobes, and her arms were folded expectantly in front of her navy cardigan vest.

"I can't seem to *not* manage it," I said. "It's hardly an answer, but it's the truth. How are things with you and Stanley?"

The vertical lines around her lips deepened. "He's been having problems lately." She leaned forward, peering at me over her rhinestone glasses and lowering her voice to a whisper. "It burns when he . . . well, you know . . . passes water. And he has to do that about four times a night." Raising her voice as though on stage, she spoke loud enough to be heard deep into their apartment. "Won't go to see the doctor, stubborn man that he is." Returning to a whisper, she added, "I think he's afraid of hearing the worst. And heaven help me, I'm not ready to lose another husband."

"I'm sorry to hear that he isn't feeling well. It's important to get things like that checked out."

"It *is* important to get things checked out, Ollie," she said, again in a second-balcony voice. "You're so right about that. Take precautions so that things don't get worse. So that we don't get to a point of no return where we're wringing our hands and wishing we'd acted sooner. You're so right, Ollie."

"Take care of him," I whispered back to her.

"I plan on it." She patted her puffy-cloud hair, and dismissed me with a wave. "Have a good night."

Delectable scents enveloped me as I stepped into our apartment. "Honey, I'm home," I called, dropping my keys into the bowl by the front door and peeling off my fall coat.

Gav came around the corner. He was wearing a striped apron and he carried a wooden spoon. Leaning down he gave me a kiss on the lips. "Got home early, hope you don't mind that I started dinner."

"Mind?" I kicked off my shoes and followed him into the kitchen, marveling at how wonderful food always smelled when it was being cooked with love. "What's on the menu?"

"Nothing fancy," he said. "A little steak, a little salad, baked potatoes . . ."

As we enjoyed the meal, I brought Gav up to speed. He'd been briefed as to all that had happened and asked me, almost word for word, the same question Mrs. Wentworth had. "You were there, then?" he repeated. "When he died?"

"Right next to him. The thing is, Hector was afflicted, too, moments before Kilian collapsed."

"You find that suspicious?"

"Don't you?"

"I'm asking you to talk it out aloud."

"Yes, I find it very suspicious," I said. "And yet, Hector couldn't very well have caused his lips to go so white, nor his cheeks to go so pale. That sort of autonomic response is beyond his control. His insistence that it was all due to taking an additional dosage of medication is a valid reason, but it's too neat. Too pat. Too similar to Marcel's situation."

"Okay," Gav said. "Let's say that it was an excuse. That he made that up. Why?"

I shook my head. "I've been trying to come up with a plausible reason and the only thing that makes sense is that he's afraid."

"To admit he might be ill?"

"Exactly. Hector seemed desperate to downplay his light-headedness. But what if he is really sick? What if there is something amiss?"

"What could it be?" Gav asked.

I raised my hands into the air. "That's the thing: I have no idea. There could be a substance or ingredient that we're all coming in contact with that's knocking us out one by one. It could very well be that Tibor and Nate have both had similar incidents but that they've been able to hide them from me."

"Are they ever out from under your supervision?"

I shrugged. "Occasionally. With four of them—well, three now—and two of us, we can't hover over their shoulders constantly. They aren't allowed onto the first floor without an escort, but they have the run of the kitchen and portions of the ground floor. No one accompanies them when they go to the washroom, or retrieve something from storage, or move between us and the pastry kitchen."

"Okay," he said. "Maybe both of the other men have fought off some illness and you've missed the signs. But then why haven't you or Bucky been afflicted?"

"Good question." I thought about it. "Could someone have a grudge against our Saardiscan guests?"

I could tell the thought jolted him. "Are you suggesting that someone inside the White House might be behind these incidents?"

"Why would it have to be someone on the inside? The men go back to their hotel every night. They have the run of Washington, D.C., and they don't have a security detachment that I know of."

Gav stroked his stubbly chin. "How do you account for Marcel's incapacitation then?"

"I can't," I said. "If he accidentally ingested something meant for one of our visitors, he did it while on duty at the White House."

"I hate to say it, but that means that we may have to look at the possibility of it being one of our own."

I didn't like this line of reasoning. "Someone in the White House?"

"Or at least someone who visits there regularly."

"Aren't American leaders supposed to be above this kind of thing?"

Gav nodded. "Supposed to be, yes."

We were both silent a few moments. Neither of us ate.

"Poisoning, if that's what's going on here," he said, "is the sort of crime one can commit without requiring the perpetrator to be present when the victim is stricken."

"What are you getting at?"

He held up a finger. "First of all, keep in mind that we don't *know* that anyone was poisoned. What I'm about to suggest is purely speculation on my part."

"Got it," I said. "Go on."

"The Saardiscan government has made a lot of enemies over the years. It's possible that there are people—American, homegrown terrorists—who will act against the Saardiscans, and do their utmost to see that their trip is cut short."

"I don't like that," I said.

"It's not out of the realm of possibility."

I knew that. I also knew that, despite the fact that it made me seem naïve, I wanted to believe that no true-hearted American would stoop to such measures. To target visitors who couldn't, and shouldn't, be held responsible for the actions of their government, visitors who may have even disagreed with their powerful regime, was simply wrong.

"What you're saying, then," I began, slowly, "is that the person who poisoned Marcel, Kilian, and Hector could be anyone. Could be one of the laundry ladies. Could be one of our Secret Service agents."

"Ollie," he said, and there was a warning in his voice, "we can't even begin to think along these lines until we find out how Kilian died."

"And it still doesn't explain Marcel."

He made a so-so motion with his head. "Unless, as you said, Marcel ingested something by accident—something that was intended for one of the Saardiscans." He tapped the side of his fork against the table, staring at it as he did so. "It bothers me that the chocolate is gone. Another mystery. I admit that at first I doubted Marcel's theory, but after today, I'm not so sure." The two vertical lines between his brows deepened, and he looked up at me. "Having that chocolate tested might have helped us out. Now, we have nothing."

"I don't like it," I said again. "Not one bit."

"I'll talk with Tom about it in the morning. Let's see if there's any light he can shed on the subject." Gav reached across the table. "I know you're smart, and alert. But I also know that you have a tendency to be in the middle of things. Promise me you'll be on guard every minute."

I squeezed his hand. "I promise."

"One more thing," he said as he dug back into dinner. "I'm part of the team heading up security for Kerry Freiberg's visit."

Gav hadn't received any field assignments since he'd been hurt.

"And?"

He gave a one-shouldered shrug. "It's a step forward," he said. "I won't be the agent in charge this time, though. They prefer to ease me back into action via a subordinate role."

"Will that be tough for you? I mean, you're usually the one issuing orders."

"Hardly the sort of assignment I'm accustomed to," he said, "but it's an important evening, and I'm happy they're giving me the chance to remind them of what I can do. Baby steps, I guess. You know how conservative the department can be."

"Have you worked events at Blair House in the past?"

"Couple of times," he said. "You?"

"I've toured the kitchen—part of my orientation when I took over as executive chef—but no, I've never prepared a meal there."

We both fell silent again and I knew that he was reluctant to bring up the subject that hung like a weight between us. I took another bite of my steak, sipped my water, and took a breath.

"I know this is hard for you," I said.

"Not being the agent in charge, you mean?"

"No," I said quietly. "Erma and Bill's decision about the winery."

He put his fork down, rested his elbows on the table, and brought his interlaced fingers up, covering the lower half of his face. "I never expected such a thing," he said.

"I know."

"I can't even imagine how hard this must be for you. We came into this marriage with certain understandings and now, after being together for less than six months, we're discussing fundamental changes."

I wanted to reach across and touch him, but he held his hands tight to his mouth.

"This is utterly unfair to you, Ollie."

"You told me that these changes might not happen for years."

He nodded. "Might not. Probably not." Blinking, he looked away. "What if Bill and Erma are really hoping for me to learn from them personally? To spend time with them? They want the winery to continue, sure, but I'm beginning to believe it's more than that. What if they're looking for me to take on a more meaningful role in their lives? The more I've been thinking about it, the more I've come to realize that if we continue down this path there will be expectations."

"Like what?"

"To become the son they want me to be," he said, simply. "If I'm to learn the business, they would want to teach me themselves. They're going to want to show me how *they* do things, so that I'm fully prepared to take over, if that day ever comes."

"I hadn't thought about that. You're right."

I didn't know what to say. He was clearly so distraught on his own that any of my concerns would only serve to make things worse for us both.

"What do you want, Gav?" I asked again, truly wanting to know. "This has come as a surprise to both of us, but I need to know if there's a part of you that wants to walk away from the danger and constant pressure you face in your job."

He studied the tabletop between us. "Truth is, I don't mind the danger and the pressure. I like feeling as though I'm making a difference in the world." He met my eyes. "I crave that."

I nodded. "I feel the same way."

"Erma and Bill have been there for me in ways my real parents never were." He rubbed his eyes with both hands. "For the first time, they're asking me to be there for them. How can I let them down?"

I reached across the table and waited until he placed one of his hands in mine. "You *have* been there for them," I said, "and no matter what your decision, you can't possibly let them down. They care about your happiness too much for them to want anything other than what's right for you."

"So if my happiness means that I'm likely to sell the winery, you think I should tell them that?"

"No," I said. "I think the issue is too new, and our future too important, for us to make a snap decision. Erma and Bill are good people. Let's take the time we need to think about all this."

"I can't tell you how sorry I am to be throwing such a heavy question into our lives right now."

"This is a good problem to have, don't you think? What if we both decide we've had enough of these crazy careers of ours, and we want to settle down in a quieter environment? They're handing us an opportunity with no strings attached."

His mouth twisted into a smile. "I've thought as an 'I' for almost my entire life. Thinking as a 'we' changes everything. What I want, more than anything, is for us to have the future we envision for ourselves. Not one someone else creates for us."

"As long as we keep that as our guiding principle, we'll be fine," I said. "No, we'll be better than fine. We'll be great."

"How did I get so lucky?" He stood and came over to me, pulling me up into a tight embrace. Resting his chin on the top of my head, he said. "And what can I do to make you as happy as you make me, Ollie?"

Nuzzled against his chest, I twisted my face free enough to say, "You already have."

CHAPTER 21

WHEN I ARRIVED AT WORK THE NEXT MORN-
ing, I wasn't surprised to find an e-mail marked "high
importance" from Sargeant, requesting a meeting. I could
only imagine the international chaos that he was facing.

I responded that I'd be available as soon as breakfast
was delivered to the First Family, about seven-thirty.

His terse reply, "Very well. My office."

Bucky strolled in as I clicked off. "Computer screens
don't magically deliver better news, no matter how hard
you frown at them," he said as he peeled off his jacket.
"What's wrong today?"

"It isn't right."

His joking manner was replaced with concern. "What
happened?"

I waved an airy hand at the computer. "It's no one's
fault. It's simply the reality we have to deal with. Kilian's
dead, and there's political fallout. There will be questions
to answer, and forms to fill out. There will be changes and
updates and memos and e-mails."

He waited.

I stood before him, arms out. "The thing is, a man is dead. A man we worked with. A man we liked. And even though we knew him for only a few days, he had an impact on us. Imagine the impact he had on his friends, his family."

"Ollie." Bucky's voice was a warning.

I knew what he was going to say, but I shook my head. "Sometimes it bothers me that we're all more concerned about how things are seen and explained, than how things really are."

"There will be an investigation, and an autopsy," Bucky reminded me. "No one is trying to hide anything."

"I'm not talking about hiding," I said, frustrated at myself for not being able to articulate more clearly. "I'm talking about being human. About being affected by Kilian's death. Because of what happened yesterday, we're going to be tied up with red tape and paperwork. We don't have time to feel."

Bucky didn't answer right away. He nodded, lips pressed tight. "I hear you. Being on the world stage changes everything. Every single step, every single action we take, can be scrutinized, analyzed, and criticized."

"That's not wrong, either," I said. "We *should* be held accountable for what goes on in this place. It's just that we're all so busy making certain that everything is transparent, that we don't have time—or we're too distanced from it—to actually feel any emotion."

Bucky patted me on the shoulder. "Comes with the job. And if you think we have it tough"—he pointed to the ceiling—"imagine what the fishbowl is like for them."

"Yeah," I said. "I know."

The two of us returned to getting the family's breakfast prepared.

"Speaking of reacting emotionally," he said as we finished filling the carafes of orange juice and coffee, "do you expect our chef friends to report back here today or do you think they'll take time off?"

The three remaining members of the Saardiscan contingent marched in before the question had a chance to die on Bucky's lips. Hector, first through the door, answered for all of them. "We are back."

Behind him, Nate and Tibor mumbled a greeting.

"How are you men holding up?" I asked.

Hector looked as though he hadn't gotten very much sleep. His eyes were puffy and his nose red. "We have spoken with our liaison. He told us that Kilian had many health issues and that his"—Hector pointed to his own chest as he fought to find the words—"valve needed surgery. He was scheduled for the operation upon our return to Saardisca."

"I'm surprised they allowed him to make the trip," I said.

Hector shrugged. From behind him, Tibor said, "This was an important opportunity, and Kilian was the best in his province."

"Will all of you remain here to finish your visit or will you be returning to Saardisca?"

Nate answered that one. "We are to stay."

I couldn't help myself. "And are all of you okay with that?"

Tibor practically glared. "Why would we not be?"

AT TWENTY-EIGHT MINUTES AFTER SEVEN I stepped into the anteroom outside Sargeant's office. Margaret sat back as though surprised to see me. "I'm sorry, Mr. Sargeant is tied up this morning," she began.

I remembered my vow to be less snippy, but was tired of her belligerence. "He set this meeting up," I said with a glance at my watch. "For two minutes from now."

"I know that," she said, "but he's in with someone else at the moment. An important visitor."

"All right," I said. "Perhaps he forgot to update me."

"Mr. Sargeant never forgets anything."

Argumentative little thing, wasn't she? Trying again to smooth things over, I said, "Then the meeting he's in now must have come as a surprise."

She opened her mouth to answer, but I cut her off. "Whatever the case, I have a kitchen to run and can't wait around until he's free again. Would you please let him know that I was here?"

Sargeant took that moment to open his office door. Seven-thirty on the nose. "I thought I heard your voice, Ms. Paras." He stepped deeper into his office and held the door wide. "Please join us."

A gentleman who had been seated across from Sargeant rose to his feet. He was rather tall, probably in his early fifties, with dark hair and a high forehead. His uneven skin and flat nose gave him a rough-childhood look, but in his crisp suit he cut a dashing figure.

"You must be Olivia Paras." His voice was deep, rumbling, and thick with a Saardiscan accent. "Mr. Sargeant has told me a great deal about you."

I didn't quite know how to take that. "Pleased to meet you . . ."

Sargeant had taken a moment to speak with Margaret. He was less than thirty seconds behind in the conversation, but apologized for delaying introductions. "Yes, please sit down, Ms. Paras. I'd like you to meet Cleto Damar. He has recently arrived from Saardisca to assist us during this trying time."

"I'm so sorry about Kilian," I said. "He was a lovely man. His family must be distraught."

He nodded gratefulness for my condolences. "We did not expect that Kilian's condition would worsen during his visit here."

"So, it *was* his heart then?" Turning to Sargeant, I asked, "The results of the autopsy are in already?"

Sargeant began to shake his head as Cleto answered for

him. "We have made arrangements to return Kilian's body to Saardisca. If the family wishes to have an autopsy, it will be performed there by Saardiscan doctors."

I opened my mouth to ask why it wouldn't be done here, immediately, but a pointed glare from Sargeant stopped me before I could utter a word.

"Protocols and practices vary in other countries," he said. Knowing Sargeant as well as I did, I could tell that he was striving to keep me contained.

"I see."

Cleto turned his body toward me. "I have been dispatched to work with you and your staff."

Confused, I chanced a quick look toward Sargeant. No help there. Returning my attention to Cleto, I asked, "You're a chef?"

He smiled, making the corners of his eyes crinkle. "Unfortunately not."

"I don't understand."

Sargeant took up the explanation. "As is to be expected, this recent turn of events is of great concern to the Saardiscan government," he said. "With Kilian's untimely death, it has lost one of its own. As team leader, Kilian was entrusted to oversee this diplomatic endeavor. In order to continue the chefs' visit without interruption, the decision was made to install Mr. Damar as liaison."

Cleto scratched the side of his face, near his ear. "Mr. Sargeant is being exceedingly polite. What I have told him, and will now share with you, is that Kilian was a highly regarded individual. I was fortunate to have been able to work with him. And while all the chefs we sent are upstanding and honorable men, none is qualified to serve as leader." He held out both hands. "This is why I am here. I will be joining them in your kitchen."

"Oh," I said, for lack of a better response. Was Cleto saying that the Saardiscan government didn't trust Hector, Nate, and Tibor? Pulling thoughts together quickly, I asked, "Why, then, didn't your government simply pull the men back?" I smiled to soften my words. "I mean, Kilian's death was a shock to us all. If the Saardiscan authorities have any doubt about the remaining chefs . . ." I let the sentence hang.

"No doubt about their abilities," he said. "No doubt about their characters, either. They are simply unschooled on procedures and on how to file reports." He leaned toward me and lowered his voice. Sargeant and I could hear him, but I doubted Margaret could, even if she had her ear pressed to the door. "What you may not understand, Ms. Paras, is how very important this diplomatic mission is to our country's future. We desperately want this to succeed."

Sargeant was smiling so tightly, wearing an expression that practically begged me not to blow this, that all I could do was nod.

Cleto continued, "That is why I'm here, and why I wished to meet with you before talking with the Saardiscan chefs in your kitchen. Kilian made regular reports to me, but I would like to also know *your* assessment of these men."

I couldn't remember the last time I was at such a loss for words. "Um . . . right now?"

"You've worked with them for a week, Ms. Paras," Sargeant said. "Surely you have formed an opinion."

"I suppose," I said, feeling my back grow stiff from being put on the spot. To Cleto, I said, "I've been impressed with their work ethic. All three men like to keep busy."

He nodded. "And individually?"

"Hector is genial and pleasant. That said, he seems to be the least mature of the group. Nate has been very quiet. I get the impression that he hasn't had a lot of practical experience."

"Go on," Cleto said.

"From what I understand, Hector and Nate come from two provinces that aren't as well supplied as Kilian's and Tibor's are."

"That is correct. And Tibor," Cleto said. "What do you think of him?"

I'd been trying to come up with a diplomatic way of describing the unpleasant man. "He's probably the hardest worker in the bunch," I said.

Cleto waited. "Is that all?"

I debated a moment, but figured that if Cleto had read Kilian's reports, there was no reason to pretend I was unaware. "Tibor seems angry," I began, "most of the time, in fact. I haven't been able to determine if he chafes at my authority because I'm American or because I'm female."

Cleto nodded sagely. "I have been cautioned about this man. He is extraordinarily committed to the old-school way of thinking. Saardisca is entering a new era and many are not happy to see the change." He offered a small smile. "Thank you for your insight."

"When you say 'cautioned,'" I asked, ignoring Sargeant's flash of panic, "are you suggesting he could be dangerous?"

Cleto's hand flew to his brow. "My apologies. A poor choice of wording. When I say that I was cautioned, I meant that others who have worked with him in the past have told me that the man can be temperamental. That is your assessment, too, yes?"

"It is," I said.

Cleto had dark, expressive eyes. "Forgive me for asking, but I hope *you* do not believe Tibor is dangerous. Do you?"

My own fault for opening that door. Put on the spot once again, I strove for an answer that was accurate but not likely to send Sargeant into spasms. "I have seen no evidence to lead me to consider him dangerous."

"I am glad to hear of it. I will be joining your kitchen, and meeting with my charges, shortly. If, at any time, you have concerns about them, their work habits, or their personalities, please feel free to bring such matters to my attention."

"And mine," Sargeant said.

Standing to leave, I forced out a fib. "I look forward to working with you."

I WENT STRAIGHT FROM SARGEANT'S OFFICE to the West Wing to see Tom. I was fully prepared to hear that he was busy, and to set up an appointment to return another time, but this matter wasn't something I cared to put into an e-mail, or discuss over the phone, knowing that the Saardiscan chefs were nearly always within eavesdropping distance.

Tom happened to be returning to the Secret Service office from the West Wing's ground-floor lobby as I came down the stairs. He stopped and waited for me to descend. "Ollie," he said, "what are you doing here?"

"Do you have a minute?" I asked. "It won't take long."

He gestured me in, past his receptionist and into his office, shutting the door behind us. Without preamble, I launched into what was on my mind. "You're aware that they've brought in a liaison to work with the chefs from now until Kerry Freiberg's visit?"

He sat behind his desk. "Yes, I was there when Mr. Sargeant was handed that directive yesterday."

"Given that one of their team died under suspicious circumstances, given all the fainting going on in the kitchen lately, it seems odd to me that they would dispatch a new leader for the group, rather than pull the remaining men back."

Tom nodded. "These visits—both that of the chefs and the candidate's tour—are very important to the Saardiscan government."

"So I keep hearing," I said. "But I have to tell you, I am not feeling comfortable with them working for me anymore. Especially after that chocolate disappeared."

"Have any of them done anything you would consider suspicious?"

"Individually, no, but—"

"But the situation feels wrong to you, and you believe it your duty to share those feelings with me."

"That about sums it up," I said, waiting for him to chastise me for wasting his time. "What about Kilian's body? I know they didn't do an autopsy, but did they find GHB in his blood?"

Tom shook his head. "No tests. Their government wouldn't allow it. Said it would be sacrilege to have it done here rather than at home."

"What about Hector? He got tested, right?"

"He refused. Swears it was a mistake with his medication and wouldn't let us near him."

"Are you kidding me?"

"Keep your voice down," Tom said. "Please." He picked up a pen and tapped it against his desk. "I do agree with you that something isn't right."

I took advantage of the moment, talking quickly. "This new liaison, Cleto, told me that he'd been cautioned about Tibor. When I pressed him, asking if Tibor was dangerous, he backpedaled very quickly."

"What would you expect him to say? That yes, they put a devious criminal in our midst?"

I ignored the jab. "He seemed particularly interested in Tibor's behavior. Given all that we've been through with these men, I find that curious."

"What do you want from me?" he asked.

That was the precise opening I'd been hoping for. "I know I've asked you this before, and you've refused me, but I believe that we would be best served by having a translator join us in the kitchen."

He didn't shut me down, so I went on. "The cover story could be that we're bringing on another chef to help prepare for Kerry Freiberg's dinner. And when the Saardiscans chat among themselves, the translator can listen in and report back to us later." I took a breath and kept talking. "That way, we find out what they're really discussing. If we discover that it's all banter and innocuous conversation—great. We were wrong to suspect them. But wouldn't it be nice to know there's nothing sinister going on?"

"And what makes you suspect there's anything sinister about them at all?" he asked.

My hands shot upward—fistfuls of frustration. "I don't know. There is simply too much going on here and I need to get a handle on it. This is the best solution I can come up with. If you have any other ideas, I'd be happy to hear them."

He pinched the bridge of his nose and closed his eyes. He chuckled. "Oh, you would, would you?"

"I didn't mean it that way," I said.

"I swear, Ollie, if it were anyone else asking this, I'd be sending them for a psychological workup."

"Does this mean I can get a linguist?"

He leaned forward, plopping his elbows onto the desk with a *thud*. "I'll see what I can do." He tilted his head slightly to keep me silent while he continued, "Budget constraints being what they are, I can't guarantee that I'll be able to keep an operative in the kitchen for more than a day or two."

I'd expected more of a fight. Delighted that he was willing to help rather than toss me out the door on my backside, I said, "Whatever you can do is better than what we have now. I really appreciate this, Tom."

He nodded, wrote a note on a legal pad, and said, "I'll be in touch."

Thus dismissed, I headed for the door. "Will you let Sargeant know what's going on so he can back me up on this new chef cover story?"

"I will." He waved me off as he picked up the phone.

CHAPTER 22

WHEN I RETURNED TO THE KITCHEN, I IN-formed Bucky and the Saardiscan chefs about Cleto's arrival. I let them all know that we were bringing on another chef as well.

"Another chef?" Bucky asked, clearly surprised by the announcement. "To take over the dessert end of things?"

"Assuming all the paperwork goes through," I said, happy for the cover story. I'd tell Bucky the truth about the "new chef" being a translator, later. Continuing to address the group, I said, "With Marcel out and Kilian gone, we're shorthanded. I'm hoping this temporary assistant will guide us and come up with an appropriately fabulous dessert."

Bucky seemed confused by this turn of events. "Is this someone we've worked with before?"

"I don't know," I said, wanting to change the subject before he pressed for too much clarification. "The request is in, and I think it will be approved. We won't know who we get until that person shows up."

"I hope it's Marcel's first assistant," Bucky said. "She's great."

"Fingers crossed," I said.

Tibor had waited for us to finish our conversation before asking, "What did you say the name of the Saardiscan liaison is?"

I told him, "Cleto Damar."

I couldn't tell whether the name seemed familiar to Tibor. "I do not understand why they have sent him to the kitchen if he is not a chef."

Providing the same explanation I was given, I said, "He's to be a liaison between us and your government."

"Bah," Tibor said, thrusting both hands down in disgust. "He is here to report on our progress. If we fail to impress this man, we will suffer for it." Turning to his colleagues, he spoke in Saardiscan.

"Do you know Cleto?" I asked.

Tibor flexed his jaw before answering. "I have not met him, no. He is the man Kilian submitted reports to." Shaking his head, he turned away. "Kilian led us to believe that this Cleto Damar is a harsh critic. Kilian made sure to always write his reports to give us the best advantage."

I hadn't talked with Cleto long enough to get a read on his true personality, but I thought Tibor's fears might be exaggerated. "You've all worked very hard, and gone above and beyond—especially in light of all that's happened these past few days." I felt a momentary wash of guilt about telling Cleto that Tibor was unpleasant, but I brushed it off. "I've told him how impressed I am with all of you. Let's not worry about his reports just yet."

Tibor had crossed the kitchen while I was talking. I expected him to add more to the discussion, but he folded his arms and remained silent.

"Cleto will join us later. For now, let's get started on our next project, shall we?" I said. "Bucky, what's on our schedule for today?"

He grabbed a handful of the papers strewn before him. "You mean the newest new schedule? Or the newer newest one?"

WE WERE IN THE MIDDLE OF MAKING A BATCH of homemade granola when Margaret arrived with Cleto. He'd been outfitted with a White House smock that matched all of ours and as I welcomed him to the kitchen, I pulled out an apron and handed it to him. He seemed confused about how to tie it from behind, so Margaret did the honors.

I introduced Cleto to Bucky, but as I began to present the three chefs, Cleto stopped me. Turning to the men he said, "I have studied all your dossiers. You are very talented individuals. It is my pleasure to meet you in person."

One by one, the men shook hands with their new leader as he addressed them by name. Tibor was the last to greet our new guest. It may have been my imagination, but I swore Tibor winced when he and Cleto shook hands.

"I need to head back upstairs now," Margaret said. "If you need anything further, Mr. Damar, you know where my office is."

He thanked her warmly. "It has been my pleasure to work with you."

Her cheeks were pink, her smile wide. "I feel the same way," she said. She wiggled her fingers at all of us and left the room.

I hoped no one noticed Bucky roll his eyes.

Cleto was the tallest of the Saardiscans and when Margaret was gone, he folded his arms and studied the others. "We were saddened to hear of Kilian's death," he said somberly. "He was a fine man and an admirable Saardiscan. He served his country proudly and well."

There were murmurs of assent from the other men. Cleto went on. "He and I had been in constant contact since your arrival here, so I am fully apprised of all your skills and I have been kept informed of your progress." He nodded to me and then Bucky. "We owe a debt of gratitude to Ms. Paras and her staff for welcoming us into their kitchen."

"Please, call me Ollie."

His eyes crinkled up as he smiled. "I have now completed my speech, which means that I should probably get out of your way."

"You're welcome to help out if you like, but don't feel pressured to do so. Before you arrived, we were in the process of making homemade granola. It seems to be a new experience for your chefs, and it's a particular favorite with the president's children. We'd be happy to show you how it's done."

Nate, Hector, and Tibor exchanged uneasy glances.

I decided to add a boost. "These chefs have been a wonderful addition to our kitchen." Okay, that was a stretch, but it wouldn't hurt to let them all think I was on their side. "They have very generously taught us how to make a few traditional Saardiscan dishes and we have been delighted to learn."

Cleto's eyebrows rose. "I am happy to hear that, despite the tragedy of losing Kilian, this diplomatic mission is shaping up to be a success."

"It most certainly is."

Bucky kicked me in the ankle. I ignored him.

THE NEXT MORNING, THERE WAS A MESSAGE from Tom telling me to meet him in his office at eight o'clock.

I'd finally had a chance to bring Bucky up to speed on the news that we'd be getting a translator. When I let him know that I'd been summoned to talk to Tom, he wished me luck. "I hope he hasn't had a change of heart."

"Me, too."

The Secret Service's receptionist ushered me in the moment I arrived. Tom was behind his desk, a young woman seated across from him.

Tom said, "Ollie, I'd like you to meet Stephanie Zhang. Stephanie, this is Olivia Paras, the White House executive chef."

Stephanie Zhang was young. Younger, even, than Cyan. She had a narrow, angular face, jet-black hair pulled into a sleek ponytail, and a timid smile. She offered her hand and we shook. "Nice to meet you," she said. Her voice was soft and clear.

Tom continued. "Stephanie has agreed to join your kitchen for a couple of days to monitor your Saardiscan guests."

"Wonderful." Turning to Stephanie, I asked, "Are you an agent with the Secret Service, too?"

"No."

Tom piped in. "Stephanie is a freelance interpreter. She's fluent in eight languages and comes with the highest of recommendations. The service has used her talents in the past. She can be trusted to keep matters confidential."

"That's great," I said. "When will you be able to join us?"

Her shy smile grew a fraction. "I can start immediately," she said. "But I do need some direction as to expectations." Glancing between me and Tom, she added, "I've never translated in this manner before—where the subjects didn't know they were being understood. I confess to being a little worried that I'll be able to remember everything they talk about without being able to take notes."

Tom and I assured her that she wouldn't be expected to recite, verbatim, every Saardiscan interchange throughout the day. We gave her several key topics to listen for, including discussion about chocolate, or drugging, or poison, and anything regarding death.

"Use your instincts," I said. "If something feels important, I'm sure it will be."

She nodded uncertainly. "I'll do my best."

I had a thought. "Let's come up with a code word." Pretending not to see Tom's look of derision, I went on. "If something does seem important, or they discuss a matter with details you may not remember later, use a word to alert me. I can call you out of the kitchen and you can tell me what it is immediately."

The idea seemed to alarm her. "Are these men dangerous?"

I smiled, wishing we'd gotten a more seasoned individual for this job. "That's what we're trying to find out."

BY THE TIME I RETURNED TO THE KITCHEN, the Saardiscan chefs and Cleto had arrived for the day. I greeted them all, then turned to Cleto. "How was your first evening in Washington, D.C.?"

"I had a great deal of paperwork to complete," he said with a wry smile. "And I was exhausted from travel, so I have not had the opportunity to do much more than sleep. I am told by my colleagues, however, that there is much to see in your fair city."

"I hope you find time to explore," I said.

"As do I."

Niceties behind us, I called an impromptu kitchen meeting. "I have good news to share," I told the group. "The assistant I requested will be joining us this morning."

"Is this Marcel's first assistant?" Tibor asked. "You believed it was she who was to be assigned here."

"Unfortunately, she wasn't available. Instead, we're getting someone new."

"New?" Tibor's tone conveyed his skepticism.

"Her name is Stephanie, and I hope you will all make her feel welcome."

"She is a specialist in desserts?" Tibor asked.

"No," I said. "Not especially. In fact, she'll serve as more of a helper than an actual chef."

He narrowed his eyes and I could sense the question that was on all four Saardiscans' minds. If she wasn't a pastry chef, why were we bringing her on board?

Once I'd met Stephanie, I knew there would be no way to pass her off as a trained professional. The young woman would be exposed as a fraud within minutes. Taking a deep breath, I launched into the cover story Tom, Stephanie, and I had settled on. "Stephanie is, unfortunately, very new at this. In any other circumstance, I would never allow her to join us in the kitchen. She is, however, the niece of a high-ranking official here in Washington. She will be assigned to us temporarily, as a favor to that official. I'm not at liberty to say who her relative is, but Stephanie is eager to intern with us, even if it is only for a few days."

"So this is being done as a courtesy to the high-ranking official?" Cleto asked.

"Exactly," I said. "The timing works out very well, as Bucky and I are learning how to prepare Saardiscan dishes while we're sharing our favorites with you. I can't think of a better opportunity for a new chef than to have so many instructors at once."

When Nate said something under his breath to Hector, I wondered if I'd oversold the story, thereby making Stephanie's sudden hiring even more suspect.

Hector replied to Nate in Saardiscan. The two men shared a knowing look, as though some suspicion of theirs had been confirmed. Or maybe I was so on edge that I was imagining things.

Overhearing the two men, Cleto turned to them. "While you are in the White House, you should speak only English." He held a hand out toward me and Bucky. "It would be rude to leave our hosts out of our conversations, would it not?"

I knew my face betrayed my surprise. The very thing I'd been working toward—knowing what was being said in the kitchen at all times—was now being handed to me via direct order from Cleto.

Nate ducked his head, then nodded. He answered in English. "My apologies."

Hector murmured assent.

Cleto turned back to me. "I hope Kilian did not allow such behavior."

I chose not to answer the implied question. "I appreciate your perceptiveness," I said. Returning to the matter at hand, I began providing additional instructions about what we intended to accomplish today. As I was talking, two Secret Service agents arrived, escorting Stephanie Zhang.

As prearranged, I acted as though this was the first time we were meeting. "Welcome to the White House kitchen, Stephanie," I said, after one of her attendants introduced us. "Let's get you a smock and apron, and get you started."

The Secret Service agents left us to make further introductions among ourselves. Cleto greeted her warmly, but the rest of the Saardiscan men provided perfunctory handshakes and a cool reception. They'd done the same with me their first day. Whether it was because they were naturally reticent, or because Stephanie was female, I couldn't tell.

To me, Stephanie seemed nervous. That wasn't entirely out of character for a person's first day at a new job, but I worried that her tension would hinder her ability to listen and translate accurately.

With Cleto's directive to refrain from speaking Saardiscan in the kitchen, however, Stephanie's talents might not be needed, after all. Nor the use of our code word. We'd settled on *pencil*, an innocuous-enough word that wouldn't sound out of place.

AN HOUR LATER, AFTER A ROCKY START, I WAS instructing the group on the steps necessary to make pecan-crusted pork tenderloin with orange-maple glaze.

After slicing the pork into one-inch-thick medallions, I flattened them with the heel of my hand. "This happens to be one of the president's favorite dishes," I said. "I think part of the reason is because we use pure maple syrup and freshly toasted pecans."

I went through all the steps necessary for preparing the pork entrée, discussing how we juggled preparing multiple courses while ensuring everything was perfectly done and ready to be served at the appointed time. "I'd like you all to get a chance to try browning and turning these. It can get messy, and we can all use the practice."

As I plated my finished example, I turned to Stephanie, who was farthest away from me and closest to the counter-top. I had a supply of chopped pecans next to the stovetop, ready for use, but I'd kept a spare container of pecan halves, for garnishing the finished dish. "Could you hand the pecans to me?" I asked her.

"The what?"

"Pecans."

She turned, looking directly at the container of nuts. "Aren't these walnuts?"

I bit my lip to keep from reacting. Any chef, even an aspiring one, ought to know the difference between pecans and walnuts. "Pecans," I said stiffly.

Recognizing her gaffe, perhaps, she hurried to grab the container and hand it to me.

Bucky tried to cover. "I used to make that mistake all the time, too," he said, which I knew was a complete fabrication.

Tibor scowled. "How long have you been studying to be a chef?" he asked Stephanie.

"Oh, I'm only starting out. It's what I . . . uh . . . always wanted to do, always . . . uh . . . dreamed of doing but I never had a chance before." Panicked, she glanced at me, her face growing red. She tried to laugh it off, but it came out more as a stammer. "I'm learning new things every day."

"Oh? Even a beginner has mastered some skills." Tibor

crossed his arms. "What is your preferred method for making a roux?" he asked her.

"Now, now," I said, before this could go further. "This is Stephanie's very first day. We shouldn't put her on the spot." I shot Stephanie a smile of encouragement. The girl looked like she wanted to bolt.

Nate and Hector exchanged a glance.

Cleto seemed oblivious to the food references, but tightly attuned to the men's observations. He lifted his chin as though about to ask a question, when Bucky chimed in, "Who wants to try it?" Pointing to the slices of raw pork on the platter before us, he said, "We all need to practice."

"Tibor, how about you go next?" I said.

He huffed, but stepped up to take over and I stifled a deep breath of relief. Backing up, I allowed the other chefs to move in closer, giving me a chance to stand nearer to Stephanie. With everyone else's back to me, I surreptitiously patted her on the arm. "It's fine. Just relax."

Her jaw was clenched, but she nodded.

For the next few interminable hours, Stephanie stumbled through task after task, proving her ineptness in the kitchen with every misstep. I'd assumed that she was a woman living on her own. How she could exist and feed herself with so few basic culinary skills boggled the mind.

I could tell it was similarly baffling our Saardiscan guests. They regarded her with blatant interest and I couldn't help noticing their expressions of disbelief when she struggled with simple things like releasing blades from a hand mixer, or being able to distinguish zucchini from eggplant. Her cover story was failing fast.

With all the Saardiscans speaking English, eliminating the need for a translator, I was tempted to say the code word, *pencil*, take her aside, and absolve her from her responsibilities. Instead, as long as she was here, I asked

Bucky to take Cleto and Tibor up to the pastry kitchen, on the pretext of doing an inventory.

I didn't have a solid plan. All I knew was that Nate and Hector had been the two who had most often lapsed into Saardiscan when we were all working in the kitchen. With Cleto out of the main kitchen, I hoped to give them the chance to converse freely again.

Stephanie and I were on one side of the countertop, Nate and Hector on the other. The two men were hard at work slicing zucchini into uniform wheels, while Stephanie and I went over a recipe we planned to use later.

She and I kept our voices low, and it wasn't long before Nate and Hector started talking between themselves. In Saardiscan.

Stephanie gave a little start. I was half-turned away from the men, so I couldn't tell if they'd noticed her reaction. If they had, I hoped they assumed she was responding to something she'd read.

"Easy," I whispered. I didn't want to confuse her, or mask the men's conversation with words of my own, so I pointed to the recipe, as though we were both reading silently together.

Nate and Hector continued to converse, their voices growing slightly louder. Whatever they were saying had both men riled up. I thought I detected the name *Cleto* in their discussion, but I couldn't be sure.

I stole a quick glance at Stephanie, who had straightened up, her back rigid. Her body language practically broadcast that she was paying attention. I wanted to bump her sideways, but there was no way to loosen the girl up without bringing attention our way.

Nate said something to Hector that caused me to take extra notice. Perhaps it was the change in inflection. He slowed his words down, and raised his voice ever so slightly, almost as though striving to be overheard.

I made a pretense of needing to retrieve a spoon from

across the room. Walking over, I was able to watch all three at once. Nate continued to talk. Hector looked confused.

Nate's body language, however, spoke volumes. He continued to slice zucchini, speaking Saardiscan as he worked. What was obvious to me was that he was paying little attention to Hector, yet watching Stephanie's every move.

Keeping his voice steady and calm, he said something that caused Stephanie to react. She gave a little gasp of surprise and her cheeks flamed bright red. Flustered, she glanced over to me. "I need a pencil," she said in a quavering voice. "Do you have a pencil?"

"Sure," I said, letting her know I'd heard the word. I then reached for one, intending to hand it to her while I came up with a credible reason to call her out of the room.

"What are you doing?" Her voice was high and thin. "I said I needed a pencil."

"I heard you," I said in as soothing a tone as I could muster. "Give me a minute, okay?"

She bit her bottom lip, sent a furious glare toward Nate, and then stomped out of the kitchen. "I didn't sign on for this."

I pressed my hand against my forehead for a precious second, then excused myself and took off after her. I didn't like the idea of leaving the two chefs in the kitchen without supervision, but there wasn't much choice.

Stephanie stormed south down the corridor that led to the Center Hall. "Wait," I said.

She turned and slowed. I had no idea where she thought she was going. I got the impression she didn't, either. When we reached the Center Hall, I tapped one of the Secret Service agents there on the arm. "I had to leave the kitchen, and two Saardiscan chefs are all alone in there. Could someone please stay with them until I return?"

The agent acknowledged me with a nod, conferred briefly with his counterpart, and spoke into his microphone as he made his way back the way we'd come.

"Stop," I said to Stephanie. "What do you think you're doing?"

She spun, her dark eyes searching behind me, as though worried we were being followed. "They are not nice men," she said. "You said you wanted me to listen to see if they knew anything about that other man who died."

"Did they?" I asked. "Say anything, that is?"

"They said too much." She pressed the fingers of both hands to her brow, then clasped them against her lips, her body jittering with what could have been nervousness, or perhaps even fear. Finally clasping her hands together tightly at her chest, she took a long breath.

Slightly more composed but still shaking, she pursed her lips, took another breath, and said, "They talked about me." She patted a high spot on her breastbone. "Me," she repeated. "The two of them were discussing what they would like to do with me. If they had me alone."

Although she'd started out in hushed tones, her voice had risen to the point that I worried we might be overheard. I led her into the Diplomatic Reception Room. "What, exactly, did they say?" I asked.

She shook her head. "I refuse to repeat it."

"I'm sorry you had to hear that. I'm sorry to have put you in that situation."

Her hands had stopped trembling. "I'm not going back in there," she said.

"Of course not." I grasped her by her forearms. "Truly, I am sorry. No one should be subject to that. I can't apologize enough."

She breathed in deeply through her nose, staring across the room. "I think," she said, much calmer now, "they were testing me, to see if I understood."

I'd come to the same conclusion.

"I should be apologizing to you," Stephanie said. "I've blown the mission. It seems I'm not cut out to be much of a spy, doesn't it?"

"It's all right," I said, though the untruth came out lame. If Nate and Hector had, indeed, engineered their conversation to ascertain if Stephanie understood, they'd achieved success. At this poor young woman's expense.

"I am sincerely very sorry to have put you through that," I said, apologizing yet again.

"I'm better now, thanks. Although I don't know how they knew, I think they suspected me right away. I'm sure this was a test. And I failed."

"I'll call Secret Service to have you escorted out."

She flashed one of her timid smiles. "If there was any other way to help, you know I would."

"Thanks," I said. "My guess is that there won't be a great deal of Saardiscan chatter in the kitchen now that they're aware we're interested in what they're saying. You helped us in that way, no question about it. I'm sure we were all worried for nothing." That was another lie, but it was the only way to make her feel better about how things had turned out.

CHAPTER 23

GAV MET ME AFTER WORK ON 17TH STREET, just outside the southwest appointment gate. We had tickets to see *Peter and the Starcatcher* tonight and had decided to grab dinner in the Foggy Bottom area beforehand.

As we made our way to the restaurant, I told Gav about what a mess the day had turned out to be.

"How did you explain Stephanie's sudden departure to the Saardiscans when you returned to the kitchen?" he asked.

I took a deep inhalation of the fall air. A gentle breeze carried the heady scent of soft carth and fallen leaves. It was the time of the year I'd loved as a child. I'd always been an indoor kid, and cooler weather meant books to read and cooking projects to tackle. "I can't wait until these visitors are gone," I said, staring up at the overcast sky.

He waited.

Returning my attention to where I was walking, I shrugged. "To answer your question, though, it didn't really matter what I said. There's no doubt in my mind that

Nate and Hector, at least, knew that Stephanie was an interpreter. When Cleto and Tibor returned, I made an excuse about how Stephanie had decided that perhaps she didn't want to follow a career as a chef after all, and how amazing it was that one day's experience in the kitchen had opened her eyes."

"That probably didn't convince anyone."

I waved a hand in the air. "Oh, they had plenty to say on the subject of young people. You know, how they don't appreciate the opportunities they're granted, and how they possess an overblown sense of entitlement, and how they— Stephanie in particular—must be a disappointment to the relative who stuck his neck out on her behalf."

"You didn't argue the point, did you?"

"How could I?" The aggravation I'd been feeling all day rumbled in my chest again.

"That had to really bother you." Gav's eyes narrowed as he glanced down at me. "I know how much it upsets you when people make sweeping generalizations."

I ran a hand through my hair. "I know. I feel as though I single-handedly painted all twenty-somethings as a group of ungrateful slackers. You know as well as I do that there are many wonderful young people out there. Strong, energetic, smart youngsters, poised to do great things in this country."

He grabbed my left hand with his right. "Slow down," he said.

It took a split second to understand. "Oh, right," I said, and decreased my pace.

"The more you talked, the faster you walked. You tend to do that."

"Pent-up frustration makes me jittery."

"I know."

I bumped my shoulder into his arm and laughed at myself. "One of the perks of the job. Unintentional exercise."

We walked for a few minutes in silence before I thought

to add, "There is some good news, though. Marcel called. He's been given the okay to return to work."

"Wow. That poor guy has been through so many ups and downs—he's in, he's out, he's in . . ." Gav said. "But won't the broken arm prevent him from being any real help?"

"Marcel will do what he can, with the Saardiscan chefs assisting him, for casual dinner meetings. When the time comes to prepare for the big Saardiscan dinner, however, Sargeant will be bringing back one of Marcel's assistants to lend a hand. Hallelujah."

We arrived at the restaurant, a tiny Italian place that smelled of garlic, basil, and comfort. We gave the hostess Gav's name and were seated at a shiny cherrywood table for two tucked into the room's far corner. The walls were buff-colored stucco, the lighting indirect and warm. As I settled into my chair and accepted a menu from the hostess, I thought about how it might be best to cast off the day's stresses and concentrate on the here and now. Yet, I knew myself well enough to know that until I came up with a plan of action, I wouldn't be able to completely relax.

After we'd made our selections, and our waitress brought us the chianti we'd ordered, Gav lifted his wineglass and waited for me to do the same.

"What are we toasting?" I asked, holding my glass aloft.

"The plan you're hatching." He pointed to his head, and then to me. "There's something generating in there."

This man knew me well. "You're right."

We both took a sip, and when I placed my glass back down, I folded my hands in my lap and leaned forward, whispering, "Before Stephanie left, she said that she'd be willing to help me, as long as it didn't involve her facing those men. You know that mini tape recorder I use when coming up with recipes at home? What would you think about me taking that in tomorrow to catch some of what they're saying?"

The look on Gav's face made me talk faster, as though doing so would convince him that my hare-brained scheme was actually a great idea.

"If I can record some of their conversations, Stephanie can translate without her ever having to step foot in the White House again."

He nodded. "You, as an individual, can probably get away with it. The government, on the other hand, is required to clear specific legal hurdles before it's allowed to tape individuals' conversations."

I shot him a skeptical look. "And we all know that the government has always adhered to those rules, without exception."

"I'm no lawyer, but it seems to me that if your expectation is that kitchen communications remain open, then you're on solid ground. That, and the fact that you don't intend to introduce your recordings as evidence against these men in a court of law." He took a sip of his wine. "Do you?"

"All I want to know is if there is something going on behind the scenes that I'm unaware of. I need to know."

The waitress brought us our steaming first course and we halted our conversation until she'd retreated.

"The Secret Service can't possibly sanction this." He dug into his linguine and raised one eyebrow. "Not officially, of course."

"Understandable," I said as I took a deep whiff of my ribollita. "This smells wonderful," I said. "I may need to ask the chef for the recipe."

We ate in silence for a few minutes, until Gav said, "In other news, I talked with Erma."

"Bill is improving, I hope?"

"He is," Gav said, "and we discussed the winery again. As well as our plans—yours and mine—for our future."

I felt the delicious bread soup do a flip-flop in my stomach. "What did she say?"

"She understands how much of a bombshell this is for both of us and completely agrees with our decision to put off a final decision until we've had time to fully digest it all."

"And?" I asked, because I could tell there was more.

"She also suggested that we take time to learn the business from them directly, which is exactly what you and I talked about. She was quick to clarify that they don't want us to devote all our free time to them. She is suggesting, however, that it might help us make our decision if we understand what's involved in running the place. And the only way to learn is to involve ourselves."

"What do you think?"

He took another bite of linguine as he considered his answer. "I always prefer having more information rather than less."

"Same here."

He smiled. "I'm not opposed to spending more time with Erma and Bill. If I happen to learn some basics about running a winery while I'm there, so be it."

"That makes perfect sense."

"I know how little time off you get from the White House, Ollie. Which is why I don't want to put this burden on you." He stared at me across the table. "I can do this on my own. Visit there from time to time, I mean. I don't want to eat up your free time with this. Not unless you and I decide this is something we want to pursue."

"How will *we* know what we want," I asked, "if *you're* there learning the business on your own?"

He patted his napkin against his lips. "I don't know."

"The idea of spending time with people who are important to you is a good one," I said carefully. "And if you warm to the notion of owning a winery, well—stranger things have happened. Who knows? The more I think about this, the more potential I see. Not that I'm ready to pack up and move this minute, but we could open a restaurant there, couldn't we?"

Gav's eyes lit up.

I continued, "What I want you to know is that I'm willing to consider the possibility. There are options we haven't yet considered, and amazing potential. We could turn this into a real opportunity that works for both of us. But before we go there, I have to ask: Is this what you want? Or are you going down this road because you don't want to disappoint Bill and Erma?"

He rubbed one side of his forehead. "I really don't know. I'm saying that a lot tonight, aren't I?"

"I'm going to give you some advice," I said.

"Please do."

"Someone I care deeply about always tells me to trust myself."

He smiled. "Anyone I know?"

"I'd say you do. Seriously, Gav. Does being a surrogate son to them feel like the right thing to do?"

He stared at the table for a moment, but when he looked up his eyes were clear. "It does," he said. "Whether that's because I want to keep Bill and Erma happy a little longer, or whether it's because I'm actually intrigued by the opportunity, I'm not entirely positive. But this feels like the right step right now."

"Then that's all that matters," I said. "And while I may not be able to go with you every time you visit them, I do hope to join you as often as I can."

"You'd do that?"

"Last time I checked we were in this together," I said. "And you know me. I'm always up for an adventure."

CHAPTER 24

"YOU'RE KIDDING ME," BUCKY SAID THE NEXT morning when I told him my plan to record the Saardiscans. He'd seen the tiny tape recorder many times before. The silver device was a little taller and a bit narrower than a pack of playing cards. I'd received it as a gift from a good friend. Bucky, Cyan, and I had made great use of it over the years as we'd conjured up new dishes for our First Families.

Today, however, I had a whole new use in mind for my trusty tool.

"You think I'm overreacting?" I asked. "After the stunt they pulled yesterday, I have to believe these guys really do have something to hide."

"We all have something to hide," Bucky said. "But to answer your question, no. I don't believe you're overreacting. I just didn't see *this* coming." He pointed at the recorder, then added, "Remind me never to do anything even slightly suspicious around you. You're tenacious."

"So I've been told." I placed the mini recorder in my breast pocket, where I usually kept a couple of pens. I moved those to the pocket of my apron so that the pens wouldn't clatter against the recorder's plastic casing. "What do you think?" I asked.

"Nope," Bucky said.

"Why not?"

He pointed. "You can see the recorder's outline bumping from inside your pocket."

"Darn."

"There's no way to tell what it is, precisely," he said, "but you always carry pens up there, and I'm assuming you don't want anything to look out of place."

"You're right," I said. "Good thing I considered that possibility."

"You did?"

"Yep." I handed him the recorder as I crossed the kitchen. "The smock I have at home doesn't have a breast pocket, so I couldn't test how it looked there."

"What about keeping it in your pants pocket?"

"Thought of that," I said, tapping the side of my leg. "I gave it a test last night, but the fabric of my slacks must be too thick. I could barely make out my words, and I knew what I had said."

He turned the device over in his hands. "This is ancient equipment," he said. "Do they even make tapes for these anymore?"

I pulled my purse out and began digging in.

"Gav offered to get me one that's more sophisticated. He said they have models that can run all day and pick up everything."

"You turned him down?"

I grinned as I pulled out my cell phone armband. "Voilà," I said, holding the hot-pink Velcro strap. "I use this when I go to the gym." Grinning wryly, I added, "Which means I had to dust it off. But to answer your question, no. He's planning to bring one home tonight. I'll start using that one tomorrow. But I'm impatient."

He waited, with a skeptical look on his face, as I returned to the other side of the kitchen and laid the armband and the recorder on the counter.

"Is that going to fit?"

"This is supposed to be a universal type for all sizes of phones. I can adjust it."

"I don't know," he said as I placed the recorder into the holder.

Designed to snug around the edges of a cell phone, it featured small Velcro tabs that allowed me to adjust the width with some degree of precision. The recorder, however, was too tall.

"I have a backup plan," I said, pulling out a rubber band from my pocket. I affixed it around the recorder and the back of the holder frame. "Can you tell that I worked on this a little bit at home last night?"

"I don't know," Bucky said again.

I removed my smock long enough to wrap the band around the upper portion of my left arm. I tucked the short sleeve of my shirt behind the top of the device, to add stability. Gingerly, I donned my smock again, its sleeves wide enough to easily conceal the fact that I was wearing the mechanical device underneath.

"See?" I turned side to side. "What do you think?"

"I think it's perched a little precariously."

"So do I," I admitted, "but I need to be able to turn it on without digging into my pants pockets, or fudging at my belt. That, I think, would be a dead giveaway."

"Try turning it on," he said.

I reached over with my right hand as though pretending to scratch my left arm. I felt for the small nub of a button and flicked it on.

"You really have been practicing," Bucky said with approval.

"I'll need to be careful not to move this arm too quickly.

But I think it's solid enough to withstand a day in the kitchen, don't you?"

"You're the ace detective here, not me."

"Ha-ha."

"By the way, is the Secret Service in on this little caper?"

I opened the oven to check on the family's breakfast casserole. "I had to tell Tom about it, because I needed to get Stephanie's contact information from him."

"And he's allowing you to do this?"

I kept one eye on the doorway, in case the Saardiscans showed up soon. "'Allowing' isn't exactly the term I'd use. He can't grant permission, but he stopped short of forbidding me from trying."

"More power to you, then," he said. "I swear, you've become a force to be reckoned with in this place."

I had to chuckle. "Don't tell the Secret Service that."

"What? You think they don't already know?" He didn't wait for me to answer. "And what about Stephanie? Is she in?"

"Yep." I pulled the casserole out. "She's on another assignment today—nothing to do with Saardisca—and won't be available until late. I'm going to her house after work so that she can translate whatever I manage to catch today." I placed the steaming dish on one of the stovetop burners. "If Gav gets me the better equipment, I'll be able to simply upload and e-mail the recordings to her. Ah, the wonders of the Internet," I said. Tapping my arm, I added, "For today, however, I'm limited to twentieth-century technology."

"You don't waste any time."

"I already feel as though they've been here too long. Too many oddball happenings since they arrived. Yet there's no way to blame any one of them. I'm hoping to find out what's really going on."

"And if there's nothing?"

I shrugged. "Then I'm wrong."

Bucky passed me the first of the family's plates. "Which you usually aren't."

We finished preparing breakfast just as the butlers arrived.

"Thanks, Jackson," I said as the head butler covered the dishes and placed them on the serving cart.

When Bucky and I were alone again, I lowered my voice. "I'll need you to pull Cleto out of the kitchen from time to time. The rest of them know better than to drop into their native language around him."

"You got it, boss," he said.

Ten minutes later, our visiting chefs and Cleto arrived. "Good morning," I said to them. To Bucky, I whispered, "Here we go."

We spent the first hour or so going over plans for lunch and organizing ourselves for Kerry Freiberg's visit. The menu had been set, the ingredients identified, and we now waited for the Secret Service to procure all the particulars on our list of supplies so we could get started on preparation. Some grocery items would arrive tomorrow, with the bulk of our needs coming the following day. A few last-minute items would be flown in fresh the day of the dinner itself. With the lion's share of our tasks identified and settled, the only thing left to worry about was dessert.

I glanced at the clock. Marcel said he'd be here this morning. I hoped he'd show up soon.

"We were very sorry that the chefs were unable to meet with Kerry Freiberg during her first visit here," I said to Cleto, "but we're delighted to be able to entertain all of you as our guests when she returns. Are you taking Kilian's place at dinner?"

"I hope so," he said, bobbing his head with enthusiasm. "It is a shame the way it came about, but I would be honored to be invited to dine with our esteemed candidate. I have been wishing to meet her since her candidacy was announced."

"I'm sure she would be pleased to meet you as well."

"We all hope to make a favorable impression on her," Cleto said. He didn't see Tibor scowling behind his back.

Marcel came around the corner. "Bonjour," he said, with a wide smile that didn't reach his eyes. "I am so happy to be returned to my favorite home away from home. Have you missed me, *mes amis*?"

I crossed the room to give him a hug, being careful not to smash his broken arm, telling him that he had, indeed, been missed. Bucky laid a gentle hand on Marcel's back. "Good to see you, sport," he said. "The place hasn't been the same without you."

When Marcel had been informed about Kilian's death, he'd called me at home to tell me that just because the man had died, it didn't prove his innocence. Although Marcel had agreed to return to the pastry kitchen, he warned me that he'd be watching the remaining Saardiscans' every move.

Once we'd finished catching up with our most welcome pastry chef, conversation naturally turned to the Freiberg dinner at Blair House. Even though Nate and Hector were the two Saardiscans most likely to speak in their native tongue, today's schedule (at least, the most recent iteration) called for Bucky to work in the pastry kitchen with the two of them this morning. I couldn't come up with a plausible reason to impose a change on such short notice, especially since the three of them had identified specific tasks they planned to accomplish up there. Bucky would do his best to keep them speaking English, and at our earliest opportunity, he'd hand that pair off to me and pull Cleto and Tibor upstairs.

In the meantime, I'd keep tabs on Hector and Nate, and tape them if need be. Although Cleto had originally insisted that everyone keep to English while we worked

together, he occasionally forgot himself and lapsed into
Saardiscan to address his men. Every time he did so, he
made a big display of apologizing to me and to Bucky,
assuring us it wouldn't happen again.

With Nate and Hector out of the room, I handed the
Blair House notes to Marcel and told him I'd be right back.
I scurried into the refrigeration area, where I double-
checked the stability and positioning of the recorder one
final time, then turned it on. I returned to find Cleto and
Tibor deep in discussion—speaking in Saardiscan. My
excitement level skyrocketed.

Marcel, for his part, kept busy scanning the documents
I'd provided, using the fingers of his uninjured hand to flip
pages as he diligently went over details. Now and then he'd
pick up a pen and scribble a note, having to lean awkwardly on the sheets as he did so, in order to write one-
handed. With any luck his tasks would keep him quiet for
as long as Cleto and Tibor talked.

The tension between the two men was palpable. Tibor's
scowl was as pronounced as it ever was; his back was rigid
and straight, while Cleto regarded the angry chef with
what appeared to be amused disdain.

I held my breath as their quiet conversation grew more
animated, but they paid me little attention. Less than five
minutes later, both men fell silent. Tibor flexed his jaw.
Cleto arched a brow.

"I gather from these notes that I have a magnificent dessert to create and mere days in which to do it," Marcel said.

Perfect timing. "Are you up for the challenge?"

He tapped his temple with the fingertips of his free
hand. "Good thing I continued to dream up ideas while I
convalesced." Using that same hand, he dug into his pocket
and pulled out a stash of papers, which had been folded
into quarters. "I have a wonderful plan for a centerpiece of
orange poppies."

"Poppies are the flower of the southern province," Cleto

said. "And Kerry Freiberg is from that province. He turned to make eye contact with me. "Is he saying that the dessert will resemble an orange poppy? Is that possible?"

"He is, indeed." I couldn't have asked for a better opening. "Marcel, I think Cleto is overdue for a visit to your pastry kitchen. He hasn't had a chance to see all your fabulous creations."

"Of course." Marcel's eyes lit up. "I will need to begin experimenting to achieve my desired results. And the sooner I am able to start, the more likely success will be." Marcel gestured for Cleto to join him. "Come, I will show you some of my magnificent artistry. We will tell Bucky and the other men that they are to report back down here."

When Marcel and Cleto were gone, I slyly shut off the recorder. I waited for a while, then decided to engage my companion in conversation.

"Now that we're getting closer to the dinner for Kerry Freiberg," I began, "I was wondering if you were beginning to look forward to the event."

He rolled his eyes. It seemed that no matter what country people hailed from, emotional reactions transcended language barriers. "Why is it important to you to know this?" he asked.

I wanted to ask Tibor if he was always this intractable, or if there was something about me that brought out this special side of him. I was ready to pose that very question, in fact, when Nate and Hector returned. Swallowing my snippy remark, I put forth my best upbeat attitude. "I know from personal experience that as an event gets closer, my enthusiasm level ramps up."

"Ramps up?" Tibor asked.

"Becomes stronger," I said, aware that Nate and Hector were watching, clearly curious about what we'd been discussing. Addressing them, I said, "I was asking Tibor about the upcoming dinner with Kerry Freiberg."

Tibor shook his head with such sustained vehemence

that I got the impression he was more concerned with convincing his colleagues that he hadn't been telling stories out of school than in addressing the question. "I have said this before: We should remain in the kitchen," he said. "It is not right that we dine at the same table as one of our candidates. We do not belong there."

"What makes you believe that?" I asked.

"We are workers. We do not belong at a fancy dinner."

Nate chimed in. "Kerry Freiberg was a worker once, too."

"She makes people believe she is one of them," Hector said. "She tells them she will give them a voice."

"Then I can understand why she's so popular," I said, treading carefully. "I would imagine it would be a great opportunity to have dinner with her. A chance to get to know your candidate personally. Not to mention that I'm sure she'll be very interested to hear how this visit went for you."

"We should be preparing the dinner, not sitting at the table," Tibor said again. "It is not my place."

"I'm sorry you feel that way."

"This candidate is attempting to Westernize Saardisca. She is bringing America's way of thinking to our people. She tries to make citizens believe that everyone is equal."

"Aren't they?" I asked.

Tibor scowled. It was a look I'd grown used to, so much that it didn't unnerve me anymore. "Of course not."

Hector and Nate seemed to find Tibor's outbursts comical. Nate tried to conceal a smile but Tibor noticed. "I should be the chef to help Marcel," he said with a haughty look at his colleagues. "Kilian was the most accomplished of us all. Now I am at the top." He stared at all of us in turn, as though daring us to contradict him.

Hector gave him no more than an indifferent glance. Nate continued to smirk.

"I will join them in the pastry kitchen where I will be of most value," Tibor said. Then, almost as an afterthought, he turned to me. "If that meets with your approval, that is."

"Be my guest," I said, ignoring the condescension in his tone. "Go ahead. I'm sure Marcel will be grateful for the help."

The moment the cranky chef left the main kitchen to head upstairs, I turned my back to the men on the pretense of checking supplies in one of our cabinets. Once I made sure no one was paying any attention, I flicked the mini recorder back on.

"Bucky," I exclaimed when I turned back around and found my assistant chef sauntering in, "Tibor just left to go upstairs."

Bucky hitched a thumb toward the corridor. "I passed him on my way. Perfect timing. Marcel is wrapping up his dessert demonstration for Cleto and is about to get down to serious work."

"Great," I said. "We've been pretty quiet down here." That was a complete contradiction, given Tibor's fiery outburst, but neither Nate nor Hector seemed to care enough to correct me.

Across the central countertop I met Bucky's curious gaze. He was silently asking me if I'd turned the recorder on. I pulled in a shaky breath and gave the briefest of nods. He winked.

With the device humming against my left arm, I smiled. We were live, once again.

CHAPTER 25

WITH MY FINGERS CROSSED AND RECORDER running, all I needed was for our Saardiscan friends to get chatty.

It didn't take long.

Nate and Hector began slowly. Judging from their cadence and the occasional name they dropped as they spoke, I got the impression that they were discussing Tibor. Whatever they were saying—and after a week I was still too lost to pick up more than moods to help me discern context—led me to believe that neither man was overly fond of the other chef.

We all kept busy with our individual tasks for the day, so the fact that Bucky and I worked in silence apart from them was not something that might arouse suspicion. At least, I hoped not.

When the two men appeared to drop Tibor as a topic, they yakked amiably for a little longer. This time it sounded like they were trading good-natured insults. They eventually lapsed into an extended silence.

When they had been quiet for longer than I could stand, I pulled up one of the planning pages I'd been working on and turned to Bucky. "I'm wondering if you and I should go over to Blair House today rather than wait. I'm really itching to get a closer look at the kitchen."

Hector and Nate glanced up at me when I mentioned Blair House, but otherwise didn't seem interested in our conversation.

"Sounds like a good idea," Bucky said. "You never know what surprises there are in store."

"We don't need any more surprises," I agreed. "The sooner we have a handle on all aspects of this event, the better we can deal with last-minute changes." Looking over at Nate and Hector, I added, "Believe it or not, all these updates aren't unusual for us. We're used to working around constantly shifting plans."

"This week has been normal?" Nate asked, aghast.

I hastened to clarify. "I'm talking about dinner plans. Marcel's and Hector's fainting spells, and Kilian's collapse are not normal in the least." I tightened my eyes. "Poor Kilian. I know he would have created a wonderful dessert with a traditional Saardiscan flair to it. I'm sorry he never had the chance to show us the depth of his talent."

Hector kept his head down. "Kilian was a good teacher. I am sorry, too. He should have been more careful."

"Careful?" I asked. "What do you mean by that?"

Nate patted his stomach, then answered, "You saw Kilian. He did not pay attention to what was good for him."

"There are a lot of overweight people in the world," Bucky said. "Kilian didn't strike me as a particularly sickly person."

Nate shook his head solemnly. "Many graves are filled with people who have much forewarning of death. Kilian was one of the most unfortunate who did not pay attention that he was in trouble." Shrugging, he finished with, "I am sorry he is gone, too, but Kilian has only himself to blame."

"From what I've heard, he had some heart issues," I said. "Is that what you're talking about?"

Nate, who had been the quietest of the bunch since the chefs had first arrived in our kitchen, seemed to be embarrassed to find himself thrust in the limelight. "It no longer matters for Kilian, does it?"

The kitchen grew quiet after that discussion. Bucky worked at his end of the room and I at mine, with Nate and Hector across from me. My goal, originally, had been to bring up Kilian's name in conversation, hoping that would spur a discussion between the two Saardiscans in their native language. I wanted to know, once and for all, if they had any knowledge of—or even suspected—foul play.

I returned to working on the spreadsheets, hoping the two men would pick up the thread of conversation.

They both watched me for longer than I would have expected. From time to time I looked up, making eye contact and smiling. They kept working as they watched, and in what seemed to be an unspoken agreement, Hector turned to Nate and asked him something in Saardiscan.

I didn't even look up. I could tell from the faint trembling against my arm that my mini tape recorder was still running. It took all my willpower not to hold my breath as Nate answered Hector with a harsh rebuke. Hector made apologetic noises.

A moment later, Nate started the conversation again, this time calmly, in a voice that was so low I feared the recorder might not catch it.

In an effort not to listen, I strove with all my might to keep my movements and body language communicating oblivious indifference. I also did my best to work as silently as possible, recognizing that noises I made near the machine could risk drowning the men's conversation out when we finally listened in.

Keeping my eyes on the pages before me, I nonchalantly tugged at my smock while I pretended to study my notes, hoping to convince them of my deep concentration. Mostly I hoped they didn't notice me at all. How they couldn't hear my pulse pound in my ears, or notice the heat that crept up from my chest, I didn't know.

Even though I operated in stealth, even though there was absolutely no way for them to know what I was attempting, the awareness that I was stalking them in this way made me nervous. Perhaps I'd simply had one too many close calls in my life, but the fact that we had three fainting incidents and one death on our hands this past week made me leery.

Gav always encouraged me to trust my gut. Right about now it was ringing like a semaphore, warning of an oncoming freight train. The problem was that I couldn't find my way off the tracks to safety. To say I was unsettled was an understatement.

I managed to find a reason to shift positions and work a little closer to the men. They'd relaxed quite a bit, or so I gathered from their casual gestures and the easy rhythm of their words. Yet, whatever they were discussing—in fits and starts—seemed to be of great importance to both. There were a few consonant-heavy syllables that they repeated again and again.

Marcel, Tibor, and Cleto returned to the main kitchen a bit later. We'd kept busy while they were gone, Bucky and I working in silence while Nate and Hector carried on like two buddies meeting for a beer after work.

Marcel fairly sailed into the room, using his good arm to gesture grandly behind him, toward Cleto and Tibor, who followed him in. "I present my prototype," Marcel announced. "Tell me what you think."

Cleto carried a small plant in his large hands. If I hadn't known better, I would have assumed it to be a real flower in a ceramic bowl. A spherical pot of bright blue housed a single, vivid orange bloom atop a delicate green stem adorned with diminutive leaves. Lifelike, and quivering with graceful elegance, its austere beauty took my breath away.

"Oh, Marcel," I said. "You've outdone yourself."

"It is merely a first attempt," he said. Though he waved my praise away I could tell my reaction had pleased him. "I will admit that creating these prototypes was exceptionally difficult given my impairment." He raised his casted arm, slightly. "Fortunately, however, my fingers remain unaffected." He made a pincer motion with his index finger and thumb to demonstrate, then nodded at Cleto and Tibor. "Together with able assistance from these two gentlemen, I have managed what seemed impossible." Marcel then picked up an empty tray, but clearly had no reason for doing so other than to make himself look busy and pretend to be utterly unmoved by our collective admiration. His eyes, however, expectant and bright, scanned our faces, eager for more.

The look of pure awe Cleto displayed made me smile because I knew precisely what he was feeling. "Marcel is a master," he said in a soft voice. "I have never encountered such a beautiful dessert." He turned to me. "Despite the fact that he created this work of art right before my eyes, I still am unable to believe it."

Even the stubborn Tibor's eyes shone with appreciation for Marcel's talent, and perhaps, too, for his kind words. He said nothing, however, and turned away when I looked at him.

"We need to put the finishing touches on plans for Kerry Freiberg's dinner," I said once we'd all sufficiently cooed over Marcel's lovely sugar poppy. "Time is running short. Bucky and I were thinking about walking over to Blair House later today, to get a feel for where we'll be preparing your dinner. Would any of you care to join us?"

Nate looked over to Hector with a "How about it?" expression. Hector seemed to answer with, "Whatever."

"We will accompany you," Nate said. "We would like,

very much, to see how the United States houses dignitaries." His smile grew wide. "I cannot imagine the accommodations being more luxurious than what we have at our hotel, but your country continues to astonish me with what you have to offer."

Tibor's gaze flipped from me, to Hector and Nate, then to Cleto, then back to me. He didn't say a word, but I could read scorn in his eyes. Why he was so opposed to this dinner, I couldn't imagine. Even if Kerry Freiberg's world views were different from his, Tibor had made it clear that he would do as he was told. The only thing that I could think of was that he didn't support her as a candidate, and knew that his hair-trigger temper could get him into trouble.

"I'll have to clear the visit with Peter Sargeant," I said, "but I would imagine we could walk over when we're finished for the day. I'll be sure to keep you both informed."

The matter settled, I started across the kitchen, through one if its narrowest sections, making my way to the computer to e-mail Sargeant with my request.

"I would like to accompany you to Blair House as well," Marcel said. "Would that be agreeable to you, Olivia?"

I turned to answer, too late noticing that Marcel had taken that very moment to squeeze behind me. The two of us collided, but not before he had a split-second chance to swing his injured limb out of harm's way. He lost his one-handed grip on the tray he was carrying and as it clattered to the floor, his cast slid up along the arm of my smock, bumping the bottom of the miniature tape recorder.

The rubber band broke, stinging as it snapped against my forearm.

I reacted instinctively, grabbing my arm with the opposite hand, doing my best to keep the tape recorder from springing from its perch. My fingers came up empty, save for a handful of sleeve. I could feel the solid mass tumble against my arm and I grasped again and missed, cognizant of the attention I was generating. I must have looked like a crazed person, fighting to free a bug from under her clothing.

In a surge of brilliance, I jerked my hand up, hoping gravity would drop the recorder into the elbow of my sleeve. The movement, however—centrifugal force at its finest—served to jettison the device out my cuff like a missile. It shot away from me, dropped to the floor, and broke into two pieces, one of which slid across the room like a hockey puck.

The entire episode took less than ten seconds, but by the time the tiny tape recorder was exposed, everyone in the room had his eyes on it. And me.

Thinking fast as I crouched to retrieve the device, I assumed the most nonchalant air I could muster. "I guess I won't be listening to my favorite music anytime soon."

My heart all but stopped in fear that I'd broken the thing, thereby losing whatever Saardiscan conversation I'd recorded, and panic that one of the visitors would recognize the slim gadget for what it was.

To my relief, the recorder's back had simply separated from the body, but to my horror, Nate leaned down to help me pick the pieces up.

He beat me to the working half of the recorder as I wrapped my hand around the plastic backing. Nate turned the little machine over in his hand, then tightened his fist around it as he took a step closer. Metal cracked. Or was that terror splitting my gut? Bucky, Marcel, and the others waited, as though every single one of them understood what was at stake here. I knew Bucky did. I prayed the rest were oblivious.

"This is not from an iPod," Nate said with a curious look on his face. "Even in Saardisca, we have iPods." He reached for the rest of the recorder, still in my hand, but I pulled away. The look on his face read perplexed, but the gleam in his eye made my pulse shift into high gear.

"Thanks." I reached to snatch the recorder from his hand, but he held tight.

"What is it?" he asked.

When he tilted his head just so, I knew he knew precisely what it was.

"Mine," I said, because I couldn't come up with a convincing lie fast enough. "For music. It's old." My brain ordered my mouth to stop explaining, but I blathered on. "Had it forever. I should probably invest in a new one."

"One that doesn't fall out of its hiding place so easily," Nate said. "New ones are far better for that." He squeezed tight, cracking it one more time before handing it back to me, pressing into my palm with more force than necessary, and holding a moment too long. "You say this type of device is for music, yes? So you may play back everything later?" When he finally let go, he did so with a humorless smile. "You will find that your recordings are of poor quality. And perhaps this one is now broken for good."

"Um, thank you," I said.

But he wasn't finished. "You would be better served to purchase downloads," he said, "if it truly is *music* you're after."

Bucky had remained silent, but piped in now to help. "Ollie, Ollie," he said in a high, chastising tone. "I've been after you to get a new player for years." Turning toward Nate, he gave an exaggerated wink. I knew my assistant was trying to cover for me, but we were coming across like a clumsy scene from a bad B-movie. "With any luck this one is broken so you'll be forced to buy a new version."

"Yeah," I said, agreeing weakly. "With any luck."

SARGEANT, UNFORTUNATELY, WAS UNABLE TO arrange for our visit to Blair House that day. Part of me was sorely disappointed, part of me was relieved. After the incident with the recorder, I nearly shook with craving to get away from our Saardiscan guests.

When they finally left for the day, I watched them depart, making sure they were through the far doors and out of earshot before I turned to Bucky, exploding with the only thought that had occupied my mind for hours.

"Do you think they knew I was taping them?"

My assistant was drying a stainless steel bowl, using a cotton dish towel to wipe, dry, and wipe the utensil again and again. The fact that he clearly didn't want to answer made my stomach squish. "Hard to say, really." He pressed the towel into the bowl's rim and ran his fingers along the edge.

"Hard to say?" I repeated. "Nate practically called me out on it in front of everyone." I pointed to where the recorder had taken its tumble. "He had to know." I began pacing the small area.

Bucky stopped his busy drying. "For all they know, you could be recording conversation so that you remember all the steps we took to prepare for this dinner."

"That's a good excuse," I said. "I wish I'd thought of it at the time."

He *clanged* the bowl onto the counter. "Seems to me that they have more to worry about than you do. Why would an innocent person care if he was being recorded?"

I gave him a look. "Really, Bucky? Did you seriously just say that?"

He gave a sheepish smile. "Fine. Recording private conversations feels wrong. Perhaps they have reason to be upset. But even if that's the case, what can you do about it now? Erase it all?"

"I guess I'm not willing to go that far."

"So you hurt some feelings," Bucky went on. "They'll get over it."

I pulled out the recorder and tapped it against my palm. "The part that's bugging me most of all—if you'll pardon the pun—isn't that we're taping them without their knowledge.

It's that I'm the one who's doing it. Like I'm stooping to a new low."

"Didn't you ask them to keep to English while they were working here?"

"Yes."

"And did they?" Bucky asked.

"No."

"And don't you believe that they were testing Stephanie to see if she was listening?"

"I do."

"I've known you for a few years now, Ollie," he said. "If anyone chooses to take the high road, it's you. You drive me up a wall sometimes with your insistence on doing what's right, versus what's easy."

"So then—"

He didn't let me interrupt. Pointing to the recorder, he said, "If that's your greatest transgression, then you're way ahead of most of the world. Your goal is to keep everyone here safe, right?"

"Right."

"And, let's say that when you listen to the recording, you find out that Hector and Nate have an illegal gambling operation they run back in Saardisca."

"They can't. They're from different provinces."

Bucky rolled his eyes good-naturedly. "I'm using that as an example. What I'm asking is this: If you discovered that the men were discussing a sensitive matter that didn't threaten anyone's life, would you alert the authorities?"

"Probably not."

"And even if you wanted to, you couldn't. These recordings wouldn't hold up in court."

I took in a deep breath. "I may not even have recordings to listen to. Nate sure did a number on this little thing."

"Another reason to go with your gut." Bucky tapped the recorder. "Your instincts tell you that something is amiss. And your instincts haven't failed you yet, have they?"

CHAPTER 26

INSTINCTS WERE ON MY MIND LATER THAT evening, as I made my way to Stephanie's house with the little machine tucked tightly in the front pocket of my slacks. When Nate had handed it back to me, I was afraid it had been irreparably broken. To my surprise, however, a few minutes of attention were all the device needed to get it up and running—or whirring—again. Its technology might be woefully behind the times, but this little gem was sturdy, having been manufactured before planned obsolescence became industry standard. I was delighted that it had survived both the fall and Nate's attempt to crush it.

At this time of the day I could have taken either the Blue or Orange lines toward Largo Town Center, because extra trains ran for a few hours. On the return trip, however, I'd have only the Blue line option from Stephanie's Maryland location. That was okay with me. Hopping on the Blue line meant no transfers to Crystal City. I was very much looking forward to being home tonight. I'd left Gav a message about my errand, in case he tried to call, but I knew he'd be in meetings until late.

Stephanie's home was in a residential area, about six blocks from her Metro stop. Dusk was settling on the D.C. area earlier these days as the seasons shifted and crisp fall winds twisted crunchy leaves. It was unexpectedly chilly and I'd been caught in one of those between-season moments where outerwear chosen in the morning proved unsuitable by the end of the day.

Today's jacket was a navy windbreaker, and although it fell to mid-thigh, it was far too light against the brisk wind. The air smelled of wet ground, molding leaves, and car exhaust.

I walked along the avenue that, according to online maps, would lead me directly to Stephanie's street. As I pushed forward, head down, I had the notion that I should have waited to make the trip until someone could have come along. More for companionship than for protection, though the fact that I was on an investigative mission made me a little more skittish than usual.

Stephanie lived in a neighborhood that was neither upscale nor downtrodden. Homes here were older and lived-in—a few of them practically begged for upgrades. As I strode past, I questioned my motivation for making this trip. It wasn't as though I suspected any of the men of intending to do President Hyden any harm. Our commander in chief had been in and out of the kitchen on occasion—granted, always with a Secret Service escort— and I'd detected no negative vibe, no undercurrent of anger.

Even though there was nothing that implicated the Saardiscans in Marcel's injuries or Kilian's death, I couldn't shake the feeling that these men were hiding something from me. That was what I couldn't tolerate. I was determined to find out what they didn't want me to know.

As I trudged forward, blinking in the wind, it occurred

to me that the Saardiscan men could very well have been discussing my leadership in less-than-glowing terms. Pulling my cross-body purse tight, I tucked my hands in my pockets and chuckled softly. Wouldn't the joke then be on me?

I zigzagged along the uneven sidewalk, watching my footing without slowing down. I wasn't fearful, exactly. Uneasy, perhaps.

Three roads converged at a quiet intersection. No cars, but plenty of scraggly leaves dancing along the curb. Stephanie's house was down the small side street to my right. From my pre-planning on MapQuest I knew she was about four houses down from her closest corner—the intersection after this one. The area was clear—desolate, even. No pedestrians, no noise, save the wind. Even though I couldn't hear vehicles approaching on the wide avenue, I stopped at the corner and checked before I crossed, looking right, then left.

That's when I noticed him.

The man hadn't been there moments ago. I knew that for certain. He had either recently exited the Metro and happened to be going in my direction, or he'd just emerged from a house. I'd had so many run-ins with those intending me harm that I'd become hyper-vigilant about keeping mindful of my surroundings. People who didn't know me could view my attentiveness as nothing short of paranoia, but I subscribed to the old axiom about being safe rather than sorry. Politeness flew out the window where my well-being was concerned.

The guy was about a hundred yards behind me and moving at a quick pace. He wore a dark jacket, dark pants, and a hat that reminded me of Indiana Jones's, pulled low, covering his eyes. In the dusky evening I couldn't get a good look at his face. The best I could manage was a sense of how he carried himself. His bearing struck a chord of familiarity, but I couldn't determine why.

When he noticed me notice him, he stepped up his pace. Not a good sign. I hurried across the street—running now—at the same time trying to gauge how far down Stephanie's house was, and calculating the odds of making it there before the guy caught up.

Maybe he wouldn't follow me across the street. Maybe he was out for a jog, or rushing for some other legitimate reason. I wasn't about to count on that, though. Pushing myself to move faster, I stole a glance behind me.

He'd broken into a full-out sprint.

I didn't hesitate. Adrenaline and fear kicked in, giving me the boost I needed to speed faster than I ever had in my life. My chances of making it to Stephanie's front door before he made it to me, however, were slim.

As I ran, my breath coming in short, panicked bursts, the calmer, logical portion of my brain sorted through my options: keep running, turn and fight, or start screaming for help.

Though the thought process had consumed all of two seconds, I couldn't believe it had taken me that long to remember to scream. "Help!" I shouted as loudly as I could, given my breathlessness. "Rape! Fire! Help!"

In the terror of the moment, I couldn't recall which of those words was supposed to be the most effective at garnering assistance. I kept running, kept shouting.

The street remained dead as my shrieking pleas for help were lost to the wind.

Seconds passed like hours. I tried to make out the homes' addresses as I raced by them.

There. Two houses away now. Short, white, rickety front fence. Address on the open gate. Maybe I could—

I caught the sound of his breathing a hard second before he pushed me to the ground. I skidded against the sidewalk, my left leg and elbow taking the brunt of my weight, as breath rushed out of me with a *whoosh*.

Instinctively, I curled up, protecting myself with my

arms tight. Rolling to my back, I kicked at my assailant with my feet, knowing I was in a wholly vulnerable position. I had the presence of mind to keep screaming, "Fire! Rape! Help!" desperate to be heard.

The man leaned over me. Up close I saw that he wore a nylon stocking over his face, the way thieves in the movies often do. Smashed against the silky fabric, his features were unrecognizable.

When I screamed again, he grunted, but didn't speak, smashing his hand against my mouth in an effort to keep me quiet. With his free hand, he grappled for my purse and tried to tug it away. If I hadn't been wearing a cross-body version, he'd have easily been able to grab it and go.

I was still on my back, doing my utmost to scramble by using only leg power. I knew I should probably let him have the bag, but a white-hot anger flared in my chest and I stubbornly held tight.

He was so intent on getting my purse strap over my head that he resorted to using both hands, thus freeing my mouth. I bellowed again, doing my best to inch away, my hands scraping against the sandpaper surface of the pavement as I rolled to keep the purse out of his clutches.

When I landed a punch directly to his nose, he yelped. I had no leverage, so I was sure the blow did little more than sting, but it was enough to startle him. He tensed up, giving me the tiniest of openings. I grabbed it.

Ignoring the bite of the pavement against my knees, I scrambled away, stutter-stepping into a crouch. He lunged for me, but I jumped out of his reach. His momentum carried him flying past me, giving me a precious chance to run. Fully on my feet now, run I did, still screaming for help, plowing my way through panic toward Stephanie's house.

I banged on her front door, spinning to see how close the mugger was, hoping she'd answer before he could tackle me again.

He was gone.

One hand against my drenched forehead, I leaned out, looking up and down the quiet street, breathing with such effort that I couldn't believe no one could hear me. There had been no response to my pleas for assistance, and the man who'd come at me had disappeared into the gray night as quickly as he'd appeared. For all I knew he was hiding behind one of the massive trees that lined the road, but I wasn't about to check to find out for sure. I decided that I'd call a cab for my return trip, no question about that. First things first, however. I needed to call the police.

Stephanie answered the door with an alarmed look on her face. "Ollie, are you all right?"

I was still hanging tight to my purse, like a toddler might cling to a blankie. My breath was coming in ragged gasps, and I willed my heart to slow down. It had no intention of obliging me. When I nodded to Stephanie to assure her I was fine, I wasn't surprised to find that she didn't believe me.

"What happened?" she asked, stepping back to allow me to enter. She leaned forward and checked up and down the street, the same way I had. "Did someone bother you?"

I nodded again, allowing myself a little longer to decompress. With one hand on my chest, I used the other to wipe the sweat from my face. "You didn't hear me screaming?" Hip-hop music coming from Stephanie's living room speakers provided my answer before she had a chance to reply.

"No; oh my gosh, no. What happened?"

My words came out fast and breathless. "A guy. Tried to take my purse." Looking down, I relaxed my death grip on the bag, and pulled in a shuddering breath in an effort to calm myself. "I don't carry a lot of money, so he wouldn't have gotten much."

"Let's get you settled," Stephanie said, shutting the door behind me. "You're shaking."

I didn't want to tell her that shaking after an attack was

normal for me, or that, based on past experience, this alter-
cation had been fairly mild. The poor girl wouldn't have
understood.

"I'm fine," I said. "Really. But I do want to report this to
the police."

She shut off her music as she led me through a tidy living room that looked like a transplanted IKEA display.
Her furniture featured lean lines, sharp colors, and a television storage system built into the wall.

I used her landline to report the attempted mugging.
The dispatcher efficiently took down my information and
told me that she would send an officer as soon as one was
available.

"You're not hurt?" the woman asked, for the second
time.

"No, just shaken up."

"And nothing was stolen?" she asked, also for the second time.

"Yes, that's correct."

"We're experiencing a high volume of calls tonight,
some of which are more urgent circumstances. An officer
will be out tonight, but I can't promise that it will be soon."

I sighed, even though I understood. "That's all right," I
said. "I plan to be here for a little while anyway."

Stephanie had her arms folded across her chest. "By the
time they get here, the creep will have escaped."

"I'm sure he's long gone."

"Have a seat," she said, pointing to a chair at her kitchen
table. The room was small, but updated in a spare, very
modern style. Green glass door cabinets, stainless steel
appliances, shiny black countertops. Except for a block of
knives in one corner, there was nothing out. No coffee-
maker, no utensils, not even dish towels. The place was
Spartan and spotless. She either didn't cook very often, or
she was a master at hiding her tools. Based on her perfor-
mance in the kitchen, I'd guess she ate out a lot.

"I'd never be able to identify him, other than by his clothing," I said as I sat. The table, too, was shiny and black. The chairs, pristine white, were molded plastic on metal legs. Not particularly comfortable. "I almost wish I hadn't bothered the police. This will probably be a waste of their time."

"It's worth it to have it on record. Do you want something to drink?"

I realized I was thirsty. "Water, if you don't mind." I dug the recorder out of my pocket and placed it in the middle of the table.

"I'm really sorry that happened," she said as she filled a glass and brought it to me. "If you want, we can go over this recording another day. Or you can leave it here and I'll let you know what's on it."

"No, I'm fine, really," I said. "I'm here now; I'd like to get this done. Plus, it would be wrong to leave before the police get here."

She brought out paper and pen, and took the seat opposite mine. "In case you want to take notes," she said, pushing the instruments across the table. "Once I get a feel for their word choices and tendencies I can give you phrases to listen for, if you like."

"That would be great," I said sincerely.

"All right, let's get started."

I picked up the tiny device and rewound it to the beginning of today's recording. "There are quite a few conversations on here," I said, "but only a few of them seemed important enough to translate."

"Important, how?" she asked. "I thought you didn't understand the language at all."

"I understand body language, and tone."

"Got it."

I hit Play and the Saardiscan men's voices immediately came through. I recognized Cleto speaking to Tibor. This was when I'd returned from visiting the refrigeration area.

Stephanie listened for a bit, then stopped the device. Looking up, she translated Cleto's words: "I think the waitress in the hotel is attracted to you."

She then went on to translate Tibor's reply: "She is attracted to the fact that we are working in the White House. Nothing more."

"I don't know," Cleto said. His voice held the playful, singsong lilt I remembered hearing this morning. "She seemed to pay you special attention last night."

Tibor made a noise of dismissal.

Stephanie continued to translate Tibor's words: "Why are these citizens so wild about this building, this residence?" he asked. "They find the president's house exciting and exotic, but I cannot understand why. It has the right name. This is nothing more than a white house. Compared to the palaces our leaders live in, this is no better than a shack."

Cleto chastised him, reminding Tibor that American officials weren't revered the same way as leaders in Saardisca.

Tibor said: "The chefs in this kitchen are very loyal to their president."

Cleto: "As we are to ours, yes?"

Tibor, sounding affronted, said: "You doubt me?"

Cleto: "No, my friend. But how will you feel if this new candidate wins the election?"

"She will not."

"You sound very sure of yourself."

Tibor didn't answer.

Cleto: "What do you know about her?"

"She travels with her dog."

"You have nothing more to add?"

"Should I?"

Cleto: "Do you keep dogs? I cannot abide them. They are dirty and smell bad."

Tibor remained silent.

Cleto went on: "I have always hated dogs. Cats as well. Does the candidate's affection for her mongrel make you believe she is more worthy? Have you, too, bought into the Western belief that filthy pets are to live indoors and be treated like people?"

Tibor surprised me by continuing to remain silent. Cleto's opinions about the Americanization of Saardisca were similar to those Tibor held dear.

Cleto: "Have you nothing to add?"

Tibor: "You talk about dogs and cats and your hatred for them. What is there for me to say?"

Stephanie stopped the recording. "This is a whole lot of nothing."

"Keep going, please," I said. "A little bit more."

The two men went on to discuss what I would call a lot more nothing for a brief period of time, before Cleto finally brought up Kilian's name.

Stephanie's eyebrows arched as she translated Cleto: "Poor Kilian," he said. "What did you think about his plans to defect?" Even though I couldn't understand the words until Stephanie spelled them out, I could tell that Cleto's tone, while conversational, was almost too nonchalant.

I leaned forward. "What does he say?"

Stephanie was already listening to the next part. This time it was Tibor talking. "Kilian would never seek asylum here," he said. "That is nonsense."

Cleto asked: "Are you sure?"

"He was a proud Saardiscan. He would never relinquish his ties to his country."

"And you?"

Tibor made a noise that led me to believe he was appalled by the question. Spluttering, he spoke fast, and Stephanie had to replay that section twice to get it right. I remembered this moment in the kitchen. I'd seen the anger on Tibor's face, and I'd wondered what had put it there.

"How dare you?" he asked Cleto. "I have never given

our leaders any reason to doubt my loyalty. How can you make such an accusation?"

Cleto's voice became more soothing. "I make no accusation, my friend," he said. "I simply ask the question. I know too well how tempting life in this country can be. Not all men are so strong to resist."

Tibor: "And you? Are you tempted?"

We replayed Cleto's answer several times but couldn't make out what he'd said. He'd moved out of the range of my recorder.

More voices joined the chatter, along with the accompanying sounds of people moving about, utensils clanking into the sink, and generalized greetings.

"That will be Hector, Nate, and Bucky returning from the pastry kitchen," I said, by way of explanation.

When she began translating again we listened as the Saardiscans conversed among themselves a bit in their native tongue. Nothing they said veered beyond polite chatter and good-natured ribbing.

We listened to a few more uninteresting exchanges.

"Here," I said. "This is where I thought there might be something worth listening to."

I recalled the scene in the kitchen that we were listening to now. I remembered how they'd been too quiet, too long.

I heard myself address Bucky: "I'm wondering if you and I should go over to Blair House today rather than wait. I'm really itching to get a closer look at the kitchen."

We fast-forwarded through the discussion in English.

Silence again until Hector spoke to Nate in Saardiscan: "She talks about last-minute changes and how efficiently they work around them. What happens if one of these last-minute changes she speaks of prevents our goal?"

Nate answered: "Nothing will stop us. We will be successful."

I sat up. Even Stephanie seemed startled. She stopped the playback and listened to it again. "Yes, that's what they said."

"Keep going," I said.

Hector talking: "It is getting more difficult to plan with Tibor always around."

Nate: "You are correct. And we can no longer freely converse because of Cleto."

Hector: "It would be best if we were allowed unrestricted access to the ingredients, but one of them is always watching."

My skin prickled. They'd had unrestricted access from the very start. Although there were never long stretches where they were on their own, we didn't police them when they ran to the refrigeration room for an ingredient, or visited storage. We hadn't started restricting access until after Kilian's death.

That had been my call. Bucky and I hadn't made a big deal out of it, but together we'd ensured that the men weren't unsupervised when they were working with food. They'd noticed, which I supposed was to be expected. But I wondered why they cared.

Stephanie translated the next part. Even though they spoke in Saardiscan, I noticed that the men's voices lowered as though to keep from being overheard.

Hector: "They promise my brother will be treated well." Heavy sigh. "I can only hope that they keep their word and release him once this is over."

"Complete your job and you will have nothing to worry about."

"I do not understand why we are to be served as guests at this dinner. How are we to ensure the candidate's dish contains the ingredient if we are not allowed in the kitchen?"

Nate chuckled: "We will have to create one of our own last-minute changes."

Stephanie clicked off, staring at me. "What does that mean?" she asked.

"Nothing good," I said.

We listened to a few more of their exchanges, but

nothing more sinister came to light. Although I would have preferred to go over the entire day's worth of Saardiscan conversations, Stephanie was getting antsy. Didn't matter. I had enough to take to the Secret Service at this point.

"I'm sure Tom will call you in to go over all this, officially," I said.

She nodded. "I imagine so. Is any of this admissible in court?"

"That doesn't matter. These chefs are here as our guests. If keeping them away from Kerry Freiberg is what we need to do to ensure her safety, that's what we need to do. Prosecuting them would be a nightmare. But if our people talk to their people, I'm sure justice will be served."

"Let's hope."

I was about to call Gav when Stephanie's doorbell rang. "Speaking of justice being served," she said, "it looks like the police finally showed up."

I followed her into the living room and waited for her to unlock the door. The moment she did, two officers stormed in, nearly knocking the young woman to the floor.

"Hey," I shouted. "There's no emergency here."

One skipped heartbeat later, I realized how wrong I was.

CHAPTER 27

THESE WERE NO POLICEMEN.

They both wore panty hose over their faces the way my would-be purse-snatcher had, but this time recognition dawned. Their builds, their movements, and the sounds of their guttural exclamations—precisely the same as those I'd heard on tape moments ago—told me all I needed.

Alarmed, I backed up, preparing to run.

"What are you doing here?" I demanded.

Behind them, Stephanie stood, her hand against the wall for support. She stared wide-eyed and open-mouthed.

One of the intruders tried to grab me, but I ducked away. "Run," I screamed to Stephanie. "Out the door. Get help."

Either she reacted too slowly, or I'd shouted too late. The first attacker, who I recognized as the purse-snatcher, was Nate. He lunged at me as Hector turned for Stephanie. Her warbling scream shot chills up my back. I tried to sidestep Nate—to leap out of his grasp the way I had earlier, but he anticipated my maneuver. Seizing hold of my wrist, he spun me backward.

Stephanie's home was not large, and as I wheeled my free arm to maintain balance, I crashed against a nearby table, knocking over a lamp and a handful of framed pictures.

My backside hit the corner of Stephanie's television storage system, sending a hot zing of pain up my back and down my leg. But the anchored wall unit was just what I needed. Using it as a brace, I regained my balance. My right arm was still pinned in Nate's grasp, so I swung my left fist at his head, putting as much weight into it as I could.

I connected hard. So hard that my hand hurt. I stunned him, but not for long enough.

I could hear Stephanie begging to be released, but with Nate blocking my view I couldn't see her. I pounded another blow to my attacker's face. This time it barely glanced his chin.

He growled at me, throwing me onto the floor. I landed hard on my seat, crab crawling backward away from him. There was nowhere to go. Nate blocked my way into the kitchen. I could see Hector had Stephanie pinned against the wall, but his large form prevented her from escaping through the open front door.

It was then I realized that neither man had spoken a word. Could it be that they didn't know I'd recognized them? If that was the case, then we might have a better chance of getting out of this alive. As long as they believed we hadn't listened to the tape yet.

Hector pulled Stephanie over and sat her down next to me. She covered her face and sobbed into her hands. "Let me go. Let me go. Please."

"What do you want?" I asked, upping the panic in my voice for effect. It wasn't difficult.

Nate pointed to my purse, and gestured for me to hand it over. Both the recorder and my cell phone were in there.

I feigned ignorance. "You're looking for money? I'll give you money."

Nate growled at me, pointing to my purse with obvious rage. I continued to pretend to misunderstand.

"Give him the stupid purse," Stephanie shouted at me.

Nate reached for it, pulling me to my feet to negotiate the strap over my head. I started bellowing for help again, beating at Nate with both hands. I couldn't give up without a fight.

"Help! Rape! Fire!" It hadn't worked before, but maybe this time luck would be on my side.

I held tight to my purse, doing my best to wrangle both it, and myself, out of Nate's grasp. "Let go!" I shouted. "Help!"

He backhanded me across the face, sending me to the floor so hard I bounced. I yelped in pain and in disappointment. He pulled the straps over my head.

Triumphant, Nate handed the purse to Hector, while keeping watch over me, practically daring me to come at him again. Hector upended my bag, dropping my possessions onto the seat of an upholstered chair. He pawed through it quickly, finding the recorder in no time at all.

Nate pointed to my wallet and cell phone, which I knew they'd have to take, too, if they wanted this to truly look like a robbery rather than an ambush.

I wiped at my mouth, my fingers coming away bloody. That slap must have caused a cut inside my mouth. My cheek was stinging hot from where Nate's hand had connected with it.

He continued to watch me closely while Hector finished his inventory.

I knew I'd probably get only one more shout out before he silenced me completely, but I had to try. "Somebody help us! Help! Thieves!"

Nate spun away. I didn't know why.

Not until I heard the most wonderful command in the world: "Freeze. Police."

The two Saardiscans rushed the surprised officer, knocking the gun from his hand as they wrestled him to the floor.

I jumped to my feet, bent on assisting the fallen cop, but at that moment, another officer—the first guy's backup, I assumed—ran through the open front door. He took a beat to get a read on the scene and, from the expression on his face, I could tell that his first priority was to assist his fallen comrade. ·

Instinctively, I stepped back, hands up, nearly tripping over Stephanie, who hadn't moved. She sat there, tears streaking her face, eyes wide, as though she couldn't believe all this was going on in her little house.

The two officers struggled with Nate and Hector. In what seemed an extended jumble of arms and legs, grunts and anger, they managed to get both Saardiscan men to the floor, and their hands cuffed behind their backs.

The cops had ignored us during the scuffle. Now they both lasered their attention at me. "On the floor," the second one ordered.

I did what I was told.

The policeman who'd arrived first—his name badge read Lucha—appeared irked to have been saved by his brother in blue. Retrieving his weapon, he made a show of dusting off his uniform.

"What's going on here?" he asked.

I still had my hands up. "Those two men broke in here and attacked us," I said. "If you'll let me show you my ID, I think I can help clear this up."

Perhaps smarting from being caught off guard, he shook his head. "Hang on."

The other officer had pulled the panty hose from Nate's and Hector's faces. When their sweating visages were uncovered, I showed no surprise. I could tell that they hadn't expected that.

"What were you planning to do?" I asked them. "Why do you want to harm Kerry Freiberg?"

They turned away, mumbling to each other in Saardiscan.

"You know these men?" Lucha adopted a skeptical air,

probably imagining that these were our boyfriends and this was some sort of perverted domestic quarrel. "What are they saying? What language are they speaking?"

Stephanie wasn't about to answer, so I did.

"My name is Olivia Paras. I'm the executive chef at the White House."

Officer Lucha's jaw dropped, as I expected it would.

"These men are diplomatic visitors to the United States," I continued. "As I said, if you let me show you my ID, I'm sure we'll be able to clear this up quickly. To start, however, it might be a good idea to call the Secret Service."

CHAPTER 28

THE NEXT MORNING I DIDN'T EVEN HAVE TO say a word. Bucky arrived, took one look at my bruised face, and asked, "What happened?"

I brought him up to speed on the prior night's adventure. "Once Tom and his band of Secret Service agents arrived to take control of the scene, I was finally able to relax."

"Where are Hector and Nate now?"

I held up my hands. "They were taken into custody by the agents, but after that I don't know. I'm sure I'll find out more shortly. Tom called an urgent meeting this morning."

"Where was Gav through all this?"

"Working late."

"You didn't call him to come get you?"

"Once I got home, I called him, sure," I said, "but his job and responsibilities don't include racing to the scene every time the White House chef runs into trouble."

Bucky shook his head, chuckling. "Now that I think about it, that would be a full-time position in itself."

"He was understandably agitated that I hadn't called him sooner."

"I'll bet."

In fact, when Gav got home, his first words were, "I want to hear it all. Start from the top. Don't leave anything out."

I hadn't. His emotions at the retelling had run from furious at the assault, to being proud of me for my handling of it, to impatience at not being able to obtain updated information from his Secret Service colleagues. He'd tried, but—as of last night, at least—there were still too many layers of protection covering the chaos for even someone at his level to penetrate.

Bucky had donned his apron and was ready to get started. "What happened to the tape?"

"Tom has it." I looked up at the clock. "You're on your own for breakfast this morning." Pointing to a small batch of potatoes on the countertop, I added, "I peeled those but that's as far as I got. Tom's meeting starts in ten minutes."

"Got it." He stretched his neck, rubbing his hand down its length, his expression thoughtful. "What about the other two? Cleto and your buddy Tibor?"

"I have no idea," I said. "Stephanie and I didn't translate the entire tape, but from the portions we heard, it seemed as though Cleto and Tibor were unaware of the plot the other two had in mind."

"So," he began warily, "they're coming back? To continue working with us?"

Gav and I had talked about this at length last night. "I can't say that I have any real influence when it comes to diplomatic decisions, but I'm not going down without a fight. I cannot allow either man in this kitchen ever again."

"How well do you think that will go over?"

"I have no idea. The decisions made at high levels don't always follow logic." Taking a quick glance at the kitchen clock, I jumped. "I'd better get over there."

"Good luck," he said.

"Thanks. I'll need it."

I ARRIVED AT THE SECRET SERVICE OFFICE IN
the West Wing with about one minute to spare. Tom's assistant showed me in. I wasn't surprised to find Sargeant there,
but I stifled my shock at the sight of Cleto and Tibor.
Sargeant and the Saardiscan men stood as I entered. I
worked to keep my expression from betraying my disbelief.

Cleto stepped forward, offering me his now-vacant seat,
even though there was a spare one waiting for me on my
right. "Thank you, I'm fine." I sat.

Tibor's scowl, which had been such a permanent fixture
on his weathered face, was gone, replaced by a flat expression that betrayed no emotion. He sat down after I did, not
looking at me.

Cleto stepped back and as he and Sargeant lowered
themselves into their seats, Cleto shook his head. "My sin-
cerest apologies, Ms. Paras. I assure you that all citizens of
Saardisca would be horrified to learn of what those two
evil men were planning."

"Everyone here has been briefed regarding the incident
yesterday evening," Tom said, bringing the meeting to
order. "The Saardiscan government has been fully apprised
and the State Department is in discussions now with them
to determine our next steps." He took a look around the
room, making eye contact with each of us in turn.

"Nothing that is discussed is to be repeated outside this
room," Tom continued. "The only exceptions being Bucky,
Marcel, Margaret, and certain Saardiscan officials Cleto
and I have identified." He squared his jaw as he faced
Tibor. "Do you understand?"

Tibor still wasn't scowling, but the blank, unreadable
expression was gone. Wild, furtive eyes betrayed fear. "I
do not wish to discuss this with anyone." His right leg

bounced and his fingers, clasped together in his lap, were white from being gripped so tightly. "I had no knowledge of what Nate and Hector were planning. I am innocent."

"No one knew," Tom said, offering the nervous man vague absolution. "We are, however, pleased to be aware of their scheme now. As things stand at this moment, we have obtained incontrovertible proof that Nate and Hector intended to harm Kerry Freiberg during her visit. Saardiscan officials have been informed and they are cooperating. We're all very interested in discovering what the two men's motivation was. As of right now, they are admitting to very little."

Sargeant used the tips of his index finger and thumb to rub his eyebrows. "What *was* their actual plan?" he asked.

I thought it was a reasonable question.

Tom breathed in slowly through his nose, clearly impatient. "I am not at liberty to discuss specifics. What I can tell you, however, is that we have searched their hotel rooms and found enough evidence to detain them until further notice."

"Where are Hector and Nate now?" I asked.

"We have them in a secure facility in Maryland."

"They should be sent home at once to face punishment," Cleto said. He turned to Tibor, looking for support. "Our government does not tolerate such treachery."

Tibor, however, was focused on Tom. "What is to become of me?" he asked. "Am I to be sent home, too?"

"The reason I called you both here this morning was to advise you that as a result of these extraordinary circumstances, neither of you will be allowed to return to the White House after this meeting. We have already notified your government of our decision and they understand our position. I trust you both do as well."

Cleto's shoulders sagged. "But this was to be the crowning achievement of my career," he said with patent dismay. His cheeks flushed pink and his hefty hands came up, gesticulating as impassioned words spilled. "You must believe me. There was no way I could have known of their terrorism. All four chefs were assigned to me. I did not choose them. I did not know them and could not have predicted this."

Tom listened politely. I breathed a deep sigh of relief. We were done with the Saardiscans in our kitchen. Done for good with the men who had brought us nothing but aggravation and trouble. One more piece of good news and I'd be dancing disco across Tom's desk. Ducking my head, I worked hard not to allow my delight to show.

"Your government understands," Tom said when Cleto took a breath.

"And yet they allow me to be stripped of authority?"

"They didn't say a word about your duties or your authority. You'll have to take that up with them later. As you might imagine, they were far more concerned with the consequences of Hector's and Nate's actions."

"Then what is to happen to me?" he asked.

"I haven't been told," Tom said. "I hope you can appreciate the fact that our governments are scrambling to understand what's going on here. I anticipate that you will be receiving updated information as it becomes available."

A team of four Secret Service agents waited to escort Cleto and Tibor out. Both of them wore downcast expressions as they were herded away. Cleto turned to me, offering his hand. As we shook, he said, "Please express my disappointment and my great thanks to your assistant Bucky, and to the delightful Marcel. I am most appreciative of the time I spent with them. And many thanks to you for your generosity of spirit."

"You're welcome," I said. "I hope our governments get to the bottom of this soon."

"As do I."

Right behind him, Tibor glared at me. "Good luck to you," I said.

I thought he was going to walk out without responding, but he surprised me by asking, "What made you suspect Nate and Hector? Why did you tape their conversations?"

I hesitated.

Tom came up from around his desk. "Let's not get into that. All we need to know is that their plans were defeated."

One of the agents nudged Tibor's arm, but the Saardiscan didn't move. He stared at me as though willing me to shrivel and die on the floor in front of him. "As you know, I do not support this woman, this Kerry Freiberg, in her quest to become president. But to stoop to such a measure to prevent her from competing for the position is dishonorable." He continued to stare malevolently, and it dawned on me that he was trying to convey sincerity rather than malice with that incensed expression. "You have done a great service to Saardisca."

With that, he turned away.

Speechless, I watched them leave.

CHAPTER 29

THE NEXT MORNING, BUCKY AND I WERE IN
the best moods we'd been in for a very long time. Bucky
whistled as he whipped up scrambled eggs. I hummed to
myself as I flipped bacon.

"Unbelievable, Ollie," he said over his shoulder. "You
managed to save Kerry Freiberg's life without alienating
the Secret Service—for once." He glanced up at the
kitchen clock.

I checked the time, too.

He grinned. "And you managed to get rid of our Saardiscan visitors in the process. Bravo, Ace. Nicely done."

"Thanks," I said. "All in a day's work."

Not only had we been freed from our responsibilities
regarding the Saardiscan chefs, not only had I not gotten
into trouble for sticking my nose into international business, we were being rewarded. Cyan was coming back,
albeit temporarily. I glanced up at the clock again.

"I know," Bucky said. "I can't wait for her to get here."

"Marcel is thrilled to have his first assistant back in the

pastry kitchen, too," I said. "We may have our teams in place only until this dinner is complete, but I plan to enjoy every minute. With any luck," I added, "the sequester will be over by then and life can get back to normal."

"You *are* quite the optimist, aren't you?" Bucky gave me a stern look, but I could tell he felt the same way.

Cyan appeared in the doorway, arms extended high in a victory pose. "I'm baaaack!" she said with a huge grin.

Bucky and I let out happy shouts of joy as we welcomed her with hugs and laughs. She was wearing her purple contact lenses today, and a smile as wide as I'd ever seen. I hoped, selfishly, that her plans to leave the White House wouldn't materialize for a long time. Focusing on the present, however, I reminded myself that she was here now, and that's all that mattered. We were together, we were a team again. And with that thought, the tension of the past ten days dissolved.

With my hands clasping both Bucky's and Cyan's forearms, I grinned. "For the first time since the sequester started, things are looking up."

When Margaret appeared in the kitchen two minutes later, I wondered if I'd spoken too soon. "Mr. Sargeant requests your presence in his office," she said.

"Now?"

"Immediately." She thrust one hip to the side and perched a fist on it while using the other hand to slide her oversized glasses up her nose. "If it was a scheduled meeting, I'd have sent you a notice via e-mail. It's imperative that you come upstairs with me right away."

I exchanged a glance with Bucky and Cyan. Bucky asked, "Are you in trouble?"

Before I could reply, Cyan shook her head. "Looks like nothing's changed while I've been gone, has it?"

Tight-lipped and blinking with impatience, Margaret motioned me to follow. "Let's go. Mr. Sargeant has a busy schedule today."

Sargeant barely looked up when I was shown into his

office. He was standing behind his desk, fingers lightly holding the edges of reading glasses as he studied a document in his other hand. "Olivia," he said by way of greeting, which I took as a good sign. "Please sit down."

His usually orderly desk was awash with papers, most of which appeared to be printed schedules with hastily scrawled notes in their margins.

When I sat, he did, too, still reading the page. He made a noise that conveyed overburdened aggravation, then handed the paper to me.

I started to scan, noting immediately that it was a copy of an e-mail to Sargeant from the White House chief of staff, time-stamped very early this morning.

"I'll save you the trouble of reading," he said, "if you'll spare me the trouble of arguing."

I hadn't gotten very far into the actual text of the message, so I looked up at him and nodded. "I want you to see," he continued, "that this is a directive coming from above. I need you to realize I have absolutely no influence with respect to this decision."

"This says," I began, "that Tibor is still invited to attend the dinner tomorrow night."

Sargeant peeled his reading glasses from his face and tossed them onto the pile of papers. He rubbed his eyes, leaving them small and pouchy. It looked as though he hadn't slept all night.

"Correct." He rolled his hand toward me. "This is where you tell me—based on all the recent drama surrounding our visiting chefs—what a ridiculously terrible decision that is."

I bit back my automatic reply. That was exactly what I'd been about to say. I pulled in a deep, steadying breath. "And there's nothing we can do?"

"And there's nothing we can do." He sat back, looking shorter than usual, almost like a little boy reclining in a grown-up's chair. "While the chefs' visit here did not proceed as we'd planned, Saardisca is hoping to salvage the endeavor and to use this dinner as a photo-op, with Tibor their proof of the chefs' successful visit."

"Successful visit?" I repeated. "One of their chefs is dead and two others were plotting to kill Kerry Freiberg."

He nodded again.

"How can they take such a risk? What if Tibor was in on it?"

Sargeant shrugged, sitting up a little. I'd seen him out of sorts in the past, but never like this. "They assure me they've gotten to the bottom of Hector and Nate's conspiracy."

"And?" Exasperation strangled my voice.

"Tibor is absolved of all suspicion. He's completely innocent of any wrongdoing."

I arched a brow. "As innocent as Hector and Nate?"

Sargeant sat all the way up. He leaned his elbows on the desk and tapped his fingertips together. He sucked in his cheeks and seemed to chew on them for a minute. "My counterpart in Saardisca has told me, in confidence, that Hector and Nate were not strangers to each other before they were sent here. Through bribery and extortion, they arranged to have themselves named as top chefs of their provinces."

I stifled my grunt of irritation. "That explains why neither of them was particularly talented in the kitchen. Did Kilian discover what was going on? Is that why he was killed? How in the world could the two men have accomplished this? They had to have had help."

"The Saardiscan government is investigating how such a nefarious plan could have been carried out under the radar. Though they promise to keep me updated, I doubt we'll ever know the full truth of the matter." He sighed. "As for Kilian, his death was determined to be from natural causes. Their medical examiner released his findings yesterday."

"Fine. Even if I believe that, I don't understand how the government can still insist on allowing Tibor to attend the dinner. He doesn't particularly want to, you know. He's made that clear from the very start."

Sargeant glanced at his watch. "Perhaps that's an indication of his innocence," he said. "All I can tell you is that this chef visit was to be a major step in the right direction for Saardisca."

"What about Cleto?" I asked. "Is he invited, too?"

"I'm waiting for an answer to that question myself."

"And they don't think Cleto was aware of the plot, either?"

Hands spread in a helpless gesture, Sargeant said, "Apparently, Cleto was acquainted with only one of the chefs—Kilian—before their visit here. He and Kilian came from the same province and had worked together several times in the past. Cleto says that he will vouch for his deceased friend's innocence in this whole devious plan."

"But not for Tibor's innocence?"

Again, the helpless hands. Again, Sargeant consulted his watch. "One more thing—we may continue to make changes as we move forward today and tomorrow."

"What kinds of changes?"

He blinked his bloodshot eyes. "If I knew, I would tell you."

"I'd still like to get over to Blair House to scope out the kitchen ahead of time," I said.

"I have communicated your request to the staff there. When I get an answer, I'll let you know."

I stood to leave. "Thanks for bringing me up to date."

"I hesitate to admit it, but I will be very happy when we bid these Saardiscans a final adieu, and I daresay you will be as well."

At the door, I turned. "By the way, thanks very much for bringing Cyan back for the duration. She's the one silver lining in this whole mess."

He'd already donned his glasses and returned to studying the pages before him. "Don't thank me yet," he said. "We still have the next few days to get through, and I'm convinced they will be a challenge." He turned to me, staring out over the tops of his glasses. "Do try to stay out of trouble."

CHAPTER 30

MARCEL AND HIS ASSISTANT BEGAN WORKING
to create three orange poppy dessert centerpieces—one
large, and two smaller versions—for the dinner tomorrow
night. I wondered, sometimes, if Marcel and his team
weren't secretly magicians. How they managed to create
such beauty so consistently, and—this time—under less-
than-ideal circumstances, boggled my brain. He and his
assistant were also in the process of putting together a
variety of coordinating petits fours to arrange on serving
plates around the vivid poppies.

Without the Saardiscans to distract us, and with our
supplies arriving on schedule, Bucky, Cyan, and I made as
much of the meal ahead of time as was feasible. We would
be serving fourteen for dinner. In addition to the president,
First Lady, the secretary of state, Kerry Freiberg, her campaign manager, her two assistants, and Tibor, six other
high-ranking American officials had scored invitations.

We'd done our due diligence on all guests and had
memorized everyone's dietary needs. Fortunately, among

these fourteen individuals, we had only one allergy—pineapple—to contend with. Even better, we had no pineapple on the menu.

In the midst of preparations, I picked up the phone and dialed Margaret's extension. When she answered, I greeted her politely, then asked, "Has Sarg—er, Peter received any response to my request to get into Blair House today?"

"Mr. Sargeant is out of the office at the moment," she answered, pertly as ever. "I will be sure to ask him when he gets back."

"Thanks."

"No luck?" Bucky asked.

"It's not like we're feeding three hundred people," I said. "I mean, we're serving a mere fourteen guests and preparing most of the food here. And although I've never actually worked in the Blair House kitchen, I do know that it's well equipped. We shouldn't have any problem."

"Who are you trying to convince? Us or yourself?" Bucky asked.

That got me to smile.

When Margaret called back an hour later, I expected her to give us the go-ahead. "Mr. Sargeant is back," she said.

"Excellent. Has he heard from the Blair House staff?"

"Yes. Your request is denied."

Why did Margaret always sound particularly cheerful when she delivered unpleasant news?

"Did they give a reason?"

For the briefest moment, I thought she might tell me that it was none of my business. Instead, she said, "If you must know, it was the Secret Service's decision. Ms. Freiberg will be returning to Washington, D.C., tonight and before she arrives, they want to do a thorough sweep to ensure nothing dangerous has been planted there. That the house is secure."

"Will they be there all day?"

"No, but apparently the staff needs to put the house back in order after their search. You would, unfortunately, be in the way." Again, the happy little lilt.

I heaved a sigh, not caring that she heard it. "Okay, thank you."

"That's not the only reason for my call."

I waited.

"The Saardiscan government has asked our photographer to send them photos from the dinner, and they've specifically requested that he take pictures of Kerry Freiberg, Tibor, and you together."

"Are you kidding me?" I asked, knowing full well that Margaret didn't possess the capacity to joke. Tibor posing for a photo with two powerful females? I didn't know whether to laugh or to feel sorry for the guy.

Bucky and Cyan stopped what they were doing, turning to me with twin looks of "What now?" on their faces.

"Mr. Sargeant told me to inform you to be sure to have a clean smock and apron on hand for the photo-op," she went on smoothly, not bothering to address my disbelief. "He also said to tell you that the biggest Saardiscan newspaper intends to run the photo as part of their cover story about Ms. Freiberg's success in extending friendship to the United States."

"I thought she was a long-shot candidate," I said.

Margaret didn't seem to care one way or the other. "All you need to know is that you will be having your picture taken. Is there anything else I can help you with?"

Resisting the urge to grouse, I thanked her and hung up. Answering Bucky's and Cyan's unspoken question, I said, "No big deal, really. I'm to have my photo taken alongside Kerry Freiberg and our good friend Tibor."

"I wonder if he knows he's supposed to smile for the camera." Bucky turned to Cyan. "You're lucky you never had to work with that guy. What a sourpuss."

Cyan, who had been brought up to date on all the drama

thus far, seemed confused. "What? Do they want a photo as a souvenir?"

I ran my fingers up through my hair, then immediately walked over to the sink to wash my hands. "No, I guess our happy faces are to be plastered across Saardiscan newspapers."

"You're joking," Bucky said.

I shot them a look over my shoulder, as if to say, "Now you understand *my* reaction."

"I don't get it. Any of it." I dried my hands. "None of this makes any sense."

"From what you two have told me, nothing the Saardiscans have done so far has made any sense."

Bucky pointed to Cyan. "Give that woman a prize."

THAT NIGHT, AFTER DINNER, GAV AND I SAT at the kitchen table going over plans for the following day. One of the perks of our relationship, beyond the fact that we were crazy about one another, was the fact that we could share specifics about the White House and its goings-on. Gav occasionally dealt with classified situations that he couldn't divulge, but most of the time we were able to freely banter and discuss.

In fact, from the time he and I had met, back when we'd respected—though detested—one another, we'd worked well as a team. I'd come to appreciate his perspective and, even when nothing exciting was going on, I looked forward to the end of the day so that we could spend time talking.

"What time are you and the other chefs expected at Blair House?" He pointed to one of the pages I'd brought to the table. "That part of the schedule has been left blank."

"I've been trying to pin Sargeant down. Or, should I say, I've been trying to pin Margaret down."

He furrowed his brow. "I can't believe Sargeant would let something like that fall through the cracks."

"He's been under a lot of pressure," I said. "He's doing his best but with all the trouble with the Saardiscans, and the diplomatic problems he's facing, it's a tough job. Plus— this sequester is taking its toll—it's hard to maintain efficiency when we're so short-staffed."

"Defending Sargeant?" Gav asked with a sly grin. "Don't let him hear you. He'll cut Cyan again and make you put Bucky on furlough, just to make you take your kind words back."

"He's not so bad," I said. "Situations change. People do, too. I wouldn't go so far as to say Sargeant has done a complete one-eighty, but he's better. His personality still rankles and there are times I'm tempted to bait him into an argument just for the fun of it, but there's no denying he's dependable and good at his job."

"Not good enough to have provided your arrival time. When will you find out?"

"I plan to head over to Blair House by noon at the latest, no matter who complains," I said. "I'd prefer to get in earlier."

"Kerry Freiberg is scheduled to arrive at Dulles Airport around two in the afternoon. That's where our team will meet her. We have several stops to make along the way, but we expect to be at Blair House no later than five."

"We plan to serve at seven," I said. "Which means that the staff at Blair House will see to Ms. Freiberg's comforts while Bucky, Cyan, and I stay safely out of sight." I pointed to the residence's floor plan. "The home is enormous. That should work to our benefit."

"The kitchen is opposite the dining room, down a long hallway," he said, "Until everyone arrives for dinner, I imagine you'll be able to work in relative solitude."

"That's precisely what I'm hoping for."

"I know you would have liked to have gotten in there today," he said, "but there were too many agents involved. It wouldn't have been pretty. The specialists in charge of advance reconnaissance don't view your presence in quite the same light I do."

"Tomorrow will be a challenge," I said, memorizing the floor plan before me. "We've been through worse. As long as Tibor doesn't have any surprises in store for his dining partners, I think we'll be fine."

"Do you believe he might?" Gav asked. "I know you're not fond of the man, and I know that the Saardiscans and our Secret Service have done exhaustive investigation on him since the plot to harm Kerry Freiberg came to light. But that has been only a couple of days and I worry that some crucial piece of evidence has been overlooked."

"I've been thinking about that," I said. "Tibor strikes me as a what-you-see-is-what-you-get kind of guy. He has made his opinion of Kerry Freiberg clear. He's also been upfront about his displeasure at being required to attend this dinner."

"Why doesn't he beg off?"

I shared what I knew about Tibor's upbringing, concluding with, "He's a good soldier. He was indoctrinated from a very early age into a life where one does what one's told. Where, even if he disagrees, he complies with government commands."

"With Kerry Freiberg's platform of freedom and personal responsibility, that ought to make for some fascinating dinner conversation."

"He'll probably remain silent the entire time, and speak only when a response is required."

"You don't think that the real reason he's agreed to attend is because he has a hidden agenda? That attending this dinner is part of some underhanded plan?"

"I suppose it's possible," I conceded. "But I have to say I don't see that in him. He's not a nice man, but he isn't evil."

"I'll keep that in mind tomorrow night," Gav said. "Once all the guests have arrived at Blair House, two of Tom's agents will remain with the president. The rest of us will move into adjacent rooms." He indicated positions on the floor plan. "There are several ways to get from the kitchen to my position, so if you need me . . ."

He let the thought hang.

"You know I always do." I ran a knuckle along his jawline. "But in this instance, we'd both prefer a quiet evening doing our jobs."

"Good," he said, snugging me tightly against him. "Let's get through tomorrow night and hope life gets back to normal after that."

I twisted to look up at him, arching a brow. "Since when is life ever normal?"

CHAPTER 31

"RIGHT THERE," I SAID. ARMS-FILLED WITH utensils for tonight's dinner, I used a free finger to indicate the countdown list I'd forgotten to tuck into my pocket.

One of the assistants who had helped us cart food and other supplies to the Blair House kitchen leaned over to pluck the indicated sheet from the nearby counter. He folded it in half and placed it into one of the bags I was carrying. I had that information on file and could have called it up from one of Blair House's computers, but having the printout ready saved me an extra step.

I thanked the assistant, then turned to Bucky and Cyan, who were also toting armloads of supplies. "I think that's everything. Let's go."

Most of the items we needed had been transported across the street earlier this morning, but I'd insisted on these late additions. It wasn't so much doubting that the Blair House kitchen would be properly outfitted, it was more my desire to work with reliable favorites that caused me to scoop them up.

Holding fast to my burdens, as well as to my vow to get into our workspace before noon, Bucky, Cyan, and I made our way to the resplendent home known as the President's Guest House.

Though crowded with pedestrians, Pennsylvania Avenue had long been closed to vehicle traffic. That had come at the request of the Secret Service after the bombings in Oklahoma City. Crossing to get to Blair House didn't require us to navigate traffic, thank goodness, but we were required to enter the home via a service door, far off to one side.

The house manager answered, accompanied by assistants eager to relieve us of our bundles. "They will deliver these to the kitchen," he said. "I want to take you the long way, to show you around."

Freed from the weight, I shook my arms to reestablish circulation. "I'd like that," I said.

"Smells different in here," Bucky remarked as we followed the butler.

"Every home has its unique scent," I answered, taking a delicate sniff. "I'm detecting a hint of . . . citrus?"

The house manager was a middle-aged man with thinning, pale hair. He turned and smiled. "You would be correct, Chef Paras. Whenever Blair House expects a four-legged guest, we treat certain areas of the home with special cleansers that are not harmful to dogs and cats."

"That's right," I said. "Frosty is part of the entourage." I turned to Cyan. "She's a Westie, a West Highland terrier, and absolutely adorable."

"Are we cooking for her, too?"

"No; I inquired about that. Apparently she's on a fairly strict regimen and Ms. Freiberg's assistants have Frosty's needs covered."

The man led us past two staircases and through a number of back corridors, narrating all the way, providing glimpses into many of the home's opulent rooms, explaining shortcuts and instructing us which doors led where, and which should remain closed at all times.

"How long did it take you to learn how to navigate this place?" I asked him.

He gave a one-shoulder shrug. "It isn't so difficult once you understand how the four individual buildings were ultimately connected to form one large home. I'm sure that once you spent a couple of days here, you would have no trouble at all."

As we continued on our tour, I peered out a window that provided a view of the garden courtyard. It was a welcoming space featuring fountains, expertly trimmed shrubbery, and dotted with benches and wrought-iron seats.

"Gorgeous," I said.

Our guide took a slight left into a wide corridor on the main level. "The kitchen is directly to your left, as I'm sure you've noticed. We will explore that in a moment." Pointing to our right, he indicated a very long, narrow hallway. "This leads to the dining room we will be using, as you can see through the swinging door at the far end."

Bucky, Cyan, and I peered down the long, darkened area into the fraction of brightness ahead. I couldn't make out much beyond what looked like federal-blue print draperies, ivory walls, and two Chippendale-style chairs flanking a sideboard.

I remembered the floor plan from last night. "There is also access to the outside down this hallway, isn't there?"

He nodded. "You have done your homework. Yes, this corridor provides access to a small parlor as well as to the main gathering area, where the president will be entertaining his guests tonight. In addition to having access to this corridor, the two rooms are connected to one other. They're not, however, connected to the dining room itself."

I thought back to the floor plan I'd studied last night. I could picture exactly the area he was describing.

"I assume this corridor gets pretty busy during meals

themselves," Bucky said, "with the butlers traveling back and forth."

"During the day, yes." The house manager chuckled. "But once an event begins, quite the opposite. When utilizing the rooms that have been chosen for tonight's soiree, our staff stays clear so as not to get in the way of our guests. Butlers take a more roundabout path when delivering meals."

"That seems an odd decision."

He smiled. "If we had more time, I'd give you a more in-depth tour. Once you saw the space, you'd understand how well this works for us."

I thought about how often we staged courses in the Family Dining Room on the White House's first floor, even though the Butler's Pantry might seem the more logical choice. I agreed with the house manager: The best choices were not always the obvious ones.

"Makes sense," I said.

I counted three doors on the left side, so I wasn't surprised when he added, "Between them is a guest bathroom. Because there are several other lavatories available and because they are somewhat distanced from where guests will be mingling, this one doesn't get used as often as the others." Gesturing to the other side of the long throughway, he pointed to the single door centered there. "On the right is a mudroom with a door that leads to the courtyard. There is also access to another staff stairway."

"Lots of doors," Cyan said.

"As I said, this structure is the amalgamation of four individual homes. It has its quirks." He waved toward the lone door down the hall on the right. "That exit is generally not open to guests of the home. Tonight, however, one of Ms. Freiberg's assistants will avail herself of the back door whenever the pet needs to be taken out. Of course, the stairway will also be open to all of you, if you need to travel between kitchens."

We would be working in the home's "hot" kitchen. Marcel would be working in the smaller, "cold" kitchen, one floor below.

The house manager had remained in the wide corridor during his explanation and now gestured to our left. "Speaking of kitchens," he said, "welcome to your home for the evening."

"Wow," Cyan said as the three of us spread out. "It's so modern, compared to the rest of the house."

Exactly as I remembered from an earlier visit, the spacious, windowless room boasted long walls of warm wooden cabinetry, an unforgiving stone tile floor, and a huge center island with a cream-colored marble surface, providing a perfect expanse for organizing ourselves. There was plenty of oven space, but the sink was relatively small, as was the cooktop.

"Not a lot of personality in here," Bucky said. "Everything is beige and brown."

I knew he was making an observation, not voicing a criticism, but the house manager's mouth turned down. "The home is designed for the comfort of the president's guests," he said. "Not for that of the staff."

Bucky murmured something along the lines of, "Oh yes, of course," but as he turned his back to the man, he stretched his chin and raised his brows, making a face that said "Whoops!"

DINNER WAS TO BE SERVED AT SEVEN, AND BY six o'clock we were precisely where we needed to be. The citrusy smell that had met us when we'd first arrived, and that still lingered ever so slightly in the long hallway across from us, had been replaced by the savory aroma of roasting meat.

A Secret Service agent had been positioned nearby to prevent unauthorized persons from entering the kitchen.

Several members of the Blair House staff had visited to introduce themselves, but for the most part we'd been left alone, which is how we preferred things.

The kitchen's position directly across the staff hallway, however, meant that I'd been distracted by movement all day. Butlers and assistants scurried back and forth, setting the table and preparing for guests.

Despite the fact that I was immersed in preparations of my own, I'd found myself glancing up every time a person entered that far hallway, or crossed my line of sight. I envied Bucky and Cyan, who had been able to tune out the activity far better than I had.

As was my habit before an important dinner, I'd imagined every step of the process in advance. Now, standing with my back to the stovetop, I took a quick look around the kitchen, reassured to see the meal progressing as planned.

Cyan was putting finishing touches on the salads. "Cyan, how soon does the roast come out of the oven?" I asked.

"Twenty minutes," she said with a quick glance at the clock. "I checked the temperature before you asked. Looks to be right on schedule."

"Fabulous," I said.

From the other side of the kitchen island, Bucky added, "Marcel called from downstairs. He wants us to let him know when the first course is served so that he can gauge when to bring his poppies up here."

"Got it," I said. "That shouldn't be a problem. Believe it or not, after all we've been through, it looks like we're going to pull this dinner off without a hitch."

The house manager appeared in the kitchen doorway, looking slightly agitated. "Chef Paras," he began, "there has been a change for dinner this evening."

"Change?" This came mere seconds after I'd predicted success. When would I learn? "What's wrong?" I asked.

Cyan and Bucky stiffened, waiting for the worst.

"Nothing is wrong," he said, quickly. "I didn't mean to

alarm you. It's just that this change has a bit of a ripple effect on the evening's agenda, and I will need to discuss alternatives with the photographer."

"And the change is?" I prompted. I wanted to hurry the man along. Unless he was about to tell us that dinner was canceled, we had work to do. We were getting into crunch time.

"One of the guests, a gentleman you are acquainted with," he said, "by the name of Tibor . . ."

"Yes?" *Come on, guy. Spit it out.*

"He will not be in attendance this evening after all."

My mouth dropped open. I closed it quickly. "Do you know why?"

He slid a sideways glance toward the front of the home, where the president and guests were enjoying pre-dinner cocktails and passed hors d'oeuvres. "There was some excitement, initially, because another gentleman arrived in Mr. Tibor's place, to deliver the regrets."

"Cleto?" I asked.

"I didn't catch the man's name," he said, "but he is, apparently, a member of the Saardiscan contingent."

"It is Cleto, then," I said. "Did he give any reason for Tibor's absence?"

"I was not informed. In any event, I wanted to let you know that dinner is now for thirteen."

"Thank you," I said. When he left I turned to Bucky and Cyan. "I wonder if Cleto discovered Tibor planning something and forbid him to come tonight?"

Bucky frowned. "You said yourself you don't believe Tibor was in on the plot to harm Kerry Freiberg."

"I've been wrong before."

Out of the corner of my eye I noticed a young woman emerging from the single door at the center of the long hallway. I didn't recognize her and she wasn't dressed like one of the servers or staff. I stepped forward, around the center island, to get a closer look. It was then I noticed that she was accompanied by Frosty, on a leash.

The young woman was no more than twenty, pale-skinned, heavy at the bust and hips, with a pixie cut the color of dark chocolate. I didn't hear her words, but could tell that she was cooing gently to the small dog, urging the pooch along. A moment later, she disappeared through one of the doors on the left, presumably to return to the party.

Cyan drew my attention back to the kitchen when she said, "I thought you both told me that this Tibor didn't want to be here tonight. Sounds to me like he was planning to duck out of this dinner all along."

I explained to her, as I had to Gav the night before, that Tibor didn't strike me as the type to say one thing and do another. "He wasn't thrilled to be invited, but he had every intention of being here. I can't help but believe that there's more going on that Cleto has opted not to share."

"After tonight it won't matter," Bucky reminded me. "Tomorrow, they're all flying home to Saardisca. And good riddance to the lot, I say."

"I can't wait," I said, with a despondent nod toward Cyan, "although that also means the sequester guidelines will be back in force."

"I'll be okay," Cyan said with forced cheer.

"Any prospects on the horizon?" Bucky asked.

"Nothing that excites me. Not yet. But it's early. And I have enough savings to carry me for a few months."

"Let's hope they put an end to this well before then."

Ten minutes later, the house manager returned. "Another change," he said with a smile. "We are serving fourteen after all."

"Tibor showed up?"

He shook his head. "The gentleman who conveyed Mr. Tibor's regrets was invited to remain for dinner in his stead."

"But," I sputtered, "but . . ."

"I discreetly inquired as to any dietary concerns you might need to be aware of, and you'll be happy to know that our new guest has no food allergies or specialized requirements."

"How did that come about?" I asked. "Who invited him to stay?"

"Apparently, when Cleto showed up to deliver Tibor's regrets, the agents notified the president immediately. He, in turn, relayed the information to Ms. Freiberg. I believe it was she who made the request for Cleto to join them for dinner. Caused no small amount of commotion, as you might imagine," he said. "Ms. Freiberg said she was sorry that Tibor wasn't able to make it, but that she would be happy to have this gentleman take his place."

At that moment, Gav showed up in the kitchen. The house manager, having delivered his message, disappeared.

"What's going on?" I asked, aware of the apprehension in my voice. I welcomed Gav's sturdy presence, even as I sought to make sense of recent changes. "How did this come about?"

He didn't waste words. "The decision was made to invite Cleto to stay. I strongly advised against it, but the agent in charge overrode me. As you know, the Saardiscan candidate's platform is one of inclusiveness, and she insisted. The secretary of state is eager to make nice with her, in the event that she's elected. Cleto was wanded and searched before he was allowed in, so the president gave the okay."

I didn't like this last-minute change and I could tell that Gav didn't, either.

Bucky stepped forward, keeping his voice low. "You're not suggesting that Tibor skipped out because he's planning to attack from the outside?" His gaze bounced from me to Gav and back again. "You don't think he's got a bomb, do you?"

Gav glared. Bucky backed away.

Drawing a deep breath, Gav calmed himself enough to address Bucky's concerns. "No one will be able to get close enough to set or detonate a bomb. All agents have been provided Tibor's description. No one will be allowed within the emergency perimeter we've established, and if Tibor attempts to cross it, he will be apprehended."

"Did Cleto give you a reason for all this?" I asked.

Having fully adopted his agent demeanor, Gav gave a brusque nod. "Cleto told the president that Tibor is feeling unwell and is too fatigued to leave his hotel room." He sent me a pointed look. "I've got to get back. I just wanted you to know what was going on. Keep your eyes and ears open. Let's hope this is nothing."

"Wait," I said, catching Gav by the sleeve of his suit jacket. "Has anyone confirmed Tibor's story?"

Another abbreviated nod. "Two agents from another team were dispatched to check on him. If he's there, then we can probably stand down. If not . . ."

He didn't finish the thought. He didn't need to.

"Okay," I said. "Let me know if you need anything."

That got him to smile, however briefly. "I will."

CHAPTER 32

THE THREE OF US TENDED TO WORK WITH A minimum of chatter. Tonight, however, we went far beyond mere quiet. Breathlessly silent, we spoke only when necessary, jumping at every incongruous noise, or the hint of raised voices coming from the front of the house. Most outbursts were accompanied by laughter or a jovial retort. Occasionally a guest would express good cheer by applauding. From time to time, Frosty barked.

My neck was sore from laboring to listen in, and I could tell the strain was taking its toll on my assistants, too.

"This is silly," Cyan said in a whisper as we began plating the first course. "If there was going to be any trouble, don't you think it would have happened by now?"

"I'm starting to wonder," I said. "Not that there's anything we can do." To Bucky, I asked, "Did you let Marcel know that we're beginning to serve?"

His brows jumped. "No," he said. "Thanks for the reminder. I'll do that now." He crossed the room to the phone and picked it up.

The two butlers assigned to serve dinner arrived in the kitchen. The tuxedoed men offered no perfunctory greeting, no smile, nothing.

Bucky called over to me. "The phone to Marcel's kitchen is busy, believe it or not."

One of the somber butlers turned to me. "The phone in the cold kitchen has been acting up lately."

Bucky overheard. "I'll run down there," he said. "Won't take a minute."

Cyan and I moved quickly, setting up each first-course plate to picture-perfect standards before handing it over to the waiting men. When I asked the butler nearest me how the party was progressing, he informed me that the guests had been seated. No embellishment, no detail. Had this been the White House, I would have been able to wrangle a tidbit or two out of our head butler and his staff.

When we'd finished arranging the final plate, the butler covered it and loaded it onto the serving cart. At the same moment, I glimpsed movement from down the long hallway opposite us. It was Bucky, emerging from the basement doorway. He hurried back into the kitchen, taking up a position to begin plating dinner's second course.

As the butlers disappeared around the corner to the left—on their roundabout path to the dining room—I asked Bucky, "Everything okay with Marcel?"

"Fine," he said. "He's ready to go whenever we're ready for him."

DINNER PROGRESSED EXACTLY AS IT HAD BEEN designed to. When each course's plates were returned to the kitchen, we inspected them to see how our offerings had been received. From the looks of the scraps left uneaten by the diners, tonight's meal had been a rousing success.

The butlers returned to the dining room to clean off the table in preparation for serving dessert. Marcel and his

assistant had sent up the poppy centerpieces and petits
fours via dumbwaiter, moments ago. The two chefs arrived
shortly thereafter and began arranging the masterpieces
for presentation to the guests.

I stepped back from the central island to allow them to
work more freely. Now, with the tough part behind me, I
allowed myself a moment to relax, enjoy, and savor. Bucky
and Cyan apparently had the same idea. They leaned
against the far wall, chatting quietly.

Movement in the long hallway caught my eye again.
The young woman in charge of Frosty made her way
toward the center door on my right, her obvious goal to
allow the pooch another outside visit during the lull
between dinner and dessert. The agent positioned at the
mouth of the hallway nodded acknowledgment as she
pointed to the back door. I watched her disappear through.

I glanced over at Marcel and his assistant as they bent over
their creations, heads together, speaking softly as they rever-
ently positioned each petit four into place. When I turned
back toward the long hallway, I was surprised to see Cleto.

The agent stationed at the mouth of the hallway straightened, having noticed the Saardiscan man, who'd just
caught sight of me. Cleto waved hello. I waved back.

Cleto stepped through the bathroom door. The agent
relaxed.

Moments later, the young woman returned with Frosty,
the little dog pawing and prancing against the constraints
of her leash. One second later, Cleto emerged from the
washroom across the hall from her. The timing couldn't
have been more perfect.

The agent took note of both appearances, but did not
abandon his post.

I watched as Cleto expressed delight at Frosty's bouncing excitement. To my surprise, he crouched to greet the
pup, vigorously rubbing her head and scratching behind
her ears, cooing praise loud enough for me to hear.

This was a man who professed to hating dogs? Or was this elaborate display of affection meant to garner favor with Ms. Freiberg? Although the candidate wasn't present to witness it personally, her assistant would no doubt convey how kind Cleto had been to little Frosty.

If that was his goal, Cleto was putting on quite a show. He continued to ruffle the dog's white coat. He held himself awkwardly, leaning away as he reached. His lips were pressed tight. I remembered his comments about dogs being dirty, and I wondered if he was afraid of getting licked in the face.

Frosty sneezed, twice.

Cleto's coos became ever more ardent and he kept his joyful attention on the dog. He was so effusive, so ceaseless in his devotion, that it got to the point where the young woman grew noticeably uncomfortable. Shifting her weight, she said something to Cleto, then tugged at the animal's leash. Frosty was having none of it, however, clearly wanting to stay where the petting was good.

Finally, the woman insisted, convincing Frosty to follow her back into the dining room. Cleto rose to his feet, rubbing his hands together as he did so. Again, he caught me watching, but this time I didn't wave. We locked eyes across the distance, and he gave a quick smile before disappearing back into the washroom.

I could have sworn I saw dust dissolve in his wake. A small glittering cloud that *poof*ed and vanished behind him like Tinkerbell's sparkling trail.

At the same time, the chatter level increased in the kitchen. Bucky and Cyan heaped compliments while Marcel and his assistant feigned modesty.

Over the commotion of their conversation, Bucky called to me. "Take a look at the finished product before these are taken out, Ollie."

Holding my hand up in a gesture to wait, I didn't answer, didn't turn to face the group. The Secret Service agent stationed in the corridor watched me with curiosity.

When Cleto stepped back into the hallway from the washroom, I called to him.

The Saardiscan man raised his hand in greeting, then began heading back toward the dining room.

"Do you have a moment?" I asked, a little louder.

He turned to face me with a quizzical smile, then started across the expanse between us. The Secret Service agent spoke to us both. "No guests allowed in the kitchen," he said.

Cleto stopped mid-stride, raising his hands. Their palms were bright pink, as though chafed from being scrubbed too briskly. Or was I imagining things?

"Of course," Cleto said.

I stepped past the agent into the long hallway.

"Exquisite dinner, Chef," Cleto said. "I cannot even begin to express my deep admiration for your talent." He closed his eyes as though experiencing ultimate bliss. When he opened his eyes again, he pressed his hands together and gave a slight bow. "It has been a pleasure getting to know you."

"I'm worried about Tibor," I said.

Though he tried to mask it, I didn't miss the relief that washed over him. As though he'd been confused by my sudden interest in conversing and that my inquiry about Tibor had quelled some inner panic. "I will be sure to let him know of your concern."

"After what happened with Kilian," I said quietly, to make Cleto believe I was sharing a confidence, "I'm especially wary. Are you absolutely certain that Tibor is all right? Shouldn't someone check on him? After all that's happened, I'm tempted to suggest that."

"Not necessary," Cleto said. He glanced around the hallway before bringing his lips close to my ears. "I did not want to say this to Ms. Freiberg, because to do so would hurt her feelings. The truth is that Tibor refused to attend tonight's banquet."

"Oh?" I said noncommittally.

With a moue of distaste, Cleto went on, "You know Tibor well enough to understand. He made no secret of his plan to avoid attending."

That wasn't exactly accurate, but I let him go on.

Continuing to whisper, he said, "Tibor does not know how to control his anger. We have seen this ourselves. He is angry and spiteful and, because of that, has chosen to turn his back on this invitation."

The agent behind me said, "The staff wants me to tell you that dessert is ready to be served," he said. "All guests should return to the table."

Cleto bid me good night. I turned and headed back, not bothering to stop in the kitchen to explain. I gave the Secret Service agent in the hall the most minuscule of updates. "I need to speak with Special Agent Gavin," I said. "Right now."

Whether he knew that Gav and I were married, or simply knew that as a member of the White House staff I was allowed a measure of freedom, he didn't stop me.

Happy not to have to fight a battle on that front, I raced around the other way, toward the front of the house. I slowed as I encountered the butlers wheeling Marcel's gorgeous poppy centerpieces and delectable petits fours. The men and their tray blocked my path, but I decided there was enough clearance to get by. Ignoring their curious glances, I edged past to find myself in what I recognized from its warm vanilla walls and peach furnishings as the Blair Front Drawing Room.

I didn't have time to admire the architecture, paintings, or even consider the room's historic significance. My goal was to get as close as possible to the dinner party while remaining out of sight. From what I recalled of the floor plan, I still had a handful of areas to traverse before I'd even get a glimpse of the guests. Gav, I knew, would be in the room adjacent to that of the diners.

The agent stationed in the Drawing Room was a fellow

I'd met before but didn't know personally. He held an arm out, blocking my way. "I need to see Special Agent Gavin," I said. "Immediately."

The wheels of the rolling cart gently vibrated the floor as the butlers pulled up behind me.

"So I understand." The agent narrowed his eyes. "Why do you need him?"

Yeah, in ten words or less, right?

One of the butlers cleared his throat. "May we get by?"

I twisted to face them. "No." Thinking fast, I amended, "I mean yes. I intend to accompany you."

"Into the dining room?" the nearer butler asked.

The agent on duty rumbled his displeasure. "That is not part of the program," he said. "I can't allow it." When he spoke into his microphone, I assumed he was connecting with Gav. Good.

A brilliant thought came to mind. "I've been requested to visit the table. By the host."

"I thought you said you needed to see Special Agent Gavin."

"That's right," I said, building on my charade. The lies were piling up. "He's the one who is supposed to escort me in."

The agent spoke quietly into his radio again, then listened to a reply. "I'll take you in."

Gritting my teeth, I politely thanked him.

I hurried through the rooms pressing ahead, moving as quickly as I could. This house was huge, and even though I remembered the basics of the floor plan, it was like traveling through a maze. In essence we would be making a giant jagged *U* in our path to the dining room.

"No, the other way," one butler whispered when I took a left that should have been a right. I was suddenly grateful for my Secret Service escort. His presence—and the fact that he'd notified them that I was coming—prevented me from having to repeat my story to all the other agents along the way. Each one expressed identical, subtle, looks of surprise, but made no move to impede our progress.

"Next right," the butler behind me whispered.

I took the turn as instructed, ready to spill my suspicions to Gav.

He wasn't there.

Two other agents, both of whom I'd met before, flanked the doorway to the dining room from where we could hear the sounds of cheerful conversation. The sentry agents waved me to one side, probably to keep me out of the diners' line of sight.

I walked up to the agent nearer to me, avoiding being seen. "Where's Ga—Special Agent Gavin?"

"Sent away." His words were clipped, quiet. I got the feeling this guy was the team leader.

"Why?" I asked.

"I am not at liberty to say."

While the butlers sailed in and out of the dining room with the cups, saucers, dessert plates, and silverware needed to properly showcase dessert, two agents discussed the situation. I shifted from foot to foot, clenching and unclenching my fists with growing impatience. I'd been counting on Gav's support to make this work. Now what?

"Gavin didn't leave word . . ." one said.

"He had more on his mind," the other answered.

"Listen," I said, making it up on the fly, "I made dinner. When a chef is invited to visit the table, it's because the guests want to offer their appreciation for an exceptional meal." The meal *was* exceptional, but I still felt like a conceited fool making the point right now, especially as part of this total fabrication. "If I wait until after dessert is served, the guests will mistakenly believe I was responsible for creating these." I held my hand out toward the vivid orange poppies and accompanying treats. "That puts the president in the uncomfortable position of having to clarify who made what and it will result in confusion for everyone. Not a happy moment."

When had I ever been so glib?

"So you see," I concluded, "it's now or never, and it really is very important that I get the chance to visit the table."

The butlers desperately wanted to serve dessert. "We're keeping our guests waiting," one of them whispered.

This room was the Lincoln Room. I knew from history that this was the room where Montgomery Blair had entertained Abraham Lincoln whenever the president visited for their informal chats. This was the room in which Francis Blair, at the request of President Lincoln, had asked Robert E. Lee to lead the Union Army. It was also, presumably, this room, where Lee had turned that position down.

And it was from this room that I was about to risk a ridiculous gambit that would either save Ms. Freiberg's life, or ruin both dinner *and* my career.

CHAPTER 33

THE ONE I ASSUMED WAS THE SPECIAL AGENT in charge scratched his head. "Fine," he said with clear exasperation. "But I'm going in there with you. Make it quick."

"Yes, yes," I said. Nerves made me jumpy.

He cast a glance back at the rest of the group in the Lincoln Room, then stepped through the dining room doorway. All polite chatter ceased at the sight of the large Secret Service agent. He eclipsed me, and it wasn't until President Hyden broke the surprised silence with the guarded, "Yes?" that the big man stepped to one side, rendering me visible to the entire table.

In a split second, I noted that President Hyden was at the center of the table on the left, Kerry Freiberg center on the right. Cleto had been placed at the far end, the same side as President Hyden. I could feel the Saardiscan's blazing eyes on me. That gave me less anxiety than the fact that Ms. Freiberg had Frosty on her lap, where she nuzzled the dog's head. It was all I could do not to leap across the table to grab the pup.

"Ollie?" the president said. His expression had morphed from surprised to perplexed in the space of time it had taken me to take another step into the room.

It had been no more than four seconds since we'd made our entrance, but it was already painfully obvious that I'd been lying about being invited in.

"President Hyden." I directed my gaze, my focus, and all my energy toward him. I'd depended on Gav being here, but he wasn't. It was up to me to effectively make my case to our commander in chief. "May I . . . speak with you a moment?" My voice trembled, high and thin. My knees went soft. I shook.

The agent loomed behind me, close enough that I could feel his body heat radiating against my back.

"Ollie," the president said, addressing me once again, "my guests and I have thoroughly enjoyed this wonderful meal you prepared. Please communicate our appreciation to your staff." The gathered group offered murmurs of assent but the president watched me closely.

I flicked a glance toward Cleto, then toward Kerry Freiberg, wishing desperately for the president to know, telepathically, instinctively, what I wanted to convey. What I actually said came out tight and stilted. "Thank you very much. I will be happy to let them know how much you liked it."

When I didn't depart immediately, the other guests began trading uneasy glances. This unexpected interruption clearly made them uncomfortable. President Hyden continued to maintain eye contact with me. I got the feeling he was trying to figure out what was really going on here.

"Mr. President," I began again, "before Marcel's fabulous dessert is served, may I have a moment of your time? Privately?"

Giggles—poorly muffled ones—skittered around the table. I continued to lock eyes with President Hyden.

As the president folded his napkin and began to rise, Cleto spoke up. "What is this?" he asked. "In Saardisca, the hired help is never permitted to address our leaders in such a casual manner. How is it in America that you allow such behavior?"

The president, surprised by the outburst, turned to face the other man, who had now pushed away from the table and risen to his feet as well.

Cleto bunched his napkin and threw it onto the table. "I thank you for this dinner, but I must now depart." With a hand on his stomach, he shook his head morosely. "This deficiency of propriety upsets me greatly."

"Please, Mr. Damar," President Hyden said in the diplomatic voice I'd heard him use on many occasions, "I'm sure this disruption is quite important. Chef Paras would not have stepped in here otherwise."

Cleto dismissed President Hyden's assertion with an impudent wave. He started around the far end of the table, making good on his pronouncement to leave, refusing to look at anyone in the room, including me. If I'd had even the slightest doubt about finagling my way in here, Cleto's reaction put those fears to rest.

"Mr. Damar," President Hyden said again.

Cleto kept his chin high, punctuating his obvious indignation with every furious step.

I turned to the guest of honor. "Ms. Freiberg," I said, my voice quivering with effort, "put Frosty on the floor. Get her away from you."

The Saardiscan candidate jerked with surprise at being addressed personally. She pulled Frosty closer to her chest, as though to protect the little dog.

"No, please, you must understand—"

Three Secret Service agents had gathered around me, huddling close, probably eager to eject me from the premises.

Cleto had originally begun making his way toward me, as though intending to exit through the front door. The moment I addressed Ms. Freiberg, however, he stopped in his tracks and doubled back. His goal was clear: the swinging door that led to the long hallway. He could disappear and be out of the house through the back exit in no time flat. While there were agents protecting the perimeter and preventing intruders from getting *in*, there was no guarantee they would apprehend a person exiting the home—especially when that person had been one of the esteemed guests.

Ignoring the agents' menacing presence, I pointed toward Cleto. "Stop him," I said. "Please." In that same instant, the Saardiscan man made it to the swinging door and pushed through.

The agents spoke into their microphones, but not one of them moved.

"You have to trust me," I said.

The room had gone completely still, like at the end of a stage play when the action freezes—that breathless second before the applause.

I stared at the president and he at me. No one spoke.

The stillness was broken by the barest of movements. President Hyden glanced up at the agents and gave a sharp nod. "Do it," he said.

With that, one sped off, speaking into his microphone as he raced after Cleto. The other two remained in the room.

"Thank you, Mr. President," I said. "Cleto has spread something into Frosty's coat. A poison, or toxin, I think. It's meant to harm Ms. Freiberg, I'm sure of it. Frosty, too."

It took a moment for my words to sink in, but when they did, the assistant who'd been responsible for taking the dog outside jumped out of her chair. Bringing her hand to her mouth, she said something in Saardiscan, which I had to believe was confirmation that Cleto had come in contact with the dog.

Ms. Freiberg ran a hand along Frosty's coat, bringing it up for everyone around the table to see. Flecks, like silt, dribbled from her fingertips. She turned to me, alarmed. "What is this?" she asked.

"I don't know," I said. "But it isn't safe."

She pulled Frosty ever closer, protectively, making the little dog wriggle in protest.

"Please," I said, "we need to get Frosty to a vet. And you to a medical facility. Maybe everyone to a medical facility."

CHAPTER 34

TO CHARACTERIZE THE FLURRY OF ACTIVITY
that followed as an exercise in terror would be to minimize
its impact on everyone affected. After one of the remaining Secret Service agents consulted his superiors for
instructions, all dinner guests, all Blair House staff members, and all of the chefs, including me, were immediately
hustled into one room.

It had been decided to house everyone in the Jackson
Place conference room, where we were to be quarantined for
an unspecified period of time. Joining us were all the Secret
Service agents who'd been on duty in the home as well.

The president and secretary of state conferred with a
handful of Secret Service agents in one corner, while Mrs.
Hyden, Kerry Freiberg, and her assistants sat around one
end of the room's large conference table, talking quietly.
Frosty had been taken away immediately, but I didn't know
to where. Other guests formed a half-circle around them,
everyone asking questions that no one had answers to.

For once, I was glad Gav wasn't here. I'd discovered

that he'd been called away during dinner, before Cleto had pulled out the threatening dust that had spurred my actions. I hoped that meant Gav was safe.

Cyan was seated, looking pale. Staring at the floor, she had her hands clasped around one knee while the other bounced a nervous rhythm. Bucky and I remained standing, taking up positions on either side of her chair. Marcel and his assistant sat about ten feet away. Blair House staff members gathered in groups, from which they shot apprehensive looks toward one another.

"You really did it this time," Bucky said, under his breath.

"I had to." There was nothing else I could say.

Hazmat professionals arrived. They were covered head to toe in protective gear, and did their best to ease our panic. Their mechanically distorted voices, however, served to ratchet up the paranoia rather than to soothe.

I wanted to be wrong. I wanted all this high-tech testing to turn out to have been unnecessary. Even though I knew that being wrong would cost me everything in terms of career and reputation, not to mention subject me to stinging ridicule, I wished with all my might that whatever substance Cleto had shuffled into Frosty's fur would turn out to be harmless to humans as well as to pets.

FROM OUR VANTAGE POINT IN THE JACKSON Place conference room, we watched as dozens of individuals in protective gear carried in screens and equipment, along with microscopes and metal trees like the ones used to hold IV bags.

Hazmat specialists explained the next steps, letting us know that everyone would be tested for toxins. We were assured that it was extremely unlikely that any of us had been exposed to a lethal substance, and that this was all simply precaution.

Someone asked what toxin they suspected, but the hazmat guy in charge wouldn't elaborate.

Kerry Freiberg, President Hyden, and the First Lady were the first to be escorted out for examination. They were followed by the secretary of state and then on down the line until no more dinner guests remained.

Cyan's voice was so quiet that I had to ask her to repeat herself.

"Are we going to die?"

"We're all going to die," Bucky said. "Let's just hope it isn't tonight."

I glared at him across the top of Cyan's head. He shrugged but his eyes were tight with worry.

"I don't know, Cyan," I said. "I'm only guessing here, but if Cleto was comfortable enough to handle whatever the toxin was, it has to be something that's safe in small doses, or after short exposure. We were nowhere near him, except for that brief moment when I spoke with him in the hallway. You and Bucky should be fine."

"What if it's airborne?" she asked. "What if we've all breathed it in?" She flung a hand out. "These people didn't show up in protective gear because they think it's fun to dress up, you know."

"The only argument I can offer is that Cleto was here the whole time. I don't think he'd release a pathogen into air that he was breathing."

"Unless he was on a suicide mission," Bucky said.

"Bucky!"

This time Cyan glared up at him, too.

Just then, four hazardous materials specialists tramped into the Jackson Place conference room, carrying what looked like sensors, which they waved in the air above our heads. When they finished, the four conferred near the doorway, clustering close together, making them look like something from out of a sci-fi thriller film. After a few minutes they left, without having spoken a word.

Cyan looked up at me. Her eyes were red. She pointed to where the hazmat professionals had just exited. "If the air is so safe to breathe, then how do you explain that?" Standing up, she began to pace, arms folded tight against her middle.

Kerry Freiberg and Frosty hadn't returned. Neither had the president. No one who had been called away had been brought back to this room. Time had been moving so slowly I'd stopped consulting my watch. Through it all, hazmat-clad officers continued to call people, sometimes two, three, or four at a time, escorting them out to who-knows-where.

As Cyan paced, Bucky stared out the window. Marcel and his assistant looked dejected and forlorn.

Everyone else in the room: butlers, maids, miscellaneous staff members and Secret Service agents, did his or her best to maintain decorum and remain calm. I took a seat, resting my elbows on the shiny table. Dropping my head into my hands, I couldn't help but wonder if there was something I could have done sooner to spare us this terror, this misery.

"Olivia Paras."

I looked up. A team member at the doorway reading from a clipboard had summoned me for examination—whatever that entailed. I stood, making my way over to the Tyvek-clad official.

I asked the agent—a woman whose bright hazel eyes seemed to convey sympathy through the helmet's plastic guard—to take Cyan in my place, then Bucky, and the other chefs, before taking me. She agreed.

Little by little, the room's numbers dwindled. I worried for Gav. I worried for the president and Kerry Freiberg. I worried for my team. And ultimately, I worried for myself.

WHEN THERE WERE FOUR OF US LEFT, WE WERE motioned to follow by the same agent who had originally called my name. "This way," she said.

As we traversed through the historic home, we passed machines I couldn't begin to recognize, dozens of hazmat experts poring over reports, and white Tyvek stretched over furniture and plastered against walls. All so high-tech. All so futuristic. I felt much like Elliott did when he and E.T. were confined in the makeshift hospital in the family's home.

One by one, the woman handed us off to other agents, who led their charges into Blair House lavatories that had been transformed into examining rooms. When it was just the female agent and me, she led me down a long hall into a large, ornate bathroom that reeked of disinfectant.

Closing the door, she hit me with a battery of questions regarding my health history. I answered as quickly and thoroughly as I could. She continued with questions about how close I'd gotten to Cleto this evening, how much time I'd spent in the dining room, and if I'd come in contact at all with Frosty.

"How is everyone else?" I asked. "The president? Ms. Freiberg? Frosty?"

She shook her head. "I don't have that information."

I provided a urine sample and a vial of blood. She disappeared with them both, returning a short while later.

She handed me a bright blue capsule and a paper cup of water. "Take this," she said.

"What is it?" I asked.

"Prussian Blue."

That was an accurate description of its color, but didn't really answer my question. I hesitated.

The woman pointed at the pill in my open palm. "The name of that drug is Prussian Blue. It's our best defense against thallium poisoning, which is what we're dealing with here. I'll give you information about what to expect in terms of side effects before you're released. You may develop an upset stomach. That's normal."

"Thallium?"

"Because its presence was detected early enough"—she raised her eyebrows and smiled in a way that told me she knew the part I'd played in tonight's drama—"there's little to no chance of long-term adverse effects. I'm sorry we don't have any more information at this time. But I do promise you'll receive additional information later."

Two important things rang in my mind: I'd been right about a toxin, and she'd used the word *released*.

I swallowed the pill.

She turned on the shower, instructing me to strip and scrub with the cleansers provided while she waited outside. She handed me a pair of blue cotton pants and a matching shirt, much like those I was used to seeing on dental hygienists and lab techs. "Put these on when you're finished. Your clothing will be laundered and returned to you later. Open the door when you're ready."

Although the fresh, hot water sluicing over freshly scrubbed skin felt wonderful, I couldn't help but be worried for everyone else. Especially Gav. Where was he?

CHAPTER 35

A FEMALE SECRET SERVICE AGENT MET ME AS I exited Blair House. "Ms. Paras?" she said pleasantly. "Come with me."

The entire area between 17th and 15th Streets had been cordoned off from pedestrian traffic, with D.C. Metro Police cars—lights flashing—on both sides. The area was as desolate as I'd ever seen it, save for the perimeter of uniformed cops and agents keeping curious onlookers at bay.

My cotton scrubs were no match for the chilly evening. I wrapped my arms around myself. The flat cotton slippers I'd been given slapped against the cold pavement.

Although I'd been allowed to keep my wedding ring on, I'd had to relinquish my watch until it, too, could be examined and decontaminated. "What time is it?" I asked the agent as we made our way toward the gate.

"Four A.M.," she said.

I took a long look at the sky. "Seems about right."

"Are you tired?" she asked. "Do you want me to call for a golf cart?"

"I'm fine," I said. That wasn't entirely true. Fatigue was setting in, if not in my brain, in my weary body. And the Prussian Blue—as promised—was making me queasy.

Once we'd made it through the gate checkpoint, I expected to be led around the back, into the kitchen. Instead, she kept going to the White House front door.

The front of the White House was lit up brightly for this time of night. When the agent and I stepped in, the Entrance Hall was deserted except for a few guards on duty.

"This way," she said.

The sound of quiet conversation met us as we approached the Green Room. At the doorway, my escort stepped aside. "Go on in," she said.

The president and secretary of state sat knee to knee, immersed in what looked like a tense discussion. The two men were both wearing casual clothing, though nothing quite as informal as what I had on. They looked up when I walked in.

"Ollie!" President Hyden said with considerably more cheer than he'd greeted me earlier. He got to his feet, and started toward me.

At the same moment, a figure at the far window turned. I hadn't noticed him when I'd first walked in. "Gav!"

He made it across the room, grabbing me into his arms faster than the president could close the short distance between us.

It felt so good to be held, felt so right to have the night's horror behind me that I pressed my face into his chest and stayed there a long, comforting while. When I raised my head, I noticed the president was still waiting patiently to talk to me.

I could barely get any words out. "Is everyone all right?" I asked.

"It seems so," President Hyden said. He gestured toward the room's striped couch. "You've had a busy evening again. Have a seat."

Gav released me, and the two of us sat as requested. The president nodded to the secretary of state, who came over, thanked me, and then left the room without another word.

"Where were you?" I asked Gav. "I never meant to barge in on dinner."

Gav started to answer, but whether it was exhaustion or

relief that kept me going, I blathered on. "I had every intention of bringing my suspicions to you and letting you take it from there, but . . ." I shrugged helplessly, bouncing my glances between the two men. "I had to improvise."

Gav and the president exchanged a look. Again Gav started to answer. Again I interrupted.

"And what about Tibor? I'm worried that Cleto did something to him. Has he ever been found? Is he all right?"

"Tibor is in the hospital," the president said. "He's recovering."

"What happened?"

Gav took up the story. "Cleto drugged him with what we believe was the same compound that was used on Kilian."

"What? Kilian's death wasn't from natural causes?"

Again they exchanged a meaningful look. "We have forensics teams putting pieces together," the president said.

"We can't say for certain what killed Kilian because we weren't allowed to perform an autopsy," Gav continued. "After last evening's events, however, we have been able to uncover an e-mail trail between Cleto and Hector and Nate."

"I don't understand."

"Kilian began to suspect that Hector and Nate were up to no good. Because he trusted Cleto, he shared his concerns. That was a mistake. Apparently, Cleto assured Kilian he would take care of things. He did. On his orders, Nate slipped a toxin into Kilian's drink."

"That's the same day Hector passed out," I said. "I don't get it. Was that just a ruse?"

"Again," Gav said, "we don't have all the answers, but from what we're beginning to understand, Nate was sent here to get rid of Kerry Freiberg. Because he required assistance, Hector was brought on to help him. We think Nate was beginning to doubt Hector's allegiance, so he slipped him a lesser dosage of the drug to remind him who was boss."

"Was Nate responsible for drugging Marcel, too?"

"The first time Marcel was hospitalized? No," Gav said.

"We're confident that Marcel double-dosed his medication. The second time, however, we believe Nate was indeed responsible. In order to test the potency of the drug, he needed to experiment on someone. Nate administered the drug to Marcel via the chocolate drink assuming no one would think it suspicious if the pastry chef collapsed again."

"That's terrible," I said. "So you're telling me that Cleto recruited Nate and the two of them masterminded this attack?"

Gav held his hand out toward the president.

"Ollie," President Hyden began, "I can't begin to thank you for always being so alert and for saving me and the members of my family, not to mention an untold number of innocent bystanders, over the years."

"Do I sense a 'but'?" I asked.

He smiled. "Not exactly. What I'm trying to say is that your involvement in issues of national security over the years has made you privy to a great deal of information that you would not otherwise possess."

I waited.

He went on, "You have been consistent in your trust-worthiness with regard to the truth behind classified infor-mation. You've never shared anything you've been asked to keep confidential."

"That's true. I would never."

"Based on your constancy, we are prepared to offer you a choice," he said. "It's my decision to give you that choice, but you have to decide which way you want to go."

"I don't understand."

"We can explain everything that happened, including who was responsible," he said. "Or you can walk away not knowing the whole truth."

"Why would I not want to know the truth?"

"Because," he said, "truth does not always bring justice. This is a big one, Ollie, and if I'm to tell you what went down, I need you to promise that you'll keep it to yourself."

After that warning, I wasn't so sure I wanted to hear. Yet,

if I declined, would I be able to put this matter out of my mind with all the questions that were still burning in my brain? I was tired and wanted to go home. I didn't want to have to push myself further tonight, or to make a promise that would be painful to keep. And yet, I needed to know.

"Tell me," I said. "I won't breathe a word."

And they did.

BUCKY, CYAN, MARCEL, AND HIS ASSISTANT were fine. None had been exposed to any thallium whatsoever. They were all granted paid leave for the following two days.

Although the rest of my team knew that Cleto had attempted to coat Frosty's fur with powdered thallium, they'd been sworn to secrecy on the matter. They didn't know why Cleto had done it, and I had to pretend I didn't know why, either. The other guests who had been around the dinner table had likewise been fully informed about the thallium threat, and treated according to their exposure. The same held true for my two butler friends.

The remaining staff at Blair House, however, was being fed an entirely different version. One that involved an unfortunate accident, and the subsequent need to go to red-alert on safety. Those whose thallium levels were zero were being told that the emergency measures had ultimately proved to be unnecessary. I didn't know how many people present that evening would believe the fabrication, but keeping the truth from them wasn't my decision to make.

Kerry Freiberg and Frosty, the targets of the attack, were fine. Both were healthy and recuperating at Camp David until everything could be cleared up.

What proved to be the most explosive revelation, however, was that Cleto and Nate were *not* the masterminds behind this attack. For all the trouble they'd caused, and all the risks they'd assumed, they were little more than pawns.

The current president of Saardisca, a man whose name

was nearly impossible to pronounce, had become concerned about Kerry Freiberg's growing popularity. He'd never been seriously challenged in an election before. This time, his lead was diminishing as his challenger's strength grew.

Cleto had been ordered to take her out. He'd been further instructed to have it done on American soil in the company of President Hyden, so that the United States could be blamed for its lack of control, its inability to keep a precious Saardiscan safe. That way, they reasoned, not only would Kerry Freiberg die, but the beliefs she held—so similar to those of U.S. citizens—would die with her.

The fact that the assassination directive had come from Saardisca's highest power was what I could never discuss with anyone in my life except Gav.

"But," I'd said to the president when he'd finished explaining, "won't the current Saardiscan president have to answer for this? Shouldn't he be thrown out of office?"

President Hyden's eyes tensed. "If it were up to me, he would be brought up on charges today. Unfortunately, it isn't up to any of us. Their country has a different culture and far different laws. We can't touch him."

"What if this information was made public?"

"The secretary of state is looking into that possibility right now. From what we can tell, however, this sort of bombshell wouldn't have the impact you and I would expect. Rather than hurt the current president, the mission's failure could—believe it or not—incite some of his more radical followers to take Kerry out themselves. For now, we believe it's best to keep this quiet."

"That's terrible."

"I agree."

"So what happens? This just gets swept under the rug?"

He made a so-so motion. "If we find ways to use this information to bring justice, we will. That may not be for some time, though."

My head was spinning, though no longer from fatigue.

I'd caught my second wind. "What about Kerry Freiberg's safety? Does she know all this?"

He nodded. "She does. Rather than dissuade her, it has deepened her resolve to win the election and to be an instrument of change in her country."

"That's admirable, but frightening," I said. "Nate and Hector have been sent back to Saardisca. What about Cleto and Tibor?"

The president waved a finger. "Cleto will not be returning to Saardisca. We can manage that much, at least. You need to know that we have Tibor to thank for knowing as much as we do."

"Tibor?"

The president continued. "When Kilian reported his concerns to Cleto and wound up dead, Tibor began to get suspicious of his colleagues. He wisely kept his concerns to himself."

"That doesn't surprise me," I said. "He never hesitated to spout Saardiscan platitudes, but when it came to personal matters, he was frustratingly mute."

"Cleto wanted Tibor to voluntarily step away from attending the dinner," the president continued. "Tibor refused. Despite the fact that he had no desire to attend, he believed it was his duty to do so."

I made eye contact with Gav, who picked up the story. "Which is exactly what you had asserted all along, Ollie. Tibor's absence made no sense. If he'd been planning an attempt on Kerry Freiberg, then why not show up? That's why agents were sent to take a closer look at the hotel where the Saardiscans were staying. When they reported back that they had located Tibor and required assistance, however, the agent in charge at Blair House took it to mean that the man presented a threat."

The look in Gav's eyes seemed to offer an apology for not being there for me. I laid a hand on his knee, silently reminding him that I understood. No apology necessary.

"The special agent in charge sent me to take over," he went on. "This came as a direct order with no time to let you know where I was going or what I was doing. It wasn't until I arrived on the scene—to find Tibor drugged and tied up in Cleto's room—that I realized the real threat was still at Blair House. I radioed back to warn the team that Cleto was our target, but by that time you'd sounded the alert."

"What was he thinking?" I asked. "Cleto, I mean?"

"Remember, Nate was supposed to poison Ms. Freiberg, with Hector's help," Gav reminded me. "When that plan got scrapped, Cleto took over. He had no one else here to trust."

"You said Tibor is all right?" I asked.

"He is," the president answered. "Had he been found much later, that may not have been the case. He has been a great help clearing this matter up."

"Poor Tibor," I said. "He's such a loyal Saardiscan. This must be incredibly painful for him."

"More than you realize." The president's face was grim. "Because he cooperated with us, Tibor cannot return to Saardisca. Not safely, at least. We have offered him asylum, and expect he will take us up on it."

I covered my mouth with my hand. "That's got to be devastating for him."

"It is." The president and Gav exchanged another look. "We will be doing our best to help him acclimate. Once Tibor spilled the truth, Cleto was very quick to request asylum as well. He will be facing charges here, of course. The good news is that with neither man returning to Saardisca, the government there has no idea what transpired. They only know that Cleto and Tibor have decided to stay."

"What about our diplomatic relations with Saardisca?" I asked. "How will they be impacted?"

President Hyden spread his hands. "That remains to be seen."

* * *

GAV AND I HAD THE FOLLOWING TWO DAYS off, too. We slept late both days and didn't leave the apartment until mid-afternoon the second day, when hunger drove us into civilization on a quest for quality carry-out. On our return, Mrs. Wentworth met us in the hallway. "What's with you two?" she asked, taking in our uber-casual clothing and sniffing around our aromatic bags of tacos, guacamole, chips, salsa, and practically the entire left side of the local Mexican restaurant's menu.

"Day off," I said. "How's Stan?"

"Much better." She turned toward the open doorway and spoke loudly. "He's feeling better because he started listening to me. Totally on the mend now, thanks to a lot of rest." She held a hand up near her mouth and whispered, "And some powerful antibiotics."

"Good to hear," I said.

As we made our way past her, she asked, "Not much new at the White House these days, is there?"

I turned as Gav unlocked the door. "Nope, nothing much at all."

"Except for that emergency drill they ran the other night."

"Oh?" I asked innocently.

"Didn't you hear about it? They roped off Pennsylvania Avenue in front of the White House to practice how the hazardous materials teams would perform in an emergency. I thought for sure you'd be in the middle of something like that."

"Sounds like I missed the excitement this time," I said. Ahead of me, Gav pushed the door open. I was pretty sure he stifled a snort.

"Yes, well," she said with a dismissive wave, "this was just a drill. Whenever you get involved, it's the real thing."

"Too true," I said. As I made it through my apartment door, I waved to my neighbor. "See you later, Mrs. Wentworth."

RECIPES

CHICKEN PITA SANDWICHES

1 Roma tomato, diced
1 tablespoon extra-virgin olive oil
1 teaspoon balsamic vinegar
Kosher salt and freshly ground black pepper, to
 taste
½ chicken breast (leftover works best, especially
 pan-seared; you want this to have been cooked
 already, and preferably with some nice cara-
 melization, for extra flavor)
Garlic powder
Cayenne pepper
Dried cilantro, chervil, basil, or other herbs
1 tablespoon grapeseed oil
½ white onion, diced
10 kalamata olives, pitted and halved lengthwise
1 pita (two halves of a pocket pita or one whole
 non-pocket)
1 tablespoon Italian dressing (oil and vinegar
 based, not creamy), optional

1 cup romaine lettuce, torn into bite-size pieces
½ cucumber, peeled, seeded, and diced
3 green onions, sliced (white and green parts only;
   omit leafy part)

Drizzle Roma tomatoes with extra-virgin olive oil, balsamic vinegar, and a little salt and pepper. Set aside.

Dice chicken breast into bite-size pieces. Season with garlic powder, cayenne, and herbs, all to taste. Set aside.

Heat skillet over medium to medium-high heat. Add grapeseed oil and heat until the surface of the oil shimmers slightly. Add onions and kalamata olives and sauté for 3 to 4 minutes. Add in chicken pieces and sauté until everything is hot and well blended. Transfer to a serving bowl.

If using a pocket pita, fill each pocket with a drizzle of Italian dressing (if using), then add in half the romaine, half the chicken, half the cucumber, half the green onions, and half the tomatoes. (Note that in my family, no two of us build our pitas in the same order, so mix it up. Surprisingly, you'll have a slightly different experience depending on how you build it, so experiment until you find your own preferred order.)

If using a non-pocket pita, simply build your sandwich on the pita following the same steps as above, fold it over, and enjoy.

Yield: 2 sandwiches

FALL HARVEST QUINOA AND CHICKEN SOUP

1 tablespoon extra-virgin olive oil, plus extra as
    needed
2 boneless, skinless chicken breasts, excess fat
    removed
2 boneless, skinless chicken thighs, excess fat
    removed
Kosher salt
Freshly ground black pepper
1 cup chopped onion
1 cup chopped carrot
1 cup chopped celery
1 (10 oz.) bag frozen corn
1 clove garlic, minced
8 cups chicken broth, divided
1 teaspoon dried thyme (leaf, not ground)
2 large sweet potatoes, peeled and diced into
    ½- to 1-inch cubes
½ cup quinoa, rinsed and drained
4 cups chopped fresh kale
Crusty whole-grain bread, for serving
Parmesan cheese, for serving (optional)

Heat a large (5-quart or larger) soup pot over medium-high
heat. Add oil and heat through. Lower heat to medium,
season chicken breasts and thighs, and cook approximately
8 minutes per side, until no longer pink. Remove from heat
and set aside to cool.

Add onion, carrot, and celery to pan (add a little extra oil if
necessary); season with salt and pepper, and sauté for about 5

minutes. Add frozen corn and sauté an additional 5 minutes. Add garlic, and cook for another 2 minutes. Add chicken broth and the thyme, and bring to a boil. Reduce heat to a simmer. Add sweet potatoes and quinoa. Shred chicken and return to pot. Cook for an additional 10 minutes. Add kale and cook until potatoes are fork-tender, approximately 5 more minutes. Taste for seasoning and adjust as needed.

Serve with crusty whole-grain bread. Garnish with grated Parmesan cheese, if desired.

(Note about reheating leftovers: You may wish to add more chicken broth, or even water, when reheating. The quinoa tends to absorb much of the liquid as it cools, so you may need to add more to reach the desired consistency.)

PECAN-CRUSTED PORK TENDERLOIN WITH ORANGE-MAPLE GLAZE

1 (1-lb.) pork tenderloin
Kosher salt
Freshly ground black pepper
*4 tablespoons pure maple syrup, plus more as
    needed, divided*
*1½ cups toasted pecan pieces, plus more as
    needed, finely chopped*
2 tablespoons extra-virgin olive oil

2 oranges (1 juiced, one cut in half and then cut
    into moderately thin slices)
¼ teaspoon cumin
¼ teaspoon cayenne pepper
Steamed or sautéed green beans, for serving

Slice pork into ¾- to 1-inch-thick slices, then lay flat and flatten further with the heel of your hand. Season with salt and pepper and set aside.

Place 3 tablespoons maple syrup in one bowl and the toasted pecan pieces in another bowl. Set up a station next to your cooktop with the pecans closest to where your skillet will be, the maple syrup next to the bowl of pecans, and the pork slices next to that.

Heat a 12-inch skillet over medium-high heat. Add oil and allow to heat.

Working quickly, place one piece of pork into the bowl of syrup, turning to coat thoroughly, then press into the bowl of pecan pieces, covering only one side of the pork with the pecan pieces. Carefully place into skillet, nut side down, trying to keep as many pecan pieces adhered as possible. Repeat with the remaining pork slices. (You may need some additional syrup and/or pecan pieces to cover all the pork.)

Pour any remaining syrup over the pork in the skillet, then press any remaining pecan pieces onto the pork slices, distributing them as evenly as possible.

Cook the pork for 5 to 6 minutes until browned, then flip and cook for another 5 to 6 minutes or until fully cooked. Transfer to a platter and cover lightly.

Combine orange juice, remaining 1 tablespoon maple syrup, cumin, and cayenne in a small bowl and whisk to mix thoroughly. Add to skillet and cook for 3 to 4 minutes or until slightly thickened. Pour over pork.

Serve pork over a bed of steamed or sautéed green beans, with 3 to 4 orange slices for garnish.

 ## SQUASH SOUP

2 acorn or butternut squash
Kosher salt, to taste
Freshly ground black pepper, to taste
1 tablespoon extra-virgin olive oil
1 cup onion, diced
1 tablespoon brown sugar
½ teaspoon cumin
3 cups chicken broth
2 cups Bartlett pears, peeled, cored, and chopped
     (approximately 2 pears)
¼ cup sour cream
2 tablespoons maple syrup
Fresh thyme sprigs (optional)

Preheat oven to 450°F. While oven is preheating, split squashes lengthwise and remove seeds and stringy insides. Cover a rimmed baking sheet with foil and add water to a depth of approximately 1/8 inch. Season cut sides of squash with salt and pepper. Place squash on baking sheet, cut sides down, and bake for 30 minutes. Invert squash and return to oven for an additional 15 minutes. Allow to cool, and scoop flesh from skin (This may be done up to 2 days ahead).

Bring Dutch oven to heat over medium-high heat, and add oil. When the surface of the oil begins to shimmer, add onion, brown sugar, and cumin. Cook, stirring occasionally, until onion starts to soften, approximately 5 minutes.

Add squash and broth and season with salt and pepper. Bring to a boil, then add pears, cover, reduce heat, and simmer until pears are tender, about 5 minutes.

Remove from heat. Puree with a handheld immersion blender until nearly smooth (or, alternatively, use a standard blender, pureeing small batches of the soup at a time—be careful not to fill the blender more than half full with any one batch).

Combine sour cream and maple syrup in a small bowl. Serve the soup garnished with approximately 1 tablespoon of the maple sour cream and, if desired, a sprig of fresh thyme.

Yield: 8 servings

 # MARINATED TOP SIRLOIN

2 to 3 pounds top sirloin, trimmed of all excess fat
¾ to 1 cup oil-based Italian dressing (not creamy)
Kosher salt

Fresh ground pepper
1 tablespoon extra-virgin olive oil

Place sirloin in a large, shallow baking dish. Cover with most of the Italian dressing, being careful to thoroughly coat the steak. Flip steak and pour remaining dressing over top, again being careful to thoroughly cover it (use your hands to spread it around if necessary). Cover with plastic wrap and refrigerate for a minimum of 4 hours and up to 24 hours.

Thirty minutes before cooking, remove meat from refrigerator and allow to come to room temperature. Position top oven rack so that the meat will be approximately 3 to 4 inches from heat source and preheat oven to broil setting.

Place a small amount of water in the bottom of a broiler pan (enough to generously cover the bottom of the pan, but not enough that it will be difficult to carry). Pour extra-virgin olive oil onto a paper towel and lightly brush the top of a broiler pan.

Remove steak from the marinade and place on the top of the broiler pan.

Place in oven and broil for 6 to 7 minutes (more or less depending on your oven setting and the height of your oven rack), or until nicely browned on the top. Flip steak over and broil for another 6 to 7 minutes or until fully cooked.

Transfer steak to a cutting board, cover lightly with aluminum foil, and let rest for 4 to 5 minutes. Slice into appropriately sized servings, and serve with fresh fruit and vegetables.

Yield: 6 servings

HOMEMADE GRANOLA

3 cups old-fashioned oats
1/3 cup brown sugar
3 tablespoons honey
1/4 cup grapeseed oil
1 teaspoon vanilla extract
3/4 cup toasted walnuts, chopped
1/4 cup flaxseed
1/2 cup coconut

Preheat oven to 350°F. Combine the oats, brown sugar, honey, and oil in a large bowl. (Note: If you measure the oil first, you can then use the same measuring device for the honey, which will then pour out easily and completely.) Add the vanilla, walnuts, flaxseed, and coconut. Mix and pour onto a cookie sheet covered with either aluminum foil or a silicone mat. Spread over the entire cookie sheet and bake for 10 minutes. Remove the cookie sheet and use a spatula to break up the granola, flipping pieces over to let the sides brown. Return to the oven for another 10 to 15 minutes, or until mixture is golden brown. Let the granola cool for 10 to 15 minutes, then gently break it up using the back of a spoon.

Note that this makes the granola slightly more clumpy. If you like fewer clumps, you can simply stir it more often while it's baking.

Yield: 8-10 servings

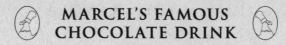

MARCEL'S FAMOUS CHOCOLATE DRINK

2 oz. high-quality dark chocolate, chopped into
  small pieces
2 oz. high-quality milk chocolate, chopped into
  small pieces
½ cup milk, plus additional, to taste
½ teaspoon ground cinnamon
1 shot espresso

Combine chocolates and ½ cup milk in a sturdy saucepan, and warm over low heat. Stir constantly, adjusting heat as necessary to melt chocolate and combine ingredients until smooth. Add cinnamon and stir well, to break up powdery chunks. Add espresso, and continue to stir until well blended.

Serve warm in demitasse cups. This drink is so rich and chocolate-y, however, that you may prefer to prepare this with extra milk.

Note: Because the cinnamon may not completely dissolve, consider straining the liquid before serving.

Serves 2